D0825440

AQUA

Nona Schrader

ALL THINGS
THAT MATTER
PRESS

Aqua
Copyright © 2022 by Nona Schrader

All rights reserved. No part of this book may be reproduced or transmitted in any form or by any means without written permission of the author and publisher.

This is a work of fiction. Any resemblance to actual persons, living or deceased, is purely coincidental. Although certain locations referenced do exist, all events are the product of the author's imagination.

ISBN: 978-1-7377671-6-9

Library of Congress Control Number: 2022934190

Author photo by: Jazzy Photo
Cover photo by Carmen Ong

For my children,
Alex and Katie

Acknowledgments

With deepest gratitude to the following people:

To my writing coach, Kathie Giorgio, for believing in Diana and Indigo from the beginning.

To my publishers, Deb and Philip Harris of All Things That Matter Press, for helping Indigo fly.

A special thank you to Deb Harris for her delightful emails and excellent editing skills.

To the members of our novel class in Kathie's writing studio. Angie, Carrie, Jeff, Maureen, and Mark provided invigorating critiques throughout this writing process.

Finally, thank you to my husband John for his constant support of my writing.

FROM THE LATIN

Aqua	Water
Aqua Fortis	Strong Water
Aqua Pura	Pure Water
Aqua Regia	Royal Water
Aqua Vitae	Water of Life

THE PROPHECY

The girl will come from the west in the land where pure water flows from the mountaintops and runs into the Earth. Her name will be Diana.

In the Wind River Mountains of Wyoming, each spring, the winter snowpack melts and trickles into rushing streams that feed the Popo Agie River. After the icy water pounds over the falls to the granite boulders in the canyon below, the roaring white river disappears into a cavern no human has explored. Quietly, secretly, the water surfaces down the canyon to form a large, deep pool and continue on as a powerful river.

Here, the girl-child will be born in the time of need, when the Earth cries for protection from its greatest enemy: humankind.

A great drought has seized the West, and, every year, the snowpack feeding the valley lessens, the source of clean water diminishes, and the time of the prophecy nears

CHAPTER ONE
THE CAVE AT SINKS CANYON

My perfect summer was ruined. A week ago, I came home at the end of my freshman year of college at the University of Wyoming. Now all I could think of was that I had to get out of the house.

Before grabbing my jacket, I checked on Grams to make sure she was still asleep. Until the broken hip, Grams had been a stable force in my life. I was shocked at how vulnerable she seemed in her sleep. Grams could ride horses, hunt, and shoot better than anyone I knew, but, this morning, she was small and fragile. The unfamiliar walker pulled next to her bedside table provided added emphasis.

I quietly closed the door to our log house and slipped outside in the early morning sun. Willy was coming in to make breakfast soon, so I had time for a quick bike ride up Sinks Canyon.

"I'm going to the cave," I told Willy after poking my head in the barn to find him brushing Blaze, his favorite horse. Willy was our ranch hand, but after working here for so many years, he was part of our family.

"I'll go inside," he said, patting Blaze on the neck.

I hopped on my bike, pedaled down the gravel road leading to our ranch, and turned left onto the highway.

Fire Season. Repeating the words in my head, I gave the word "fire" two syllables, and soon they matched the rhythm of my feet pushing down on the pedals as I rode up Sinks Canyon highway. *Fi-er Sea-son. Fi-er Sea-son. Fi-er Sea-son.*

On my right, the granite cliffs of the canyon wall gave way to charred sagebrush surrounding the occasional boulder nestled in the side of the canyon. To my left, the Popo Agie River flowed out of the canyon toward my family's ranch located at the mouth of Sinks Canyon outside of my hometown, Lander, Wyoming.

The right slope of the canyon was scarred black, a grim reminder of the fire last July. Seeing the charred sagebrush brought back last summer's fear when the fire raced toward our ranch, and my relief when the firefighters put out the blaze before it jumped the road and engulfed us.

In spite of the river roaring down from the mountains to our ranch, the canyon was dry, dry, dry. The only way we kept our alfalfa growing was to pull irrigation water from the river.

"Add Fire Season to summer and fall, Diana," Grams had said

yesterday. Already a fire raged six hours southeast of here outside of Boulder, Colorado, even though it was only the beginning of June.

I truly was glad to be back. I loved college, but I couldn't wait for summers in the Wind River Mountains with my dad and Willy. I'd expected everything at home to stay the same as it was in my childhood, and throughout the spring, I looked forward to our summer pack trip. But between May and June, my meticulously planned summer events fell apart.

It all started when Grams broke her hip in May. Dad said that I didn't need to come home then because I shouldn't miss school right before final exams. He'd take care of Grams while I finished the semester.

Last night, Dad told me we couldn't go into the mountains on horseback this summer.

The trailhead was right up the canyon from our ranch, and I'd been going on summer pack trips with Dad, Grandpa, and Willy for years. We made a living by taking families of tourists into the wilderness area in the mountains above the ranch, camping for a week at a time. The first trip this summer was important because we were going without tourists. When fall came, hunting season started, and I returned to college.

"Hunting camp is no place for a girl," Grandpa'd said when I was younger.

Even though Grandpa died two years ago, I still didn't hunt. I knew how to shoot a gun, but I didn't want to kill animals. Now Dad and Willy kept the business going.

Summer was the best because when we took families into the mountains, Willy, Dad, and I worked as a team. The tourists were surprised when I cooked breakfast each morning and served as wrangler, taking care of the riding and pack horses in the mountains.

"I have to leave for the summer and work in the oil fields in North Dakota," Dad said last night. "Our hunting business isn't making as much money without your grandpa here, and this will help us get through the winter."

So today I biked up Sinks Canyon to stand next to the river as I did every morning throughout the summer, trying to remember my mother.

Reaching the parking lot of the Sinks Cave, I coasted to the edge of the sloping paved lot, exhilarated from biking uphill. Locking my bike in the rack provided by the Forest Service, I navigated the trail to the river's edge. Winding and steep, the trail was flanked by aspens, their early June green leaves fluttering in the morning breeze. Last year's fire hadn't touched this side of the canyon, and the white bark of the slender trees gleamed in the sun.

A flash of color caught my eye as a Mountain Bluebird landed on the branch of an aspen. Surprised it had perched this close to me, I paused. I knew it was a female because she was light grey, except for the vivid blue on her wings and tail. She gazed at me with black eyes, chirped once, and flew away. I continued down the trail.

The spray from the Popo Agie River misted the air as it poured over boulders and into a cavern where the water disappeared underground only to surface a quarter mile down the road. Divers couldn't explore the underground cave because the crevices were too small. As more and more people learned about the mystery of the Sinks, I came here early in the morning to be alone in my daily pilgrimage to the river.

The roar of the river crashing over boulders drowned out the sounds of Mountain Chickadees and my footfalls on the trail. The air was cooler here, and the smell of water on limestone filled my nostrils. I stepped off the trail and stood on a boulder next to the river, my chest constricting as it did every time I stood here.

I was drawn to the river, especially in spring. The snowpack melted from the mountains so fast that part of the river forked to the left in an overflow channel. The cave entrance was buried in surging white water.

The power of the water terrified me as it crashed over the huge boulders in the riverbed, strewn about as if giants threw them long ago.

Mesmerized, I wondered why I did this. Was I here to prove that the river couldn't defeat me the way it had my mom? Did I come to find memories? Fear, mixed with exhilaration, flooded my chest, but no memories of my mom surfaced.

Thirteen years ago, when I was five, my mom, Elaina Carter, died in a whitewater rafting accident near Yellowstone Park on the Hoback River in Hoback Canyon outside of Jackson Hole. I was there, but I don't remember it, so I only knew the story now from my dad's retelling of the event.

Years ago, he'd explained what happened. "Your mom and I loved rafting. We had a rafting guide on the Hoback River. I was at the back of the raft with you, and your mother was in her favorite place up front," Dad said, looking down at his strong, tan hands. Dad was a tall man but seemed to shrink in size as he told the story.

"The river was high that year, but the guide felt it was safe, and so did we. It was a fluke when the raft hit a boulder and knocked your mom into the rapids. She would have been okay, and we could have saved her, but her head smashed against another boulder and she went under," Dad said. "We found her body downstream the next day. After that, you cried at night and told me you wanted to drown so you could be with your mom. That's when we sold our house in town and moved out on the ranch to live with your grandma and grandpa."

For as long as I could remember, the ache of Mom's absence was too overwhelming to deal with. Every time I started to think of it, tears threatened to overcome me, so I stuffed my grief deep inside. I knew that if I started to cry, I'd never stop. My tears would fill this river and pour into the cavern at a greater volume than the water flowing there now.

I wanted to cry rivers, lakes, and oceans of tears. But I couldn't. My tears were jammed up like the waters of beaver ponds in high mountain meadows, held back by the complex intertwining of twigs and tree limbs elaborately constructed by beavers.

Sometimes I felt like all it would take is the plucking of one branch and the whole dam would collapse with the force of my tears.

So I made myself stand on the boulder next to the raging spring run-off, knowing rapids like this had taken Mom. My dad and Grams told me stories about her, but those were their memories, not mine. I couldn't remember the sound of Mom's voice, and if it weren't for the photo on my nightstand, I wouldn't recall her face at all.

I was losing my memories of Mom.

I closed my eyes, reveling in the spray misting my face. The pounding of water on the boulders brought me back to the present. I spread my arms wide and high, yelling over the roar of water. Dwarfed, my yell was a relief, but didn't take away my thoughts of Mom, leaving my tears jammed up inside.

As if in response to my call, the cliff walls above the cave opened in a straight line, just like an elevator door. I jumped in surprise, falling to my knees on the boulder.

Two large black winged horses pulling a shiny black chariot flew through the opening, gliding up and over the river, forcing me to lean back to see its progress. The magnificent horses curvetted back toward the river, gliding to a stop, suspended in the air in front of me.

"You can't be real," I whispered. Did I fall and hit my head without realizing it? Or was I dreaming? Maybe I was still cuddled under the covers in my bed at home. But the spray from the river touched my face and the water roared as it crashed over the boulders. I scrambled to gain my footing, scraping my palms on the rough granite boulder as I stood up. The pain meant this must be real.

Standing in the chariot was the most beautiful young woman I'd ever seen. Her warm brown skin contrasted with her brilliant green eyes. Long, black curly hair flowed halfway down her back. A gold circlet gleamed against her broad forehead, joined in the middle by a brilliant emerald stone that matched the color of her eyes. Another emerald in the shape of a delicate leaf connected a flowing dark green cape, its sides draping over her strong shoulders. She wore brown boots that almost reached her knees, and green pants. The letter P was embroidered in green vines on a brown vest that emphasized her trim, muscular shape.

Her eyes drew me in further: emerald green, with flecks of gold. They compelled me to move forward.

A mischievous smile curved the woman's poppy-red lips, and strong white teeth flashed as her smile broadened.

"This is crazy," I said, because I recognized the woman as the goddess Persephone, daughter of Demeter, the Greek goddess of the harvest. I've loved Greek mythology since sixth grade, and even though I was in college, I still read my worn mythology books.

"Are you here to help me?" I asked, for some reason thinking the goddess must know my mom died in rapids like these.

"No," the green-eyed woman replied. "*You* are going to help *me*."

Energy radiated from the black horses as they spread their wings. The woman flicked the reins, moving the chariot next to the flat boulder, and extended her hand.

"Come," she said with determination. "We have work to do."

A beam of green light flowed from her hand. Warm and bright, it grew longer, branching into vines. Leaves appeared on the sides of the constantly forming vines. Snaking through the air, the leafy vines reached my hand and circled my arm gently, curling and twining. The leaves followed the contour of my arm up to my shoulder and then my neck. Stopping at my face, the vines caressed my chin.

I wasn't afraid, but surprised that I couldn't move. I closed my eyes, thinking this must be a dream. Before I could open them again, a sense of joy filled my heart as it does on spring mornings when I gallop through the pasture on horseback.

Bright hope caused me to inhale deeply, and I opened my eyes, expecting to wake up in bed. But Persephone, the horses, and the chariot still hovered in front of me.

Oddly drawn to her, I reached out. Energy surged up my arm as Persephone grabbed my hand and propelled me into the chariot. I landed on the padded seat behind the tall woman and the vines evaporated with a puff of green dust.

"How did you do that?" I asked. "This can't be real."

"Fly to Hades," Persephone cried.

The horses neighed in response and flew into the air, while I grabbed the edge of the chariot and looked down on the raging river, its roar losing power over me.

As the horses turned and approached the limestone cave, the cliff walls above the river once again parted in a straight line, and we flew inside.

A rumbling of stone from behind caused me to turn around. The morning sunlight disappeared as the cave walls closed. We were inside a cave where no human had been before.

CHAPTER TWO
HADES

I expected darkness when we flew through the doors into the cave, and it was dim at first. I thought the cave would be a narrow, confined tunnel in the rocks, but instead, before me was a vast, wide cavern filled with light. A pungent tang of limestone merged with the smell of water on sandstone.

"How did you get me to come with you? What did that green light do to me? How can the inside of a cave look like this?" I rattled off the questions in quick succession, letting my anger come out also. "I don't like being in enclosed areas."

"We've used this cavern as a way to reach the surface of the Earth for thousands of years," Persephone said. "Hades installed skylights so we could easily see."

She ignored my first two questions, and I let that pass for now as I heard the river cascading over rocks and hitting water far below. Looking down, I saw a dark blue lake. Rainbows shimmered as spray from the river filled the beams of sunlight streaming through the cavern from the skylights above. *This seems real*, I concluded when droplets of water misted my arms and face.

Leaning my head over the edge of the chariot, I remembered that Hades was infamous for having kidnapped Persephone and making her his queen. I was fascinated by their story.

"I wanted to be Queen of the Underworld," Persephone said, as if reading my mind. "He didn't force me to stay with him. Humans have always misunderstood. The Greeks liked to sensationalize everything about our lives." She shook her head.

We descended past ferns and flowering plants growing on rock ledges. Amidst the green leaves, vibrant blossoms lifted their faces to the rays of sunlight pouring into the cave. Nourishing water sprayed the plants, forming rainbows as it danced through the sunbeams coming from above.

"I couldn't be here this long without redecorating," Persephone said with a smile. "I had to add plants."

"You still didn't tell me how you did that vine trick to get me in here," I said.

"Plants are my power," she said. "I used the vines to remind you of the joy you feel in nature. Then I pulled you into the chariot and brought you inside the cave."

I knew the Popo Agie River flowed through a limestone cave so narrow divers couldn't enter. For years, scientists had tried to follow the path of the water as it disappeared into the cave. In the end, all they could do was put red dye in the water at the cave entrance and wait to see if it surfaced downstream where the river once again came above ground in a forceful spring.

After reading it so many times, I'd memorized the description in the Sinks Canyon Visitor Center. The dye placed in the river resurfaced two hours later a quarter mile down the canyon on the opposite side of the highway, forming a large pool. The flow of water from this spring exceeded the volume going into the cave, leading scientists to believe there was a deep, dark lake of water underground. *Well, they were right*, I thought.

As the horses carried the chariot along the path of the waterfall, the sunlight weakened to a dim light. Clinging to the rocks, the plants changed from ferns and blooming flowers to luminescent succulents, giving off an unearthly glow.

"I've been experimenting with phosphorescent plants," Persephone said. "At night, moonlight illuminates everything. These are new, hardier plants that use moonlight to grow. I call it lunarsynthesis," she said with a mischievous smile. "Instead of producing chlorophyll like they do in photosynthesis, these plants produce lunophyl, using the light of the moon. Even though the moon does not come out every night, they save up enough lunophyl to survive until the moon's cycle changes. I'm an expert in horticulture, because, after all, my mother is Demeter, goddess of the harvest and growth."

The crashing of the falls grew louder, and soon we reached bottom where the water poured into a dark lake with broad, rocky ledges on either side. On the right, a tall figure with dark hair and a silver crown stood near two high-backed golden thrones studded with rubies, jade, and sapphires. The horses whinnied joyfully before gracefully landing on the rocky ledge next to the lake.

The figure stepped forward and stroked the foreheads of the powerful black horses. They kneeled down on their front legs, bowing in respect. Persephone laughed and jumped from the chariot, and I realized this was Hades, Greek god of the Underworld.

His gaze moved from the horses to me. A dark, foreboding terror constricted my lungs, but when he smiled, the oppressive weight on my chest lifted.

"You don't have to fear me," Hades said, placing his arm around Persephone. As the young goddess leaned into his broad frame, he touched his lips to her forehead. His silver crown glimmered next to the gold circlet on her head.

He looked up and continued speaking. "I only cause panic for those who come here without invitation. You're here as our guest and can willingly leave. This is not the Underworld, but a cavern under Sinks Canyon."

Hades was magnificent, from his blue-black hair and dark eyes to his bronze skin shining in the light from torches on the cave wall. The silver crown on his head gleamed brilliantly in the torchlight. His presence was formidable. Tenderness altered his face when he smiled at Persephone, turning his dark eyes amber. His booming laugh reverberated against the cave walls, rising above the sound of the river, and the black horses whinnied loudly in reply.

Persephone grinned as he picked her up and twirled her around before gently lowering her to the ground. Flooded with the intensity of their love, I longed to experience their joy.

Hades embraced Persephone and then turned back to me, his gaze enveloping me in the cloak of their love. As the King and Queen of the Underworld stood next to the chariot, their combined power was overwhelming, but then it diminished, leaving a vibrant joy. With one arm around Persephone, Hades extended his right hand toward me, and I realized I was still in the chariot.

Taking his hand, I experienced a surge of companionship and belonging, as if I were part of this majestic couple, joined in the circle of their love. Warmth surrounded my hand, making my fingers tingle. His grip was strong, like Willy's.

"Welcome to Sinks Cavern," Hades said. "We've been waiting for you, Diana."

I stepped onto the broad rocky ledge to see a comfortable campsite with a campfire and two white tents. Torches hung on the cavern walls, adding warm light.

"What do you mean, you've waiting for me? What's going on here?" I asked. The horses seemed real, and Hades and Persephone seemed real, but this couldn't be happening. *Am I dreaming? Did I hit my head on the boulder next to the river? Am I delusional?* I pinched my arm, testing my senses. It hurt. *Is this real?*

I stepped closer to the horses, feeling no fear at their huge size and broad backs, with their wings folded neatly against their sides, as bird wings do when they're resting. Looking into the intelligent eyes of the nearest horse, it seemed I'd known this animal forever, and that he understood my disbelief. I stroked his soft muzzle, and he nuzzled my hand, blowing warm breath into my palm. Even though I'd lived with horses my entire life, I'd never seen such graceful and proud animals.

"You'll help preserve water, *Aqua Pura*," Hades said, gesturing toward the lake lapping against the rocky ledge. "This is pure water, fresh from the mountain snowpack. It's been flowing like this for thousands of years. You're the human who will help us keep it clean and plentiful, Diana."

"That's ridiculous," I said. I moved closer to the black winged horse, placing my hand on his muscular neck, seeking comfort in the familiar warmth of horses.

Hades stepped forward and pulled the long reins from where they rested in the chariot, and turned to face me again. "At the far edge of the world is Oceanus, a river of water that circles the globe and is the source of all aquifers, rivers, lakes, and streams," he said. "All water is connected by Oceanus, just as we are connected to the Earth." Pausing, he looked into my eyes. "Humans are polluting the ocean at an alarming rate, and you must help us protect the waters of the ocean."

"How can I do that?" I said. "I'm just a teenager."

"You'll travel with Persephone to Oceanus and ask Eos, goddess of the dawn, for the use of her immortal horses. The water on our planet is threatened, Diana, and you must help save *Aqua Pura*, the pure water. We have more to discuss, but first I must feed the horses. Persephone will show you around the campsite."

Hades pulled on the reins, and I moved as he led the horses and chariot away. On our ranch, taking care of animals always came first. *That's a connection to reality*, I thought.

"I know this is hard to believe," Persephone said. "We just didn't know any other way to tell you."

"I have to talk to Grams," I said.

"Come with me to your tent," Persephone said. "We'll stay here tonight and then we'll leave in the morning. We have to finish our task by midsummer, which is five days from now."

"Explain this right now." I crossed my arms and locked my legs in a defiant stance.

"Of course," Persephone said and walked back to me. "You have always been special, Diana. Why do you think Willy lives on the ranch? Why has your grandmother done all she can to protect the ranch from development? They know you will help keep the water pure and strong."

"What about my father? Does he know anything about this?" I felt trapped, as if everyone I loved knew something, but kept it a secret from me.

"No, your father is just that: your father. He loves you, but he knows nothing about us," Persephone said.

"What about my grandma?" I asked. "She'll wonder where I am."

"She knows you're here," Persephone said. "She knows about me and knows you're safe with us. Tomorrow, I'll take you to meet my mother,

14

Demeter. For now, let's go see your tent."

Puzzling over how Grams knew about this cave, I followed to where the white tents stood side by side against the cave wall. I walked into the tent on the right as Persephone held the flap open with a welcoming gesture.

The inside smelled like lemons, my favorite smell. Against the far wall of the tent was a raised wooden platform with soft white blankets on top. Next to the bed was a pair of sturdy brown boots.

"Those are bamboo. My mother can fashion incredible fabrics from bamboo. They're just like mine." Persephone extended her foot, showing her worn, but comfortable-looking, boots. "They last forever."

I stepped forward. "How did you know my size?" I asked, picking up one boot.

"Your grandmother told me. Go ahead, try them on," Persephone encouraged.

I stroked the soft boot. Sitting on the bed, I took off my tennis shoes and pulled on the boots. They were even more comfortable than my worn cowboy boots sitting in my closet back at the ranch. *Are my senses deceiving me? Well, the boots seem real. I feel them on my feet. I can smell lemon and that seems real, also.*

"These are nice," I admitted. Standing, I walked around in the tent, pausing to admire the trim boots on my calves. Then I shook my head and looked up at Persephone, unwilling to be swayed by this gift.

"This will help you understand," Persephone said as she reached under the pillow on my bed and pulled out an envelope.

I recognized Grams' old school cursive writing. Taking the envelope from Persephone, I slowly broke the seal, pulled out the single page inside, and began to read:

Diana,
When you read this, I will be safe at home with Willy, and you'll be in the cave with Persephone and Hades. You can trust them, Diana. For proof, ask Persephone to give you our code word. If she gives you the right answer, you'll know she speaks the truth when she tells you they need help saving pure water. I wanted to tell you in person, but between my hip surgery and your dad leaving, there wasn't time.
You must help them, Diana. Willy will take care of me. Come back to me when you have completed your task. I will be waiting at the ranch.
Love,
Grams

I looked at Persephone, narrowing my eyes. Would she know the code word? When I was young, Grams, Dad, Willy, and I established a code in case someone else had to pick me up in town. We chose Marilla from *Anne of Green Gables*. She was the gruff woman who adopted Anne in the story. Grams loved reading that novel to me at night, and I never tired of listening to the story over and over again. It seemed silly to rely on this childhood code word now, but the note was in Grams' handwriting.

"What's the code word?" I asked.

"Marilla," she said confidently.

I reluctantly folded the letter and put it back in the envelope, placing it on the bed. Grams *had* wanted to talk to me last night, but she fell asleep on the couch before I helped her to bed.

"Let's go eat something," Persephone said, as if she knew I was overwhelmed. "We'll have some ginger tea and honey cakes. My mother makes them. You'll love them. Tomorrow, we'll fly to the Platte River to see her."

She walked out of the tent and turned to hold the flap open with a welcoming smile. Undecided about the boots, I left them on and followed her.

CHAPTER THREE
THE BLUEBIRD REPORT
THE HEART OF A DINOSAUR

I hatched in a nest hidden in the cavity of a pine tree at the edge of the meadow on the cliffs above Sinks Canyon. My mother was beautiful, but my father was magnificently blue. Mountain Bluebirds are bluer than any other bluebird, and he was brilliant in the morning sun. Both my parents worked tirelessly to feed my brothers and me. In a nest of four hatchlings, I was the only female.

The first month of my life was an incredible insect feast. My brothers and I waited as our parents raced to and from the nest, returning with grubs and caterpillars. Later, we graduated to crickets, grasshoppers, and other bugs. My favorite was the dragonfly with its gossamer wings, delicate and fresh, coupled with the crunchy outer shell and soft creamy substance of its inner body. As we grew older, my brothers tried to shove me aside with their featherless wings when one of our parents returned, but I learned early on to fight my way to the center of the nest for food. I had a large gaping mouth and they diligently fed me, too, so I grew strong. My parents came back to our nesting cavity in the pine tree on a rotating basis every twenty minutes.

Featherless and ugly, I was born with a riotous tuft of fuzz on my head, and with my eyes sealed. When my eyes opened eight days later and I first saw the magnificence of my father's blue body filling the opening of our nesting hole, I longed to be as beautiful. At first, I thought I would be.

But, alas, that brilliant blue was reserved for my brothers, not me, for the male Mountain Bluebird steals all the color from the sky, while females like me become a soft grey with brilliant blue wingtips and tails. Our vibrant black eyes are perfect for spotting insects.

My mother's eyes were especially kind. I think she favored me because she knew that my life would be hard, dedicated to laying eggs and brooding on the nest, and non-stop feeding of the young from dawn to dusk. She named me Indigo, telling me that word means blue. Even without blue feathers all over my body, I was proud that at least my name meant blue.

What stories mother told at night when we snuggled under the warmth of her wings! Feeding time stopped when darkness took away the sun, and we huddled together in the hole in the pine tree that Father had found to attract Mother. Our home had been hollowed out years ago by woodpeckers, and my parents came early in spring when the snow still flies to claim the tree cavity before any other types of birds returned from the winter migration.

"You are descended from the greatest dinosaur of all time, Tyrannosaurus Rex," Mother said. "Never forget that inside your little chest beats the heart of a dinosaur. Every living bird is a distant relative of the dinosaurs of old."

Before the end of the month, we were all ready to fly for the first time, but Mother held me back as my brothers flew from our home to a nearby tree. In her chirping voice, she asked me to help with her next brood. "It's common for young fledglings to help feed the next batch of hatchlings," she said. "Would you do that for me?'

"Of course," I replied. The nesting instinct was already strong in my soul, and I yearned for my own little batch of bright blue eggs. More than that, I yearned for a mate as handsome as my father, even though I doubted any bird could match his brilliance.

So my brothers and I left the warm nest in the cavity of the pine tree, making our fledgling flight only twenty days after we hatched. For another month, we stayed together as a family while Father fed and protected us. At night, we huddled in a pine tree across the meadow for warmth. During that time, Mother returned to the nest to lay another batch of eggs while Father took care of us, continuing to catch crickets and grasshoppers.

We learned how to hunt by watching him hang low above the ground, grabbing the insects when they flew up from the meadow grass. My favorite pastime was watching him fly over the meadow, startling grasshoppers. As the surprised green food darted into the air, he snapped it up with his beak, racing across the meadow to feed us.

Eventually, we caught our own food in this manner, and my brothers flew away to begin their own lives. I returned to the nesting cavity to find that my mother's new batch of eggs already hatched, and five little nestlings waited with mouths gaping wide, their eyelids sealed. Father and I joined Mother in a constant rotation of finding grubs and caterpillars to feed those funny little naked birds with soft tufts of wild feathers gracing their heads.

This continued until their pinfeathers grew in after about ten days. On my third trip to the meadow one morning, a tall, beautiful creature stepped from the edge of the forest into the meadow. I was more surprised than alarmed because I'd never seen anything like this before. Deer, rabbits, mice, and other birds were now familiar to me, but this creature walking upright on two legs was different. I stopped in flight, landing on the branch of an aspen tree. By her side walked two lovely animals, larger than coyotes.

"I am Artemis," she said in birdspeak.

I opened my beak in surprise, dropping the huge grasshopper in my mouth. "You can speak like a bluebird," I replied.

"Yes," she said. "I am Artemis, protector of all animals." She moved closer so that she was eye level with me as I perched on the tree branch.

"What are those?" I asked, nodding toward the sleek animals at her side. By now they were seated, watching me with intelligent eyes. They didn't look hungry, so I wasn't worried they would attack.

"These are my hounds," Artemis said, stroking the head of one. Even when sitting, his head reached her waist. "I have a task for you, little Mountain Bluebird."

"What task?" Suddenly, I was eager to help this amazing creature standing on two legs. "Right now, I'm helping my mother with her new batch of hatchlings," I said, standing taller on the branch. "My name is Indigo."

"I know who you are," she said. Smiling, she reached out and stroked my head softly. I pushed up against her finger and warmth spread through my body like it did when I sat on a tree branch in the afternoon sun after a long morning of catching insects.

"I need your help with a new fledgling, a human. Her name is Diana. She is still young, like you. I want you to travel to the ranch where she lives just outside of this canyon," Artemis said.

"What about helping Mother?" I asked.

"You can see Diana today and then finish helping with this batch of hatchlings. This fall, you are going to migrate south to New Mexico and return in the spring," Artemis said. "One year from now, you will help Diana with a quest."

"What about babies?" I asked. "I want to find a mate and have a nesting cavity like my mother."

"That is not your destiny at this time, little Indigo," she said. "You will find a mate someday in the future, but now I need your help with Diana." She touched my head again, and I puffed up, proud to be chosen. Then I sighed, remembering I wanted to raise my own babies.

"Why do I have to help Diana?" I asked.

"Some creatures are born at important times in the history of the world," Artemis said. "You are special, Indigo, and this is an important time."

"I still don't understand. How can a little bluebird help?" I said.

"You were born with the heart of a dinosaur," she said. "Your mother told you that, right?"

"Yes, but I don't really know what it means," I said.

"You have great inner strength. You are courageous, even though you don't know your own strength of will. Helping Diana with this quest will give you a chance to understand what this means. You'll face danger and come out on the other side, finally realizing the courage you possess in your dinosaur heart."

"I don't think I have courage," I said, shaking my head.

"I am preparing forces to join together and help the planet. You represent creatures of the sky, Indigo. You represent all birds," Artemis said. "Diana will represent humans and all animals, and the third force will come from the sea, representing all creatures that dwell in water."

"You mean like fish and frogs?" I said. "What is the sea?"

"The sea is a great body of water, larger than you have ever seen. You will go there with Diana," Artemis said. "That is your destiny."

"But I don't want to leave Mother. I'm helping her with the new hatchlings," I said.

"Your path is caught up in Diana's quest, and you must help her. Destiny means you are obligated to fulfill a purpose, even if you don't fully understand it in the beginning," she said. "I want you to trust me." She smoothed my head again and the warmth of her fingers comforted me.

"Okay. I'll go see Diana today and then help Mother with this brood," I said. "Does my mother know about this?"

"Yes," Artemis said. "Later today, a meadowlark will come to your home and take you to see Diana. You'll know you can trust him when he tells you his name."

"What is it?" I asked.

"Memnon," she said. "He's named after the Greek hero who is the son of Eos, goddess of the dawn. You'll meet Eos later. When the hero Memnon died in the Trojan War, my brother Zeus, the ruler of all gods and men, gave the hero his own flock of birds that come every year to lament over his grave. The real Memnon was granted immortality by Zeus. The meadowlark Memnon is my faithful helper, and he is proud of his name."

"I am proud of my name, too," I said. "It means blue."

"And your wingtips and tail are a beautiful blue," Artemis said. She leaned down and plucked a grasshopper from the meadow grass at her feet. "Take this back to the nest and tell your mother you spoke with me."

I snapped up the grasshopper and flew away, excited to tell Mother about meeting Artemis. When I arrived at the pine tree, Father was just leaving. I stepped in the cavity to find mother inside.

"Mother, I met Artemis," I said after feeding the grasshopper to my rapidly growing younger sister. "She is sending me on a quest. I'm going to meet a fledgling named Diana."

Mother turned her head, her mouth full of white excreta pellets left by the young hatchlings. She flew out without talking but nodded at me. I knew she would return quickly. Every day, she cleaned the cavity, carrying the pellets far away from the nest so no predators would smell the waste of our young. *I'll take good care of my hatchlings someday*, I thought.

She soon returned, chirping over the loud sounds of the youngsters as they clamored for more food. "Let's go outside," she said.

Just as we flew out, Father returned with a cricket. Mother and I landed on a large branch above the nesting cavity. "Artemis said you know about the quest," I said.

Moving closer to me, Mother rubbed her head against mine. Her familiar smell and warmth moved me, and I suddenly realized I would leave her behind. "I am proud of you, my young daughter. This is a great honor. Never forget you have the heart of a dinosaur, and the blood of Tyrannosaurus Rex is in your veins," she said, her voice close to my ear. "Go now and be brave."

"But I want to help you feed the babies until they fly away in a few days," I protested.

"You will help me this summer. Indigo, the women of our family have a history of helping Artemis," she said. "Your grandmother helped Diana's grandmother years ago."

"What did she do?" I asked. "You never told us about that."

"I knew the time would come when Artemis needed your help. While I sat on the nest keeping you and your brothers warm, Artemis came to me and asked if my daughter could help with a great quest. Of course, I was honored, and asked only that Artemis protect you on your journey," she said.

"So you knew about this?" I asked. "And my grandmother helped Artemis?" I puffed up with pride, knowing I was as important as my grandmother.

Father flew out of the hole in the tree and Mother and I flew in to be near the nestlings.

"Yes," Mother said. "Your grandmother helped Diana's grandmother make Sinks Canyon a Wyoming state park so that birds and other animals would have a safe place to live. Your grandmother also waited to find a mate. But after helping Diana's grandmother, Helen, your grandmother met my father and had her own babies." Mother folded her wing around me and cradled me next to her chest, softly tweeting in my ear, "I love you."

"I love you, too," I said. "I want to stay, yet I want to go." I burrowed my head under her wing, breathing in the sweet smell of her feathers.

"You have to find your own way in the world, and you should go now to learn about Diana. I'm so proud that you were chosen for this quest," she said. The pressure from her wing increased, pulling me close to the sound of her heartbeat, steady and strong. Then she gently pushed me away. "You must follow your own destiny."

"I'll go," I said, looking into her black eyes. "But I'll be back soon."

I flew out of the cavity to find a speckled bird with a bright yellow chest and belly waiting outside on a branch. "Artemis sent me to guide you to Diana's ranch," he chirped. A black triangle on his chest highlighted the deep yellow of his belly. "My name is Memnon."

"You're a Western Meadowlark," I said. Father taught us how to recognize all the birds in the meadow. "Artemis told me about you."

"Follow me," he said. Without further explanation, he took flight. I glanced back as Mother's grey head peaked at me from the nesting cavity, and then, beating my wings double time, I flew after the meadowlark.

"Wait up!" I said.

He slowed his flight until I reached his side and, without speaking, we flew over the meadow and down into the canyon. Father never took us this far from home, so I looked around eagerly. The river roared in the canyon below as we skirted the edges of the cliffs. A black snake wound through the bottom of the canyon next to the river, and colorful bugs moved along the snake's back.

"That is a road and those are cars," Memnon said.

"Can we eat them?" I asked.

"No. They are large, fast, and dangerous. They won't stop if you fly in front of them, so don't ever get near one. If you sit on the road to catch bugs and a car comes along, you might not be able to fly out of its way before it hits you. Cars come in different sizes, so it's hard to judge how quickly you should fly away when they come," he said. "I lost several cousins that way."

"What do you mean?" I asked.

"Let's stop here," he said. Flying down to the floor of the canyon, he landed on a branch in a tree next to the river.

I followed, looking around as we perched next to the roaring water. I knew about the river because Father took us to see it last week, but we didn't fly into the canyon.

"What do you mean you lost cousins?" I said.

"You are young and have never experienced death," he said, looking at me kindly. The bright yellow of his chest gleamed in the sun. "When death comes to a bird, we stop chirping. Sometimes that happens when birds are hit by cars. They slam into the car and fall to the ground, their wings still outstretched in flight. I hope you never see that happen."

"Me, too," I said. My heart beat faster as dread filled my chest.

22

"While we're here, let me tell you Diana's story," he said. Mother told us stories every night in the nest, so I ruffled my feathers and hunkered down, anticipating something good.

"Diana is a human who walks upright on two legs. Humans drive the cars, but they don't always mean to hurt us," he said. "She's seventeen this summer and lives on the ranch with her grandmother and her father."

"Seventeen? I'm only a few months old!" I interrupted. He glared at me, so I closed my beak.

"Humans live a long time. Diana's quest is to save *Aqua Pura*, the clean water on our planet," he said, back in storytelling mode.

I knew not to ask any questions because I'd learned early on that interrupting in the middle of a story is the height of rudeness.

"Diana is going on a great quest with Persephone and you will accompany them. Next spring, you must return to this spot and wait for them. The cliff wall will open and Persephone and Diana will fly out in a chariot pulled by horses. Meadowlarks will be the escorts, but you will be allowed to fly with us as we begin our journey. I'll be there. The first stop we will make is to see Demeter, Persephone's mother," he said.

I clamped my beak shut, knowing better than to ask about horses, chariots, Persephone, and Demeter. Father whipped his beak across my brothers often when they interrupted Mother during story time, so I knew saying anything now was a mistake. *Mother would be proud of me*, I thought.

Memnon continued. "Artemis told Persephone and Demeter that you will be Diana's guardian bluebird. Bluebirds have a long tradition of serving as guardians. We all know you truly have the heart of a dinosaur and that is why you were chosen. You are also representing all birds on this quest." His eyes looked into mine, serious and intent.

"Why doesn't Artemis just go along on Diana's quest?" I asked.

"She is protector of all animals and is overwhelmed by helping other creatures around the world right now. But she knows that if a guardian bluebird is by Diana's side on her journey, success is more likely."

"But not guaranteed?" I asked. "Guardian bluebirds don't ensure complete success? How can I do anything? I'm just a little bluebird." Suddenly, I realized there might be danger involved.

"Persephone will be there also. You will encounter danger, but your blueness will help make Diana safer," Memnon said. "There is more to know about Diana."

"What?" I asked.

"Diana experienced death," he said.

"Her cousin was hit by a car?" I said before I could clamp my beak shut.

"No. Her mother died in a rafting accident. She drowned in a river," he said, without commenting on my rude interruption.

I closed my beak, horrified at his words. How could she lose her mother? I didn't know mothers could die. I pulled my head close to my chest, wanting to bury it under my wing.

Memnon must have seen the horror in my eyes because he spoke in a very kind tone. "Yes, she lost her mother. But she still has part of her flock. Her grandmother and father take care of her, and their hired hand, Willy, lives on the ranch. Let's go now so you can see her. She doesn't know birdspeak, but we can watch her. Plus, I want to teach you how to get to the ranch. If you ever get lost, you can fly along the river and then up the cliffs to find your home meadow."

Storytime was over and we flew away from the tree branch, following the river.

As we came out of the canyon, the land below widened to a broad valley. A large mountain towered on the right and between the river and the mountain, green fields glimmered in the sun, but across the road, the sagebrush and field grass was dry and brown.

"Those are hay fields on the ranch. They are lush because humans use water from the river to keep them green," Memnon said. "See those buildings below? We'll land there so you can see Diana."

I followed him down to brown square and rectangular structures. We perched on a fence next to the green fields and he nodded toward giant beasts in one field. "Those are horses," he said. "Have you seen one before? They eat grass and they won't hurt us."

"No, I've never seen one. They're larger than deer," I said.

"Yes. Humans ride them. Persephone has horses with wings," he said.

"What? Those huge creatures can fly?" I said.

"Not all of them," he replied. "Just the ones Persephone and some other gods have. Look. Here comes Diana." He nodded toward one structure as a two-legged creature came running outside.

Her head feathers were dark brown, but the rest of her body was tan without feathers. I later learned she had hair on her head, like the manes on horses. Her dark head hair was short, and she wore coverings on most of her body, but her tan skin gleamed in the sun. She ran on two legs and jumped on a blue device the meadowlark told me was a bicycle.

"I'll be back in a while," she shouted, waving at another human standing on the porch.

"That's her grandmother, Helen." Memnon said. "She takes care of Diana when her father isn't home."

"How does she eat and sleep without her mother?" I said.

"It's hard for her, but she doesn't let the other humans know how much she misses her mother," he said. "Let's follow her."

We took off and flew above Diana as she rode the blue bicycle alongside the black snake where cars that kill birds travel. "Won't a car kill her?" I said as we flew along.

"No. She knows to stay off the road where the cars drive. She's going to stop next to the river and stand on a boulder," he said.

We followed Diana as she pulled into a large patch of skin the snake left beside the road. "That's a parking lot," Memnon said.

Diana walked down the path through the trees and stepped onto a boulder next to the roaring river. We perched in a small aspen and watched as Diana spread her arms wide and raised her face to the sky. A loud scream came from her mouth.

"What is that?" I asked.

"Grief," he said in my ear. "She is grieving for her mother."

"Oh, dear," I said. "I don't want grief."

Diana stopped the terrible screaming and turned right where the river roared over boulders and then she looked left where water filled the cavern at the base of the cliff.

"The river goes into the cave and comes out down the road," Memnon said. "Humans call this place Sinks Canyon and that is the Popo Agie River. This is where you will come next spring to wait at the top of that cliff for Persephone to come out in a chariot pulled by flying horses."

I looked up where the cliff towered above the roaring river and spotted a tree at the top where I could perch and wait.

"Don't forget where this is," he said. "You'll come back here."

I nodded, looking again at Diana. She seemed better now, her arms at her side, staring out over the river.

"Indigo," Memnon said.

"Yes?" I turned to look at him.

"We all experience grief at some point," he said. "You must learn how to live with it."

I nodded, but didn't really understand how to do that. Diana's scream seemed so painful and raw. She turned and stepped off the boulder, walking back up the path to her bicycle.

"Let's go back to your meadow," he said. "You know where to come next spring. You can come see Diana whenever you want before you migrate with your family."

"Okay," I replied.

He took flight and I followed, turning for one final glimpse of Diana as she pedaled her bike next to the black snake road. We flew quickly up the canyon and over the cliff, heading back to my mother and the nestlings.

When we reached the meadow and landed in my home tree, I turned to Memnon. "Thank you for taking me to see Diana," I said. "Next spring, I'll be ready to fly with you. I'll wait on a tree outside the cave."

"I'll see you when you return from your migration," he said. "We'll talk then. Have a safe flight south." He nodded briskly and flew off just as Mother came out of the cavity.

"I saw Diana," I exclaimed. "She lost her mother and lives with her grandmother."

"I wish I could go on this quest with you," Mother said. She looked tired and I realized how much work it was for her to feed the babies day in and day out, returning every twenty minutes with food for the hungry nestlings. "I'll be right back, and you can tell me all about it." She spread her wings and flew across the meadow to scare up some grasshoppers. Inside the cavity, I heard the babies chirping, anxious for a food delivery.

I worked with Mother and Father for the rest of the summer as my siblings grew from nestlings into fledglings, taking their first flight late in the summer.

"Snow comes early in the mountains," Mother said when the leaves on the aspens turned yellow and fell to the ground. "We're going to take off soon with the flock. It's a long journey with many hours of flight each day and I want you to stay by my side."

I knew the time was drawing near when more and more Mountain Bluebirds started converging in the meadow. Caught up in the excitement, I joined the others as we practiced daily how to fly as a group and land together. We soared over the canyon and back, swooping and landing as one. At first I had difficulty turning with the others, and sometimes when the group suddenly turned, I flew the wrong way, looking back and turning when I heard Mother's sharp chirp. Embarrassed, I flapped my wings to catch up, but felt better when several other young birds flew the wrong way as well.

At last, we were coordinated as a flock, flying up and over the meadow as one, landing in a giant pine and turning its green to blue as our collective blueness covered the tree. What a joy it was to fly with the flock! I now turned instinctively when I saw the elders flying in front. I could tell by the dip of a wing when we would change course, and the lowering of a beak from the lead bird told me when we would land as a group.

Mirroring the sky and clear mountain lakes, our blueness brought us together. Excited chirping and the beating of wings surrounded me, and I laughed into the wind as I flew next to Mother. I always stayed by her side in flight.

We left the meadow on a cold day. Together, the flock flew over the rim of the canyon and headed south. We flew for days, and the air became warmer and warmer. On our last day, we landed in a group of pines at the edge of a dry and dusty meadow.

"This is the desert of New Mexico," Mother said. "Our flock has been wintering in this meadow for years. We'll stay for some time and return to Wyoming in the spring."

Throughout the winter, we lived at the edge of the meadow, catching bugs. Mother taught me how to find berries in the forest. The time passed quickly, and in the spring, our flock gathered again, swooping and diving as one. The day came when we took off together and headed north.

"We'll be back in our home meadow soon," Mother exclaimed after our third day of flight.

She wasn't wrong, and when we reached the familiar meadow, I landed on the branch of our home tree. It seemed Mother had no time for me now because she immediately gathered soft grass for the nest. I was distracted by the sounds of male birds calling enticingly from other trees. Lovely chirps drew me to the vibrant blue of a handsome male a few trees down. He flew up and around, calling my name.

"How does he know me?" I asked Mother, but she was busy building the nest and didn't answer right away.

She deposited soft moss in the nesting hole and came out again. "Don't listen to him, Indigo," she said. Rubbing her head against me, she spoke softly in my ear. "You have to be strong and resist his blueness. You are destined to help Diana."

Day after day, he sang and swooped around our tree. He was beautiful. I was drawn by his call and, before I knew it, I landed on the branch near him.

"Look what I found for us," he said, pointing his beak toward a cavity in the tree.

I poked my head inside and felt a yearning to gather moss and line the inside with soft feathers and grasses. Babies. I wanted hungry open mouths yearning for grubs. Hatchlings of my own with riotous tufts of feathers on their heads who turned from nestlings to fledglings. The pull was irresistible, and I almost stepped into the hole in the tree. The smell of bark and the warmth inside was alluring, drawing me in. I was intoxicated by the thought of babies and grubs, imagining the joy of sharing the feeding with my blue mate.

"Indigo," a sharp voice called my name.

Pulling my head out of the nesting cavity, I turned to see a meadowlark landing on the branch where my handsome male waited. "Memnon," I said in surprise.

He shoved my blue admirer aside. "Leave her alone," he said and turned to me. "Indigo, it's time for us to leave. Come with me."

"I can't come yet," I said. "I just found a mate!"

"Remember Diana." Memnon said. "Don't forget Artemis."

Shaking my head to clear away the blue fever, I looked once more at my admirer. From a nearby tree, I heard the chirp of Betty, a young bird from our flock. "Indigo is too proud to mate with one of us," she said.

Violet, another young female on the branch, added, "I'll bet she's more interested in this meadowlark. I've heard some Mountain Bluebirds are drawn to their yellow coloring. Indigo must be one of those types."

"Mating with a meadowlark?" Betty said. "Mating outside of our species is terrible. Why would she do that?"

"Maybe she thinks she's too good for us," Violet replied. "Why else would she turn down an invitation from the handsomest guy around?"

"You two don't know anything about me," I said. "I have my own destiny to follow." I wanted them to understand my desire to mate with this bluer-than-blue male, but I had to help Diana.

"Indigo, let's leave," Memnon said. He took flight, looking back to make sure I followed.

Regret weighed me down, but I spread my wings and flew after him. Looking back, I saw my handsome admirer was already swooping around Betty and Violet, trying to entice one of them into the nesting cavity that would not hold my babies this year.

I followed Memnon down into the canyon. We landed next to the river where it roared into Sinks Cavern.

"Diana and Persephone will come out of the cave tomorrow," he said. "Wait here until then. My flock will surround the chariot when it comes out and you can join us." He took off.

I flew up to the tree I spotted last spring. Throughout the night, I slept restlessly, waking up at the unfamiliar sounds of owls I didn't know.

The third time I woke up, my thoughts returned to the evening before, my last night at home with my parents. I was in the nest while Mother and Father sat outside, watching the setting sun. They thought I was asleep.

"Why didn't Artemis choose one of the boys?" my father asked. "They're strong, brilliant, and blue," he said. "Like me."

I sat up in shock but settled again, wanting to hear Mother and Father talk about me.

"Indigo is also strong," Mother replied. "And she has the heart of a dinosaur."

Thank you, Mother, I thought, shocked that my father questioned my ability. Maybe I shouldn't go. I'd assumed Father would be proud of me, but now it seemed he doubted my ability to help Diana, doubted my ability to represent all birds on this quest.

"It just seems like one of my sons should go," Father said. "I never expected a girl to go. Plus, she is our little Indigo. What if something happens to her?"

"We have to trust Indigo," Mother said. "I don't want her to go, either, but we must give her a chance to fulfill her destiny."

There it was. That destiny thing again. I was tired of everybody else telling me what I had to do. Nonetheless, I was curious about the quest, and I wanted to show Father he was wrong. I could be strong and bluer than my brothers. I heard an owl hooting again, bringing me back to the present where I perched in the tree above the cave.

"Thank you, Mother," I whispered. "I won't let you down." But inside, I was terrified, wondering if Artemis had chosen the right bird for the job. Somehow, I drifted to sleep after that.

CHAPTER FOUR
AQUA FORTIS

Leaving the tent with Persephone, I tested the comfort of my new bamboo boots by bouncing a bit as I walked. Satisfied, I followed her to a stone table built in an alcove along the side of the cave, vowing to find out if this situation was real. I intended to question their every move.

We sat, and Hades returned after feeding the horses. He walked to the tent, came back with a basket, and unpacked a plate of honey cakes. Placing bronze plates and cups in front of us, he removed a flask from the basket before sitting.

"Are you trying to trick me? I know the rules," I said. "If I eat in the Underworld, I'll be doomed to remain here forever." *Good. I have them now.* "That's how you got stuck with Hades." I narrowed my eyes at Persephone.

"This isn't the Underworld, so you're safe," Hades said. "But it's wise to question things." He bit into a honey cake with his large white teeth. "Persephone made her own decision to stay with me. She'll tell you about that later."

"What about this food?" I demanded. "Why aren't we drinking ambrosia, the drink of the gods?"

"We only drink that on Mount Olympus," Hades said. "But the pure water in this cave is nourishing. We used it to make this ginger tea." Steam rose from our bronze cups as he poured from the flask before filling his.

Persephone picked up the plate of honey cakes, extending it with a smile. I was hungry, so I shrugged and took one, but I watched her take a bite before eating mine.

The honey cakes were just as tasty as she'd promised. I still didn't fully believe what was happening. The letter from Grams helped a bit, but I still had questions.

"Why are you guys sleeping in tents down here? Can't you create a beautiful castle or something?" I asked.

"Our powers are only for protecting the planet, not conjuring magic or wizardry," Hades said, looking at me over the rim of his cup.

"I'm not buying it," I said. "Why can't you guys fix the planet? You have the power, and I don't." I sat back, pleased with my observation.

"We are stewards of the Earth, but, again, not magicians or wizards. We try to repair the destruction brought on by humans, but we don't have the power to clean up pollution or change the course of history. We can't force humans to do things," Hades said. "Each god and goddess rules in his or her domain. My brother Zeus rules the sky, Poseidon rules the ocean, and our sister Demeter is goddess of agriculture. But we need your help to change human behavior."

"Why me?" I asked.

"Your love of the mountains and your connection to water," Persephone said.

I put down my cup in horror. "That's sick," I said. "Water took my mom."

"Yes, but your connection is deep. You'll see," she said.

"Lots of people love water. And I don't even go swimming in rivers or lakes. Just swimming pools," I said. *A concrete pool with no flowing water*, I thought.

"Your grandmother, Helen, helped us in the past, and she passed that obligation on to you," Hades said.

"How did Grams help?" I asked.

"She worked to make Sinks Canyon a state park, which prevented developers from buying up the land for a ski resort or subdivisions," Persephone said.

I pictured the short ski hill we used for sledding in Sinks Canyon. It wasn't as magnificent as the Tetons in Jackson Hole or Grand Targhee Ski Resort on the back side of the Tetons, but it was a popular sledding hill. The ski lift hadn't been used for years.

"If Grams helped you, why didn't she tell me about it?" I asked.

Persephone nodded, and I knew I'd made a good point. "She was going to tell you this summer after your father left. We had to speed up our plans because an oil rig in the Gulf of Mexico is leaking," she said. "Plus, she had to have surgery on her hip and that held things up."

"Why can't Poseidon stop the leak?" I asked. Score one for me again. "He's the god of the ocean."

Hades sighed. "He's using his power to marshal the ocean currents and contain the plastic pollution. Have you heard of the Giant Pacific Garbage Patch?"

"Yes," I said slowly. "We just studied that this spring in biology." I recalled the article that described a huge area of plastic trash, twice the size of Texas, floating northeast of Hawaii.

"All of his energy is focused on using the ocean currents to contain the plastic in one area," Persephone said. "We'll see him on our quest."

At every turn, they had an answer. "But—" Before I phrased my next question, Hades interrupted me.

"We have an important gift for you," he said. He walked into his tent and returned, carrying a brown pouch. "You must stand, Diana. You're already protected," Hades said, placing his large hand on my shoulder. Warmth from his touch radiated through my shirt. "The elk teeth on your necklace are powerful. May I hold it?"

I pulled my elk tooth necklace from under my shirt. I wondered how he'd known about it. Willy had given it to me when I turned twelve.

"Always wear this," Willy'd said six years ago, holding the necklace in his weathered brown hand. Spaced one inch apart on a silver chain, two ivory elk teeth were strung between polished Tiger Eye stones, interspersed with silver beads.

"Both Eastern Shoshone and Crow people know the ivory teeth are powerful medicine. The elk is your animal, Diana," he said. "A very strong animal."

Recognizing it as a solemn moment, I'd remained still as Willy placed the necklace around my neck. "Keep it under your clothes," he said, his brown eyes looking into mine. "The kids at school might not understand. Promise you'll always wear it, because this necklace will protect you."

"I'll wear it, Willy," I promised, tucking it under my shirt. Warm against my skin, the elk tooth necklace made me feel safe, as if I were wrapped in a blanket on the couch while a snowstorm raged outside the windows of our ranch house.

I never questioned Willy's understanding of the world. His mother came from the Crow people in Montana, and his father was a member of the Eastern Shoshone Tribe on the Wind River Reservation, a few miles from our ranch. Both of his parents passed away before I was born.

Willy's wife, Sarah, died years ago, and his children were grown, but he stayed with us on the ranch, teaching me how to ride, track animals in the forest, and use a bow and arrow. He was a guide in our family outfitting business, taking hunters to places in the mountains where they could find elk and deer.

Now, at Hades' request, I removed the necklace and handed it to him. For a moment, both our hands were on the ivory elk teeth, and I found myself running on a bank next to a swift river. Looking down, I saw my feet encased in beaded moccasins, the flap of their leather on the path below thudding in my ears. I looked across the blue-green river to see a female elk keeping pace with me on the opposite bank. Or was I keeping pace with her? I laughed and ran faster, my braided hair flying behind my shoulders.

Then I was back in the cave, pulled to the present by Persephone's voice. "It's beautiful," she said.

What just happened? I looked up at Persephone and then at Hades. That was too bizarre to mention, I decided as Hades returned the necklace to me.

"That necklace will keep you safe," he said. "Now, here is our gift to you." He reached into the leather pouch and removed a silver flask, its sides covered with markings shaped like fish scales.

My hand tingled when I grasped the cool metal. The surface of the flask smoothed to a shimmering silver, and a tiny fish jumped from it into the air, like fish do in mountain rivers and lakes. I gasped and looked up at Hades. He seemed not to notice as he gazed at Persephone. *What's going on*, I wondered. *Was there something in that tea?*

"In the Greek language, the word for water is *Vεpo*," Hades said, as if nothing about the flask was unusual. "But you are named Diana, in the Roman way, so we will use the Latin terms. This is *Aqua Fortis*, which means strong water. Use it if one of you is hurt. Persephone is immortal, but, in the real world, she is not invincible." His eyes grew stern. "You are protected by your necklace."

Then Hades held up a different flask, which was golden and glowing. "This is *Aqua Vitae*, the water of life. Only I give this water." His black eyes burned with blue flame. "Come back here if Persephone is hurt. That is your job. Do you understand?" The blue flame in his determined eyes turned black again. "You're the conduit to our world. We can travel around the world, but we need you on this adventure."

Panic flooded my veins at the intensity of his gaze until Hades placed his hand on my shoulder, calming me.

"Feel the power of your necklace, Diana. It will make you strong. I also have an important gift from Artemis." He walked to his tent again and returned with a smooth brown bow and a silver quiver of arrows, which shimmered like mercury, reflecting the colors around it.

"Willy taught me how to use a bow and arrow," I said. Even though I didn't hunt animals, I used it for target practice on the ranch. By now, I was easily able to hit the center of a target. I wondered how Hades had known that.

"You'll be tested in battle," Hades said. "Artemis is your sponsor, and I give these to you on her behalf. She's in Africa now, working with rangers on the game preserve to protect elephants from poachers." He sighed. "We almost lost the battle for the buffalo, but some still roam freely in Yellowstone National Park and on the Bison Range in Montana. And, of course, you were with Willy on the reservation when they released a herd this spring."

In late May, the Eastern Shoshone Nation celebrated the return of buffalo descended from wild herds of the 1800s. I came home from college to go with Willy to the reservation for the ceremony, and I watched as tribal leaders released descendants of ancient buffalo herds to gallop across the pasture, returning to the reservation for the first time in over a hundred years.

"This is a great day for the Shoshone people," Willy had said.

As I cheered with the others, tears burned my eyes when the buffalo bolted from the corral to the freedom of the pasture, tails raised in joy. Two of the younger buffalo kicked up their heels before following the rest of the small herd.

"Look at the past," Hades said, gesturing with his palm up.

I turned as the cave wall glowed, revealing a vast herd of buffalo thundering across the prairie. The rumble of their passage created vibrations on the cave floor as dust filled the air.

The giant beasts surged over the grassland, disappearing into the distance. I remembered Willy telling me stories around the campfire about his ancestors stopping in their travels across the prairie to watch herds so large they were five miles long.

The cave wall lit up again, and the dust dissipated to reveal a blue sky filled with a flock of beautiful birds, the density of their numbers blocking the sun. They flew over a field where people bundled freshly cut wheat. Dropping their tools, men ran to a wagon and lifted long rifles, pointing them to the sky.

"No," I yelled as hundreds of birds fell to the ground while the men fired again and again, all at once. "Make them stop killing!"

"I can't control human behavior," Hades said. "The gods are stewards of Earth, not sorcerers."

The shooting stopped as the remaining birds disappeared on the horizon. I sighed in relief as the vivid scene once again became a cave wall. I didn't want to watch the farmers pick up the dead birds.

"We lost the passenger pigeon because humans hunted almost every bird," Hades said, turning to face me. "Artemis is the goddess of the moon, but she is truly the protector of all animals. The Greeks also called her the goddess of the hunt, but she now roams the forest and jungles to protect animals from humans. We can't let these magnificent animals go the way of the buffalo and the passenger pigeon."

Hades' eyes pierced mine, but I was strengthened, rather than frightened, by the intensity of his gaze.

"Her courage flows in your veins, Diana. Why else would you be given her name? Diana is the Roman name for Artemis." He gestured toward the deep, flowing cavern river. "Why do you think you confront the river every day? Why do you stand on the boulder, feeling the spray of the water that took your mother?"

"But I don't want this adventure," I said. "What can I do? I'm only eighteen. And I have lots to do this summer."

Hades placed his large hand on my shoulder. "You're stronger than you think," he said.

His energy ignited me, but warmth and compassion flowed from his touch. Suddenly, an image filled my head: I saw myself flying a chariot, alone, but not afraid, my face upturned to the sky, my shoulders thrown back in defiance.

"See?" Hades said. The vision faded and I was once again in the cave. "You have great strength and courage."

"I'm not fierce," I said, shaking my head.

"You will be when the time comes," Hades assured me.

Persephone stepped forward, putting a hand on my shoulder. "Let's go see the stables," she said. "You'll want to meet the horses."

After a last look into Hades' eyes, I followed Persephone to the stables, which were a short distance from the camp. Natural indentations in the cave wall formed a protective enclosure where the horses were happily eating hay. Without fear, I walked up to one of the beautiful black horses.

He raised his head and nickered softly, just as my horse, Daisy, did on the ranch. I stroked his powerful neck and he gently pushed against me with his muzzle.

"These animals are descended from warrior horses of long ago," Persephone said.

"Why don't we take them? I read that Hades has immortal horses," I said.

"His immortal horses are in the Underworld now, enjoying a much-needed rest. Besides, I want you to meet Eos, goddess of the dawn," Persephone said, picking up two brushes and handing me one.

This was a familiar task because I brushed Daisy every day at the ranch. I automatically began on the neck of the horse closest to me. Persephone moved to the other horse. The routine comforted me. I marveled at their strong wings and powerful shoulders.

"Tomorrow, we'll use Hades' chariot to travel to meet my mother, Demeter. She is on the banks of the Platte River in Nebraska. You'll like her. She grows the hay we're feeding the horses." Persephone paused in her brushing and looked at me. "We have only until the summer solstice to stop the oil rig leak in the Gulf of Mexico. After that, I am duty-bound to help my mother with the task of growing and harvesting crops. That gives us five days," she added in a serious tone.

I caressed the softest part of a horse, the sides of the muzzle right above the lips, impressed by the size of the beast. Surprisingly, the winged creature tolerated this, seeming to sense my need for comfort in this familiar routine. Engaging in this soothing ritual in the cave helped normalize this bizarre situation I faced. I still questioned whether Hades and Persephone were real. Was I really inside Sinks Cavern, or was this a dream?

The horse's soft nose certainly seemed real. As I rubbed my left hand over his muzzle, I automatically raised my right hand to his shoulder and

36

discovered an even softer part where the downy feathers on his wings joined his shoulders. As I gasped and looked up, the horse nodded his head and nickered softly, just like Daisy did when I stroked her neck. Hearing that friendly sound, I buried my head in his neck and inhaled his clean horse scent. I never experience smells and sounds like this in a dream, I knew, so I relaxed into the sensations of smooth horsehair and warmth.

The afternoon passed quickly as we groomed the horses and walked along the edge of the underground lake. I told myself I wasn't afraid of the deep water, but I didn't stand on the very edge of the ledge, either. Throughout the afternoon, I relaxed in Persephone's presence, enjoying the sound of her voice.

Hades cooked dinner that night, and after eating the delicious barley soup he made, we sat around the campfire, watching the flames, just as I did in the mountains with my dad and Willy.

"My mother gave us this barley. We used the last of the onions and potatoes we stored for the winter," Persephone said. "She works with people all over the nation to set up farmer's markets so people can buy locally sourced food. She's also trying to help save bees. Her hives on the Platte River produce this amazing honey. Isn't it good?"

I nodded and sipped my ginger tea, savoring the honey. After one more cup of tea, I began to yawn. At Persephone's suggestion, I returned to my tent to find a gossamer nightgown lying on the bed. I took off my new bamboo boots, appreciating the supple, but sturdy, material. Dressed for bed, I climbed under the soft white blanket. "I'll bet this is bamboo, too," I muttered to the empty tent.

Hades and Persephone talked near the campfire, their voices rising and falling in a comforting murmur. I thought about the world outside the cavern. I was relieved no one could ever buy the land bordering the family ranch because Sinks Canyon was a state park. Ours really couldn't be called a ranch by Wyoming standards. Kids at school lived on ranches that were thousands of acres in size, while our property was only nine hundred acres.

Our place was special because it was located at the mouth of the canyon. Our land began at the edge of the highway into town, which formed the border of our property. On the other side of the ranch stood Table Mountain, rising sharply up from the hay fields located between the river and the mountain.

Our alfalfa and smooth bromegrass fields were green and glorious, following the river and winding along the base of Table Mountain, so named for its broad, flat top. It was more a large hill than a steep mountain, but it offered protection from the wind during winter, and the irrigation water we pulled from the river helped make our hay fields productive.

When landowners across the highway sold out to developers, houses cropped up on five-acre lots. The hills across the highway were dry and covered in sagebrush. "Nothing but rattlesnakes up there," Willy always said. There were few rattlesnakes on our land next to the river.

My mom had grown up on this ranch, and I now slept in her childhood bedroom. My mom and dad met in college and moved back to Lander, buying a house there before I was born. Dad and I moved to the ranch after Mom died so Grams and Grandpa could help take care of me.

Grandpa, Willy, and I made a good team. Of course, Dad was always there, and Grams, too. Grandpa and Willy were true mountain men, happiest when on horseback in the Wind River Mountains above the canyon. I helped on the summer trips when they took tourists up into the mountains.

Then at the end of the summer, we harvested the fields on the ranch, selling some of the hay and keeping the rest to feed our string of riding and pack horses in the winter.

Grandpa'd had a heart attack and died two winters ago, when I was sixteen. That spring, as soon as the snow melted, we hiked to the top of the waterfall above the canyon with some of his ashes and cast them in the river, just as he'd wanted. We spread the rest on the ranch in the fields he loved.

When I was in fourth grade, Grandpa bought two horses at auction in the fall. One was a saddle horse named Bayside, and the other was a beautiful buckskin mare with a tan coat and black mane and tail. Even though she wasn't trained as a riding horse, Willy thought she'd make a good pack horse. I named her Buckskin.

Throughout the winter, her belly grew bigger and bigger.

"I'll be darned," Dad said in January. "That mare is going to have a foal. She must have been pregnant when we bought her."

In spring, in the pasture at night, without us knowing, Buckskin had a filly, a little female horse. By that time, Buckskin was part of our string of horses, and the other animals accepted her. She separated herself from the others after the filly was born, though, keeping near them, but grazing apart to protect her baby. She bared her teeth and put her ears back when the others came near. I watched from a distance as the tiny filly nursed, shoving her nose into Buckskin's underbelly and latching on to drink. The little one was tan with a fluffy white mane and tail.

"She's going to be a palomino," Willy said.

In late April, when the filly was two weeks old, Dad turned to me at breakfast on Saturday morning. "Diana, we have something important to tell you," he said, a smile on his face.

"What?" I asked. "Did something happen?"

"We're giving you Buckskin's filly. She'll be your horse from now on," he said.

"Mine? She'll be just mine?" I asked. We all had favorite riding horses, but nobody owned a specific horse.

"Just your horse," Dad said.

"You'll have to train her to be a good saddle horse," Grams said. "Willy can help you with that."

"Oh, Dad, thank you!" I jumped up and ran to him, throwing my arms around his neck. "I'll take really good care of her!"

"You can't ride her until she's three years old, but you can work with her and teach her to accept a halter and lead rope before then," Dad said.

"Can I go see her now?" I asked.

"Take this with you," Grams said, wrapping a muffin in a napkin.

I grabbed the muffin and bolted from the kitchen after snatching my coat from the hooks near the patio door. I ran to the pasture, slipping through the rails in the gate. I slowed to a walk so I wouldn't scare the horses, taking huge bites of the muffin until it was gone.

I approached the horses, who grazed on the early spring grass poking up through the ground in the pasture. Raising their heads with ears perked forward, they looked up at me with interest. Buckskin was used to me by now. She looked over and resumed grazing as I walked up to the filly.

"You're mine," I said softly. I'd been petting her for several days now, so she turned curiously and sniffed my extended hand.

After that, I spent hours with her, running to the pasture every day after school. White whiskers jutted from her tiny chin, which was no bigger than my fist. Gleaming in the sun, they danced when she rubbed her lips over my palm. She was curious about everything, my hair, my hood, my jacket, my boots, and my neck. Her nostrils were big and the hairs dotting her upper lip were always in motion as she explored the world with her nose and lips, imprinting the smells of the world in her brain.

I loved her with a fierceness I could not define, stroking every inch of her body with my hands. Her high-pitched whinny made me smile.

I agonized for days over what to name her, coming up with names and trying them out on Willy. "What do you think of Sunset?" I asked.

"She's your horse," he said. "You have to decide."

"What about Goldie? Because she's a palomino, her coat will turn golden even though she's tan now," I said one Saturday.

"You decide," he replied.

I discovered the perfect name the next morning as I walked through the pasture toward my little filly. As I came closer, she moved toward me with a high-pitched whinny, her head bobbing as she walked. The early sunlight gleamed on her coat, and her white mane and tail seemed translucent in the rays.

"Daisy," I said as she nuzzled my shoulder, nibbling on my coat, "You're as perfect as a summer flower." I hugged her fiercely, but she protested by pulling back and snorting. I laughed when she moved closer again, sniffing my boots. "Your name is Daisy."

By the time I was in high school, she was sixteen hands high, and her coat was a deep golden color with darker spots dotting her backside. In the morning sun, her white mane and tail flowed gracefully when she walked. With Willy's help, I trained her to be a perfect riding horse who responded to the commands I issued through the reins and with my heels. She looked glorious in the finely tooled saddle Dad gave me that Christmas.

There would be no pack trip this summer.

I heard Persephone laugh softly and the horses nickered. The world above the cavern seemed far away, and I was relieved to be safe and warm inside the tent. I thought back to this morning when Dad left for his new job in the oil fields.

"Selling hay doesn't make much money, and we don't have as many hunters coming here since your grandpa died," he'd said early that morning while I perched on a chair in his room, watching him pack. He stopped filling his duffle bag and sat on his bed. "I have to work in the oil fields to make money for us to live here on the ranch. We can take pack trips with tourists next summer."

"I don't want you to go," I said. I knew he had to work, but it was hard to imagine him leaving. I wanted everything to be just like it was before I left for college, but now nothing was the same.

"I don't want to leave, honey." Dad said. "But I can't pass this up. There aren't any places to rent, but Jim said I can live in his trailer. I'll make enough money to last us all winter."

Dad's friend Jim worked in the Bakken Oil Fields in North Dakota. It seemed like everyone was going up there to make money off the discovery of oil near the Montana border with North Dakota. It was dangerous work, and I was mad that Dad had to go. So this morning, I'd kissed him goodbye, refusing to cry when he left, then I grabbed my bike and headed up Sinks Canyon.

Now I was here in this tent, and I could tell from the silence outside that Persephone and Hades had fallen asleep.

Tomorrow, Persephone planned to take me to see Demeter, her mother. I wondered what she'd be like. I realized I wanted to fly in that chariot again.

A soft whinny told me the horses were going to sleep, and, as I dozed off, I decided I had nothing to lose by leaving tomorrow. With Dad gone for the summer, there wouldn't be any pack trips into the mountains. Willy would take care of Grams. We'd be back in five days and life would return to normal.

I also had to admit I really did want to see if those immortal horses existed. I already knew the power of winged horses, and immortal winged horses must be even more amazing.

I'll just leave if I don't like it, I told myself before falling asleep.

***

When I woke in the morning, I put on my new boots, determined to try this adventure. After looping the strap on the leather pouch containing the silver flask of *Aqua Fortis* over my neck and across my chest, I stepped out of the tent to find Persephone and Hades eating at the campfire.

"I'll go," I said. "I don't have anything better to do right now." I shrugged to show it was no big deal, but inside, my heart fluttered at the thought of a quest.

This time, the honey cakes had a delicious nutty taste, and the tea tasted like mint. After we ate, Persephone moved to the chariot and lifted the lid of the seat, stashing my new bow and arrows inside.

"There," she said, squeezing my shoulder. "You're ready to travel."

"You're sure my grandmother knows about this?" I asked while Hades hitched the winged horses to his ebony chariot.

"Definitely," Persephone said. "Climb on board."

I stepped in and turned to look at Hades. "Thank you for the gifts," I said, realizing I'd forgotten to say it the night before.

"You will prove yourself worthy," Hades said as he smiled and patted the nearest black horse on the neck. "You and Persephone will become a team." He stepped back as Persephone flicked the reins and made a clicking sound to the horses.

They trotted briskly on the rocky ledge and moved into the air, easily rising in the spray next to the falls. "Goodbye, Hades," Persephone called.

We flew to the high ceiling above the falls and the limestone walls opened with a rumble, followed by fresh air and sunlight. With a joyful whinny, the horses flew out of the cave.

CHAPTER FIVE
DEMETER ON THE PLATTE RIVER

A cloudless blue sky and bright morning sun greeted us as we flew up and away from the limestone cliffs outside Sinks Canyon Cave. The horses gained speed, pulling the chariot higher, while Persephone sang a clear, echoing song. From the canyon below, a flock of Western Meadowlarks flew up and around the chariot, chirping excitedly. The flapping of their wings filled the air. So close that I could see their eyes, many of the yellow-breasted birds turned to look curiously at me. Settling below the chariot, they formed a dense group. A line of birds remained on either side, flying swiftly to keep up with the horses.

Persephone laughed. "The meadowlarks will provide cover. If anyone looks up, all they'll see is a flock of birds."

At first, the horses flew close together while each spread only his outside wing. They leaned into each other, almost flying as one creature. After rising above the rim of the canyon, they moved apart and fully expanded their wings, a magnificent sight from where I sat in the back part of the chariot. My dad would call this a smooth ride, like the Cadillacs ranchers drove into town.

The birds on the right side of the chariot shifted, making room for one small Mountain Bluebird that flew next to the chariot, flapping its wings steadily to keep up with the larger meadowlarks. The bluebird turned to look at me, and I swear it deliberately made eye contact. Facing the front again, it kept pace with the chariot.

Persephone looked back and laughed. "She's determined to stay with us!"

I looked closer, realizing Persephone was right. It was a female. Rather than being an all-blue male, this lovely lady had a grey head and body with bright blue wingtips and a vivid blue tail. She glanced at me again, chirping once before facing the front as she managed to keep up with the horses and meadowlarks.

"How do we get to the Platte River?" I asked, looking down as the flock separated, providing a glimpse of our ranch before we flew over Lander Valley.

"The horses will follow the path of the river," Persephone said as she banked the chariot to the southeast.

"We're not following the Popo Agie?"

"No. We'll fly over the Sweetwater River until it joins the Platte, and we'll follow that into Nebraska. We'll explore the Yellowstone River later today after we pick up my mother's horses. Then we'll send these two back to Hades. We need her lighter chariot."

I smoothed my hand over the soft seat of the chariot. It *was* large, and although the horses seemed to carry it with little effort, I could see how something smaller would be easier to navigate.

Leaning back, I enjoyed the sensation of flying smoothly through the air. *I'll stay with Persephone until we meet her mom. Then I'll decide what to do.*

"As I said, we'll follow the Sweetwater River for a while. After that, we will cut across Wyoming to Nebraska," Persephone said.

The Sweetwater was about sixty miles southeast of Lander. Last winter when I was home on break from college, Dad took me cross country skiing by moonlight on the Sweetwater. We left the ranch on the night of a full moon as it rose on the horizon, driving for an hour on a lonely highway and parking the truck on the banks of the river. Snow-covered and frozen, the meandering river was breathtaking by the light of the moon. The only sound was our soft conversation and the swish of our skis on the fresh snow. By the time we turned around and followed our tracks back to where we parked the truck, my toes were numb. I'd loved passing the snow-covered bushes and trees lining the banks of the river, feeling unafraid on the frozen water.

My dad told me about the first time he'd come there with my mother to ski by moonlight, connecting me to Mom through the river. "Your mother loved the Sweetwater. We came here a lot before you were born. Do you know what else she loved?" he asked in a teasing tone.

We'd engaged in this childhood game often when I was younger. "What?" I said, playing along, even though I knew the answer.

"You," he replied, rubbing my head with his hand before starting the truck.

A grey bird landed in the chariot, pulling me back to the present. On the seat next to me sat the little Mountain Bluebird, fluffing her feathers as if landing in a chariot next to a human was a perfectly normal thing to do. We had occasional bluebird sightings on the ranch, but I'd never been this close to one before. I reached out my hand, expecting her to fly away. Instead, she looked up at me.

I laughed and looked up at Persephone. "We have a new friend," I said.

"She's our self-appointed guardian," Persephone said.

The little bird chirped again and moved to the side of the chariot, settling down in the corner and closing her eyes, apparently ready for a nap.

The large black chariot moved smoothly through the air, and I grew brave enough to slide to the opposite edge—and grip the side—before looking down.

"Did you know the Eastern Shoshone people used to follow the path of the Sweetwater River? Willy told me that," I said.

Persephone looked back and smiled, nodding to indicate she wanted to hear more.

"Then the French fur traders came to hunt in this area. Finally, the white man came and took over the land," I said, looking to see the snaking and curving river through spaces between the birds as they briefly separated below the chariot. "Now white ranchers own this land. It makes me sad to think Willy's people lost their ancestral lands and had to live on the reservation."

"Many things have changed over time," Persephone said. "Theirs is a sad history."

I watched Persephone, recalling the story of this beautiful young goddess. Of course, I knew every story about the gods and goddesses by heart. Persephone was the daughter of Demeter, goddess of the harvest. One day, Hades, god of the Underworld, kidnapped Persephone and took her to his underground kingdom. Demeter searched high and low for her daughter, and eventually, the birds told her what happened. Demeter's grief became so intense that she no longer cared about tending the plants growing on Earth. As trees, flowers, and fields of grain died, Zeus granted Persephone the right to return above ground and live with her mother once again.

However, because she'd eaten one pomegranate seed while in the Underworld, Zeus ruled that Persephone must spend four months out of the year there with Hades. This myth helped the Greeks explain the seasons and the cycle of growing things. While Persephone was in the Underworld, Demeter declared, nothing would grow. When her daughter returned above ground each spring, flowers bloomed, leaves unfurled from tender buds, and the Earth flourished.

Persephone controlled the huge stallions with ease. As I studied the firm shape of her chin and the youthful profile of her face, I wondered how this vibrant young woman managed to survive in the darkness of the Underworld for part each year.

As if reading my mind, Persephone turned her green eyes on me. "The Greeks had it wrong," she said. "They liked to embellish stories. I'd known Hades all my life, but when I grew older, I fell in love with him. He didn't kidnap me. I went willingly into the Underworld when he asked me to be his queen, even though it deeply saddened my mother. I still come above ground every year and remain until September when the snow flies in your Wind River Mountains."

She gestured to indicate I should stand in the front of the chariot. I looked over to see our little bluebird safely sleeping, and then joined

Persephone. When I reached her side, she continued talking. "I live in two worlds, above and below Earth."

"Will you have kids someday?" I asked, remembering the deep bond I witnessed between Hades and Persephone.

Persephone frowned at me. "How could I leave for six months to help my mom with planting? And if I give birth above ground? A child born in sunlight should not be taken to live in the Underworld."

"Couldn't you change that?" I asked. "Your child would be part of you. Couldn't he or she travel in both worlds like you do? Maybe Hades could take care of the baby when you're gone until the child was old enough to go along and help with planting. Wouldn't that work?"

"I've been stuck in old patterns," Persephone said. "You could be right." She nodded and returned her gaze to the horses.

We flew without talking for a while. "Where are we now?" I asked.

"We're flying over the North Platte River. But we're still over Wyoming, just north of Denver right now."

"Okay," I said. "My cousin Melissa grew up in Denver. She goes to design school in Chicago." My thoughts turned to Melissa.

My mom's sister, Joan, grew up on the ranch, but never moved back after she finished college. Instead, she moved to Denver where she met and married her husband, Dan. They traveled here every summer, and for years I loved it because they brought their daughter, Melissa, who was two years ahead of me in school.

Once Melissa hit eighth grade, though, our summer fun changed. As kids, we'd roamed the ranch, rode horses, had picnics on the deck in back of the house, collected eggs from the chickens in the barn, rode horses some more, and biked up Sinks Canyon. But I could tell she was different the minute she stepped out of the Cadillac SUV when they came for a visit the summer after her eighth grade year.

Instead of the normal summer shorts, tank top, and tennis shoes, she'd worn capris, sandals, and a white lacy top. Who wore white to play outside? Her hair was carefully collected in a long ponytail, and, as I walked off the porch to greet them, I could see she wore eye shadow and lipstick. Lipstick on the ranch? I knew things weren't looking good for our normal summer activities.

And I'd been right. Instead of hanging around outside, she wanted to sit in the house and listen to music while painting her toenails. Her entire personality seemed different. She'd loved Grams, the ranch, and the outdoors. She still loved Grams, but looked around our house with a lift of her chin and a disdainful sniff.

"This place is so old," Melissa said when Grams and Aunt Joan were in the other room. "Why don't you buy some new furniture?"

I looked around the living room with its large picture window, western landscapes hanging on the walls, and leather sofa and chairs in front of the rock fireplace built by our great-grandparents. I loved this room in every season. In cold winters when the wind howled outside and the smell of the fireplace scented the inside, in spring when we opened the windows again, and in fall when the cottonwoods in the back yard turned from green to gold, framed by the picture window.

"I guess it is kind of worn," I said, noticing that for the first time. "But it's still good."

Melissa sniffed again. "This place stinks like that old ranch hand. I can't believe you let him eat with you."

I looked at her in shock. Willy'd worked here for so long that he was part of our family. He didn't stink. He smelled like horses, leather, and the barn. Those were good smells. He slept in the bunkhouse that Grandpa'd built between the house and the barn. It was newer than our log home.

When we walked into my bedroom, I noticed for the first time that the quilt on my bed was faded and worn thin in some places. Grams had made it for me and I kept it on my bed year round, folding it back on hot summer nights.

Melissa moved to the nightstand and picked up the photo of my mom. "You look like your mom," she said. "It's funny how you and your mom have dark hair and my mom and I are blonde. You could be really pretty if we put some makeup on you."

I wasn't sure she realized she'd just handed me an insult. I was too surprised to reply.

Melissa rubbed the top of my dresser with her fingertips and stroked the post on my bed with her hand. "This is a beautiful antique bedroom set. Keep the furniture and get new bedding," she said. "I'm going to be an interior decorator. I'm going to design school in Chicago when I finish high school." She smiled at her image in the mirror on my vanity.

That was news. Growing up, we'd planned how we'd live on the ranch together and become forest rangers so we could always be in Sinks Canyon.

Melissa was never the same. Throughout high school, our visits became strained as there seemed to be less and less to entertain her on the ranch. To her credit, she wasn't as critical of Willy and our house as we grew older, but last summer, Melissa and Aunt Joan didn't even drive up from Denver to visit.

"Your cousin Melissa?" Persephone said, bringing me out of my thoughts.

"Yes. Last year, I visited them one weekend. The University of Wyoming is only two hours north of Denver, so Aunt Joan insisted I go there when I was at school," I said, remembering that Melissa'd come back to Denver that same weekend, but she didn't talk about the ranch. She did ask about Willy and Grams, but was more excited about school in Chicago.

In the silence that followed, I admired the strong backs of the black stallions and the glint of the sun on their wings. "Why didn't Hades come with us?" I asked.

"He faces his own challenges," Persephone said grimly. "Humans use fracking to remove the oil from the crevices in the Earth. He's trying to protect the aquifers from that."

I remembered Grams telling me about fracking, and the way the oil companies pumped water and toxic chemicals into crevices in the Earth to force out oil and natural gas. Now Dad worked in a fracking oil field in North Dakota.

"You are our conduit to the present day," Persephone said. "That word comes from the Latin word *conducere*, which means bring together. The Medieval Latin term was *conductis*. That's you, Diana. You are the channel for the transmission of our efforts to save the planet."

"Why me?" I asked, shaking my head.

"Your love of animals and love for Wyoming is strong. Wyoming is the source of four major river systems, and you love the mountains where the rivers begin," Persephone said. "Artemis is strong within you. She protects the animals and wild places, just as you will do."

I thought of the many small creatures I'd rescued as a child, and the countless times Grams and Willy had patiently taught me how to care for them, allowing me to keep them in the barn. Once they healed, Willy went with me to take the animals up the canyon and into the forest to release them.

"There have been other conduits throughout time," Persephone said. "You know about Rachel Carson, right?"

I'd learned about her in science class in high school. Rachel Carson wrote *Silent Spring*, exposing the dangers of DDT and other toxic chemicals.

"Rachel worked with my mother to stop the spread of terrible chemicals that were killing insects and birds. John Muir was another conduit. He came from Wisconsin and spent decades in the Sierra Nevada Mountains. He was responsible for the creation of Sequoia and Yosemite National Parks in California."

I nodded, recognizing his name.

"Your grandmother saved Sinks Canyon by helping to make it a state park. She is also a conduit."

Suddenly, the meadowlarks accompanying us chattered excitedly. The ones in front flew to the right and left, while more meadowlarks came in from behind, providing protective cover.

"We just entered Nebraska air space," Persephone said. "Whenever we fly over a state line, that state's birds insist on providing cover. Both Wyoming and Nebraska claim Western Meadowlarks as the state bird, and the Nebraska birds want to take their turn now. That's what all the chirping is about."

I turned to look back and met the eyes of the bluebird sitting in the chariot. She sang out a greeting, clearly taking her duties seriously now that she was awake. I smiled and sat beside her, enjoying the novelty of sitting next to a bird in a flying chariot.

"Hold on for the landing," Persephone said some time later, and I scooted to the edge of the seat, looking at the view. My heart raced as the meadowlarks departed while we flew over the Platte River.

"We're going to land on that island."

Gripping the edge of the chariot, I voiced my fear. "It's too small. We'll never make it," I shouted.

The horses flew lower, and, to my surprise, the island was large enough for us to land. It was just like landing in an airplane, except smoother and without the terrible roar of engines. We slowed with a gentle forward motion as the horses carried the chariot down, its wheels landing softly on the island. The horses trotted up to a statuesque figure waiting at the edge of a small grove of aspens.

Persephone leapt from the chariot and ran into her mother's open arms. The bluebird flew over our head toward the trees.

"My beautiful daughter," Demeter said, releasing Persephone from her embrace and placing her palms on the younger woman's cheeks. She smiled and then turned to face me, keeping one arm around Persephone's waist.

"We've been waiting for you," Demeter said. "The Earth is out of balance, and you will help restore it." In a welcoming gesture, she extended her hand, palm up.

I stepped forward, overcome with emotion as I looked into Demeter's brown eyes. Suddenly, I longed for my mother and tears choked my throat, just as they did every time I stood on the boulder and faced the surging water of the Popo Agie River where it roared into Sinks Cavern.

Demeter took my hand, drawing me into a firm embrace, and the smell of freshly cut hay from the fields of our ranch filled my nostrils. Warm sunshine caressed my shoulders as she held me close, and then the tears I held back were replaced by a joy so powerful that I began to laugh.

"Welcome to Nebraska," Demeter said, gently pushing me back, but keeping her strong hands on my shoulders.

Her skin was the color of acorns, and golden braids wound about her head, circled by a delicate green crown dotted with yellow daisies. I looked into her eyes, and a warm, velvety feeling flooded through me, as if I were cocooned in a fleece blanket. Demeter's eyes pierced my soul, but I felt no fear, only warmth and a surge of strength that made me feel invincible and safe at the same time. Deep brown, her eyes were like rich soil. They reminded me of my grandmother's eyes.

"I often visited your grandmother on the ranch," Demeter said with a smile. "She worked with us for years to keep the ranch free from developers who wanted to build houses there."

"Why didn't I ever see you?" I asked.

"I came when you were in the mountains on summer pack trips. That's why you didn't know I was there. But I made sure your hay was green and sweet-tasting for the horses," she said with a wink.

I realized I hadn't even thought of Daisy since we'd brushed Hades' horses yesterday. I didn't feel the urge to run away from Demeter, either. *I can still leave whenever I want to*, I reassured myself.

"Willy is taking care of your horses," Demeter said. "He knows you're with us, just as your grandmother does. You don't have to worry. You are safe here, and your grandmother will be waiting when you return home." She gestured as two horses approached. "Here is what you came for."

"They're like Quarter Horses," Persephone said. "Their names are Glenda and Golden. They're sisters."

I recognized the Quarter Horse traits the instant the mares came forward with their inquisitive eyes and strong hindquarters and legs above delicate ankles. Where Hades' horses were magnificent and powerful, like Andalusians, these horses were strong and calm, with the sleek golden coats of a palomino, just like Daisy. Long white manes curled and swayed against their necks as they walked. They nickered a greeting while moving toward me. Then I spotted their wings, gracefully folded against their sides, reminding me these horses could also fly. From their flowing white manes and tails to the deep golden color of their bodies, they were a perfectly matched pair. With nostrils flaring, they gave a quick whinny as they neared Hades' stallions. Even though the mares were smaller, I could see they would be strong and swift in flight.

The larger black horses bowed gracefully, dropping their heads and leaning down on their knees. At first, I thought they were bowing to Golden and Glenda, but then realized they were showing respect to Demeter, who had moved closer. Hades' horses remained kneeling, heads lowered. The sight of such humility from the giant black stallions brought sharp tears to my eyes.

"Rise, my beauties," Demeter said, rubbing their foreheads.

"Poseidon created horses for my mother," Persephone whispered in my ear.

I knew the story of Poseidon and Demeter. Poseidon was so in love with Demeter that he created horses to impress her. Even though Demeter refused to become Poseidon's queen, she loved his gift. Horses always bowed with respect and came to Demeter whenever she called them.

"I grow special grass for the mares on the banks of the Platte River," Demeter said, continuing to stroke Hades' horses. "It's nourished by moonlight and water from the Platte, and also the Ogallala Aquifer, which lies deep underneath where we now stand. It's a source of *Aqua Pura*, Latin for pure water. You learned that from Hades. But marsh hay from Wisconsin is also good in a pinch."

"These aren't immortal horses," Persephone said, patting the golden neck of one mare. "We'll fly across the ocean and ask Eos, goddess of the dawn, for permission to use her horses. They're immortal and can withstand the dangers of our journey."

As I wondered what color the immortal horses of Eos would be, Persephone supplied the answer.

"Sorrels and bays are her favorites, but she has horses in every color," Persephone said. "Eos's father is Hyperion and her mother is Theia. Eos is goddess of the dawn, sister of Helios, the Sun, and Selene, the Moon. Every morning, she rises from Oceanus, the river that circles the world, source of all aquifers, rivers, lakes, and streams. Her Roman name is Aurora, or Dawn-bringer."

"Will she let us borrow her horses?" I asked.

"Their names are Lampos and Phaethon, and they're her most treasured animals," Demeter said. "You'll convince her."

"Why me?" I asked.

"We need the help of humans," Demeter said. "Your grandmother helped make Sinks Canyon a state park, and you must carry on her legacy. This is what you must save," she said, sweeping her hand toward the sky. A shimmering screen appeared on the front of puffy white clouds hovering just above the ground. "Behold the wonder of the Platte River!"

The silver screen came alive with magnificent long-necked birds in flight, filling the sky with the sound of their wings and calls to each other. Tens of thousands of them landed on a sandbar in the river, calling with forceful beauty compounded by their immense numbers. I recognized Sandhill Cranes as they landed and gracefully stood, their elegant necks outlined by the setting sun. The image shimmered and disappeared, leaving an ache in my chest.

"This place provided sanctuary during their migration for thousands of years," Demeter said. "The Sweetwater in Wyoming flows into the Platte, and we must protect that water. Underneath the Great Plains lies the Ogallala Aquifer. Every day, humans pump great volumes of water up to the surface to grow corn and soybeans. Because they feed corn to millions of cattle to supply fast food restaurants with beef, the aquifer is diminished. One day, this will dry up if humans don't stop." She ended her tirade with a sigh. "We have work to do. Come, let me show you your chariot."

The mares moved aside to reveal an elegant brown chariot. "It's made of bamboo," Demeter said when I gasped at its beauty. "It's extremely light and strong. Bamboo must become the new plastic. Even now, Poseidon is trying to contain an island of plastic in the Pacific. People must stop using single-use plastic. Bamboo can do everything plastic does, and more. It's easily grown and biodegradable. Did you know plastic straws are floating in the ocean? Look what that causes."

She gestured to the sky and the shimmering screen cloud hovered again. This time, a wall of blue-green water appeared, and a sea turtle swam toward us. As it drew closer, I saw the terrible plight it was facing. A straw protruded from its nose; the turtle turned left and right, unable to pull out the straw with its claws. Demeter waved her arm and the scene disappeared.

Her voice rose as she continued to talk. "All those plastic bags people pick up at the grocery store are polluting the ocean. Several states have banned those things. We have to get rid of them everywhere." She looked sternly at me and I suddenly felt it was my job to do so. "Those plastic rings companies put on soda cans are also affecting the ocean. But I'm working with a brewery in Florida that makes biodegradable six-pack holders for cans. They dissolve in the ocean and can be eaten by fish as food. Now we just have to get companies to use them." She paused and stared at me again. "Let's have some lunch and then you can be on your way. We'll feed the horses first."

I helped Persephone unhitch the chariot and we led the horses to a grassy area near the grove of trees.

"They can eat while we do," Demeter said.

Persephone and I followed her into the grove of trees. I was amazed by this island in the middle of the river. I knew the Platte River was wide and meandering, with constantly shifting sandbars, but I hadn't realized it had islands.

"This is my home base in spring and summer," Demeter said as we moved into the trees. We walked along a narrow trail to a small clearing, where a picnic table and lunch waited.

Maybe I could trust Demeter. The sun on my face felt normal. Bees buzzed around while we ate.

"Don't worry, they're harmless," said Persephone. "My mother keeps beehives on the other side of the river. She harvests the honey and sells it at farmers markets in Omaha. She's helping people around the country set up beehives."

"Giant chemical companies create pesticides containing nicotinoids. In an effort to grow crops and make money, the farmers buy the chemicals to kill insects," Demeter said, pausing to watch a bee landing next to her plate. "We have to convince farmers not to use these chemicals because they kill beneficial insects, like bees. However, the people who run the companies care more about money than our planet." She reached out with one finger to gently touch the bee.

Just then a bluebird landed on the table next to my plate. "That's the bird that flew with us from Sinks Canyon," I said. She looked at me and peeped, then hopped along the table and perched on Demeter's hand.

Demeter caressed the little bluebird, who seemed to puff up in pride at the attention. "This is Indigo," Demeter said. The bluebird looked at me.

"How do you know her name?" I asked.

"I understand birdspeak," Demeter said. "The gods and goddesses understand the language of all creatures." Demeter continued to stroke the bluebird's head and then gently drew her finger across the bird's back. She held out her hand toward me. "Here. She wants to perch on your finger."

Hesitantly, I extended my left arm and the little bird quickly jumped from Demeter's hand to mine. Her feet gripped my fingers tightly and she turned to look at me, her black eyes peering into mine as she chirped excitedly.

"She's telling you her story," Demeter said. "I'll translate for you. She was chosen by Artemis to accompany you on this quest. She was born in a meadow above Sinks Canyon and left her mother and the flock just to be with you on this journey." The little bird continued to chirp while Demeter talked. "She'll be with you the entire time. She wants you to know that her name is Indigo, and that it means blue."

"Okay," I said. I was still processing the idea of birdspeak. I'd held baby chickens before, but never a bluebird. Her little feet dug into my skin, tickling more than hurting. "Why do I need a bluebird on this quest? What can she do? She's so small."

"Don't underestimate the power of blue," Demeter said. "Artemis has a reason for making her your companion. You'll see."

"Now she's asking for some food because she doesn't want to eat the bees," Persephone said and then laughed. "She doesn't want to make Demeter angry."

"I'll give her some of mine," I said, placing a small part of my honey cake on the table next to my plate. "Here you go, Indigo."

She jumped off my hand, eagerly pecking at the crumbs on the table. Soon they were gone, and she looked up at me.

"She wants more," Demeter said and chuckled. "She hasn't eaten since you left Sinks Canyon."

"Right," I said, reaching for another honey cake and breaking off a portion to sprinkle on the table. "Birdspeak?"

I didn't realize I said the word out loud until Demeter laughed. "Yes, birdspeak," she said. "Maybe someday Artemis will teach you how to understand birds."

"I don't know about that," I said. We watched Indigo pecking at the honey cake. The soft buzzing of bees filled the pleasant silence until Persephone resumed our conversation.

"Did you know beehives are being set up in cities across the nation?" she asked. "Beekeepers are cropping up all over in places like New York and Boston. They use the rooftops of buildings for the hives and bees fly all over the city, pollinating and gathering nectar for making honey. Then beekeepers sell the honey to restaurants and at farmers markets."

I swallowed the last bite of the honey cake I'd shared with Indigo, thinking that each time we ate, the cakes had a different taste. This morning, they'd been chewy like English muffins, but these lunch cakes were crisp and flaky, with the taste of oatmeal.

Demeter stood from her side of the table and moved next to me. "I have a gift for you," she said, reaching into the pocket of her dress to pull out a bronze flask. "My brother Hephaestus, the smith god, made this for you. Although he makes lightning bolts for Zeus, his real talent lies with metals. He's an excellent craftsman."

She extended her arms, resting the flask on the palms of both hands. I instinctively reached for it.

"Don't touch it yet," Demeter said. "Just look."

I focused on the flask. Made of bronze, the back was pounded to look like fish scales, but the front was smooth. In the center was a drawing of a female elk grazing in a meadow framed by the forest. The detail was extraordinarily precise, down to the blades of grass dangling from the side of her mouth.

"Here," Demeter said, interrupting my perusal of the flask by extending it to me. "This is my gift to you."

"Thank you," I said, looking into her eyes before I looked down at the flask in my hand.

I focused on the grazing elk and squealed in surprise when she looked up at me, calmly chewing the grass hanging from her mouth. "This is crazy," I said, holding it out to Demeter. "This thing moved! She's scary."

"She's yours," Demeter said and then laughed as I raised my eyebrows and opened my mouth to gulp in air. "She's magical and was made for you."

Raising the flask to eye level, I forced myself to look. The elk had lowered her head again, but as soon as I set eyes on her, she shifted her foot, lifted her head, and chewed on the grass. Nodding, she pawed the ground with her delicate right front hoof. I swear we established eye contact.

"When you and Persephone reach the source of the Yellowstone River in the Absaroka Mountains of Wyoming, use this for gathering pure water from the top of Younts Peak. *Aqua Pura* will give you strength on your journey," Demeter said.

Dragging my eyes away from the flask, I looked at her. "Thank you," I said. "This gift is truly mesmerizing. The elk looked at me!"

"Hephaestus made sure she would recognize you. She remains still for all others who hold the flask," Demeter said.

"How did he do that?" I asked.

"He added a lock of your hair when he melted the metal to form the flask," she said.

"My hair? How did he get my hair?" I leaned back in shock.

"When you were a baby, your grandmother gave me the hair," she said.

"That's cringy," I said.

"Your grandmother knew we were making gifts for you, so she gave me a tiny lock of your hair. When Hephaestus melted it with the bronze, the flask gained the power to recognize you. It's magical, not creepy," she said.

"I guess so," I said. If Grams knew about this, it must be okay, I decided.

"Let's go load up the chariot," Persephone said, rising. She picked up the lunch dishes and placed them in a basket at the end of the table. "Do you know what these are made of?" She smiled at me.

"Bamboo," I said confidently.

"You've got it right," Persephone said, and we laughed together.

"You two," Demeter said, closing the basket. "You'll thank me when plastic no longer pollutes the ocean." She softened her words with a smile.

Indigo flew along as we followed the trail through the trees.

"Here's where we'll keep our gear," Persephone said when we stood next to the chariot. Climbing in, she lifted the padded seat to reveal a storage area with clever compartments.

It reminded me of the window seat Grandpa'd built as a reading nook in my bedroom when I was in fourth grade. It also had a padded bench that opened to reveal compartments where I stored my favorite books. I'd spent hours there, mesmerized by my books on Greek mythology. Thinking about Grams, Dad, and Willy, I looked back at the trail winding through the aspen grove.

Dappled sunlight filtered through the leaves on the trees. Years ago, Willy'd told me that aspens grew in groves for a reason. "The trees extend their roots to help each other," he'd said. "They provide help when trees are sick. You'll never find just one aspen growing because they depend on each other like families do. They send out roots to start new shoots that grow into trees."

Looking at the sunlight on the leaves, I realized I missed my family, almost as much as I did when I'd first gone to college last fall. I was like an aspen removed from the grove, uprooted and alone. Could I make it without Dad and Grams? I longed to hear Willy's calm voice and feel the touch of his weathered skin. The elk tooth necklace under my shirt grew warm, a comforting reminder of him. "This necklace will protect you," his voice echoed in my head. A bright chirp got my attention, and I looked over to see Indigo perched on the branch of a nearby aspen. She flew off the branch and circled my head, encouraging me to move on.

Persephone stepped out of the chariot. "Are you ready to load up?"

"Yes," I said. Her warm smile invited me to move closer.

"Indigo and I will be with you on this journey," Persephone said, seeming to sense my hesitation.

"Did you know aspens live in groves so they can help each other survive?" I asked.

"We're all like aspens," she said, placing her hand on my shoulder. "Willy and Grams will be there when you return to the ranch. But Indigo and I are here for you now." She turned to help her mother.

I looked back at the grove and sighed. Maybe I could draw strength from a bluebird and a goddess with green eyes. I did want to see those immortal horses.

"I have something else," Demeter said. She reached into the chariot and pulled out a coiled rope. "This is made of bamboo and spider webs."

"Spider webs? How did you collect enough of those?" I said.

"I talked five hundred of them into creating enough silk for this rope instead of making webs. It's hard to get spiders to work together because they want to bite each other's heads off at lunch, but I bribed them with flies," Demeter said as she handed me the white coiled rope.

It was a soft creamy color, like the inside of trees, and smooth to the touch, the bamboo and spider silk fibers woven into a diamondback snakeskin style.

"It's strong as steel," Demeter said.

I tugged on the rope, pulling one section between my hands, and then let it slip through my fingers. Silky and supple, the rope would clearly hold up under any situation.

"Can I try it out?" I said.

"Go ahead," she said, stepping back.

Coiling the rope in my hands, I tied one end into a loop and twirled it in the air around my head with my right hand while holding the coils in my left. The rope worked better than those we had on the ranch, and I sent the loop flying through the air, intentionally aiming it to land around Glenda's head. She whinnied in surprise, turning to look at me. I tugged gently to create tension on the rope and walked to her side.

"Sorry, Glenda," I said, pulling the rope over her ears. She snorted and bobbed her head, appearing to forgive me when I rubbed her neck. "This will be useful," I said. I coiled the rope and stowed it under the chariot seat, then turned to Demeter. "You have given me valuable gifts."

She extended her arms and stepped forward to embrace me. The smell of honey and lemons drifted from her skin.

"My mother wore lemon perfume," I said without hesitation. I never talked about my mom. Why now, with Demeter?

"I knew her when she was a little girl on the ranch," Demeter said, leaning back to look down at me, but still holding me in her arms. "You look very much like her."

I hugged Demeter tightly, inhaling honey and lemon. "Thank you for the gifts," I said as she released me.

We unloaded our gear from Hades' chariot. I transferred my pouch containing the flask of *Aqua Fortis* from Hades and added my new bronze flask in a separate section of the pouch so they wouldn't clank against each other. I placed my new bow and quiver of arrows on the padded seat of the bamboo chariot. There was just enough room for two people to sit or for one person to recline.

"Here's some food for your journey," Demeter said, holding a basket. She opened it to pull out a packet. "The honey cakes are wrapped in special pouches made from milk protein. People don't have to harm the environment by using plastic baggies for lunches and leftovers. These are biodegradable."

"It's time to hitch up Hades' horses to his chariot," Persephone said. "They'll fly on their own back to Sinks Canyon and Hades will let them in the cave."

I hugged each horse after we hitched them to the black chariot and watched as Persephone stroked their strong necks. "Fly to Hades. Give him my love," she added softly.

The horses nodded their heads and flew off with a parting whinny. As the chariot moved higher in the sky, a flock of meadowlarks moved in, quickly concealing the horses and chariot from our view.

"That's amazing," I said. "It looks like a flock of birds and nothing else."

"That's how we look from the ground," Persephone said. "We have to take off. Goodbye, Mother."

As I watched Demeter and Persephone face each other, I sensed the older woman realized her daughter was also a woman now, with a quest of her own. I saw the anguish of their parting when they embraced fiercely.

"I must help the bees and you must help Diana," Demeter said firmly, as if trying to convince herself as well. Then she included me in their love by grabbing my hand and pulling the three of us together as one. The energy of growing things flowed through my veins as a surge of life poured from Demeter.

"Travel safely," Demeter said, stepping back as we climbed into the chariot. "Remember, you must return by the summer solstice."

Indigo flew into the chariot and landed on the seat next to me. *I'll wait until we get to the source of the Yellowstone River to see what happens,* I told myself, absently smoothing Indigo's back. *If I need to, I'll tell Persephone to take me home.* A little flutter of anticipation in my stomach told me the excitement of this adventure eclipsed my thoughts of going home.

Persephone gathered the reins and the palominos moved forward, trotting on the sandbar. As the horses gained speed and became airborne, I turned to wave at Demeter, who now seemed a lonely figure on the sand. Persephone did not look back, but squared her shoulders and sang out a high, beautiful song as we flew up and over the Platte River, heading northwest toward the mountains of Wyoming and the Yellowstone River, the source of *Aqua Pura*.

CHAPTER SIX
THE YELLOWSTONE RIVER:
NATURALIS UNDA FLUENS
NATURALLY FLOWING WATER

The chariot rose above the Platte River, the mares eagerly taking to the air as Persephone banked to the northwest, following the course of the river. I looked at the ground below as a flock of ducks flew up from the river with a great deal of quacking. As they neared us, the emerald green of mallard heads glinted in the morning sun. A sizeable male turned and quacked loudly, and I laughed. The ducks seemed large up close, especially after the smaller meadowlarks that had provided cover on our journey this morning.

Indigo flew out of the chariot to join the mallards, flapping her wings quickly to keep up.

Leaning back, I picked up my bow, rubbing my fingers down the smooth curve of the wood. Suddenly, a loud crack of gunfire from below caused me to jump. Indigo darted inside, landing on the floor at my feet. The sound exploded again, and the duck that had just quacked at me let out a sharp squawk before plummeting to the Earth.

"Oh, no. We lost a duck!" I said, looking over the edge to see the bird falling awkwardly, spiraling down in a tumbling spin.

"Poachers. This isn't duck hunting season," Persephone yelled. "Diana, grab your bow and stop them from shooting."

I grabbed an arrow from the quiver and placed it in the bow. I'd spent countless hours practicing with my bow and arrow under the direction of Willy. When we camped in the mountains, he'd taught me how to shoot while riding bareback, dropping the knotted reins on Daisy's neck and using my knees to maintain my balance while taking aim at targets he set up in the meadow. Before long, I could shoot a target Willy held on a long stick as he rode by on his horse. Eventually, I became skilled enough for Willy to just hold onto the target as he rode by. Our games helped hone my skills with a bow and arrow so that now I was confident, but I still had no desire to hunt animals.

"Circle back to the river," I shouted.

As Persephone turned the chariot around, I got to my feet, then leaned over the edge to take aim at the poachers below. Once we were over the river again, I spotted a man and a boy on the riverbank, their rifles pointed toward the ducks that had scattered at the sound of gunfire. I aimed carefully at the man's rifle and let my arrow fly, smiling grimly when it knocked the gun out of his hand and into the water.

The boy dropped his own rifle in surprise. As Persephone urged the horses on, the man waded into the shallow river, looking for his rifle, which, of course, wouldn't work while it was wet. The boy looked up again, his mouth forming a large O as he pointed at the chariot and shouted. By the time the man looked up, the ducks had closed ranks, once again hiding us from view. Persephone guided the horses northwest.

A soft whisper caught my ear, and I was surprised to see my arrow fly over the edge of the chariot and back into the quiver that rested on the padded seat.

"Artemis used feathers from homing pigeons in those arrows," Persephone said. "They will always come back to your quiver, so you'll never run out."

Amazed, I sat down, examining the arrows. I ran my fingers over the soft feathers at the end of one, realizing what a powerful gift Artemis gave me.

Indigo jumped up to the seat, squawking and flapping her wings.

"I know, Indigo," Persephone said. "We lost a brave duck."

I reached out my hand and gently rubbed Indigo's back. "I saw him fall to the ground," I said, wondering if she understood me. "I'm sorry we lost him." She fluffed her feathers and calmed down, as if responding to my voice.

"We'll reach the Absaroka Mountains before sunset and camp for the night," Persephone said. "Tomorrow, you'll be drinking *Aqua Pura* from the source of the Yellowstone River. We'll also take some with us for our journey across the Pacific to see Eos."

As I leaned back, the chariot rocked from side to side. I sat up in alarm, and Indigo hopped up and down.

"I didn't realize it at the time, but the poachers hit one of our mares," Persephone exclaimed. "Golden is bleeding. Diana, hold the reins."

I stepped forward quickly and stood next to Persephone. Golden, the mare on the right, faltered as she flew, moving her right rear leg up and down nervously. Blood oozed from a wound across her right haunch. Both horses began to whinny in alarm as Persephone thrust the reins into my hands.

"Take the reins and hold them steady," she said. She climbed over the front of the chariot and jumped onto Glenda's back, gripping her sides with both legs.

"Wait," I shouted. "What are you doing? You can't just jump out of the chariot while we're flying!"

Persephone glanced back at me with an impish grin. "I just did!"

"Well, get back here," I yelled. Indigo landed on my right shoulder, chirping in my ear. She moved her head against my cheek as if trying to comfort me.

"It will be okay," Persephone said. Then she leaned over to examine Golden before reaching into the pocket of her pants and pulling out a silver flask.

The ducks quacked in alarm.

"Quiet," Persephone commanded and they stopped. The sound of flapping wings filled the air while Persephone leaned over to pour liquid from the flask onto Golden's wound, causing the mare to whinny again.

Bloody water blew off her back, but in moments the wound stopped bleeding. With a final pat on Golden's back, Persephone turned around on her knees, seeming not to care that the horses continued flying through the air. She brought her legs up to crouch on top of Glenda and then jumped back into the chariot.

"I'll take the reins again," Persephone said, turning to face the front

Realizing I still gripped them in my hands, I uncurled my fingers and looked up at Persephone, who grinned.

"Now you see the power of *Aqua Fortis*," Persephone said. "It cannot heal a wound, but it will provide strength for a while until we land and take proper care of her. We have to keep going until we reach the slopes of the Absaroka Mountains, but I think Golden can make it that far."

I sat down again, weak-kneed after all that had happened. "Take a small drink of this," Persephone said, extending her flask of *Aqua Fortis*. With a peep, Indigo hopped from my shoulder onto the seat.

I took a cautious sip, immediately feeling my strength return with the clean, brisk taste of the water. I handed the flask back to Persephone, remembering the *Aqua Fortis* Hades had given me.

"Save yours for later. You'll need it at some point," Persephone said. "There are more dangers ahead of us. Now you can see why we need immortal horses on our journey."

The ducks quacked loudly and flew off to the left and right in the front of us as Western Meadowlarks took over on both sides and underneath.

"Those ducks should never have been with us in the first place," Persephone said. "I think they joined us to avoid the poachers. Now that we're flying in Wyoming air space again, the Western Meadowlarks are back."

I scooted to the edge of the chariot and looked below. Between the meadowlarks, I could see mountains. "We must be over the Big Horn Mountains now, right?" I asked while still looking down.

"You know your mountain ranges," Persephone said.

"We've camped all over the state," I said. "I know that the Big Horn Mountains are in north central Wyoming." I continued watching the mountains, which soon gave way to a broad plain.

We traveled for hours above the plains until we were again flying over forested, mountainous land. I was beginning to doze off when I spotted a large group of bears in a mountain meadow. "Persephone, look at that," I shouted, pointing.

Persephone leaned over and gasped when she saw the bears below. "Grizzlies," she said. "We're above the Shoshone National Forest where grizzlies live. Usually, a female travels alone with her cubs, never in groups like this. I'm going to land so we can see what's going on."

"There's no way I'm going down there with the bears. And what about Golden?" I asked.

"She'll be okay," Persephone said. "This is too important to ignore." She circled the horses back and the chariot landed in the meadow, some distance from the bears. "Come with me," she said, climbing down.

Indigo jumped up from the chariot seat and fluttered near Persephone.

"Grizzlies can kill you," I said. "We knew a guy who was mauled by a grizzly when he was camping. I'm staying here."

Persephone placed her hand over mine where I gripped the side of the chariot. "Diana, you'll be safe with me. And you have the elk tooth necklace. Leave your bow and arrows and come with me." Indigo landed on Persephone's shoulder.

I shook my head. "Grizzlies attack people, Persephone. We can't go over there. They'll kill us."

I felt the urge to run, but I knew that if I did, the bears would follow and maul us, just the way my dad had described his friend's death. I imagined the scene. My dad, Grams, and Willy would be devastated. Nobody would find us for a year at least. After a winter under the snow, our bodies would emerge in spring, picked clean by coyotes and crows. Only scraps of our bloody clothes would be there, stuck under our white-washed bones. Next summer, when hikers came into the meadow, or a forest ranger traveled through on horseback, they'd discover our remains and identify me by my necklace. *Maybe I should leave right now*, I thought. *I could take the chariot.*

"Diana, the animals know you're here," Persephone said. "Count them. Thirteen. They never travel in groups like this. Let's walk slowly and find out what's going on." She grabbed my hand and tugged. Her touch gave me a morsel of courage.

By now, the bears had stopped walking and formed a row, which was also unusual behavior. Moving cautiously, I got down and followed Persephone until we stood ten feet from them. I held my breath, never having been this close to grizzly bears in my life. Even though we didn't have grizzlies near the ranch, I'd seen them from the safety of a vehicle on our camping trips in Yellowstone National Park.

I stood still, my heart racing. "The bears killed my dad's friend," I whispered.

"I know," Persephone said.

"They maul you," I said. Staring ahead, I didn't realize I was crying until I tasted the salt of tears on my lips.

I turned and ran, even though I knew you should never run from a bear. Persephone yelled my name, but I kept running. Just as I feared, I heard the roar of a bear and the pounding of feet behind me. The bear came so close I felt hot breath on back. In my panic, I tripped, falling to the ground.

"No," I screamed, gulping in the smell of grass, my face pressed to the earth. Expecting sharp claws to rip through my back and tear into my skin the way the bear's ripped into Dad's friend, I wondered why my life didn't flash before my eyes as it always does to people in books when they confront death. Something landed on my back, pushing the air out of my lungs.

"Diana, turn over," Persephone said.

Wet slobber dribbled onto my neck and soft sniffing moved around my ear. The weight on my back shifted, pressing against my side. A small grunt accompanied the movement.

"What is that?" I said, realizing no claws had ripped into my clothes to pierce the skin and muscle of my back. No warm blood ran down my sides.

Instead, I turned over to see a bear cub cuddled next to me. Like a clumsy toddler, the bear opened its arms and pounced again, grunting with apparent glee.

"That's how they get us," Persephone said. "They kill us with their cuteness."

I sat up, reaching out to the adorable cub, who promptly climbed on my lap, rubbing against my chest, grunting, and slobbering. I looked up at Persephone, who stood with her arms crossed, smiling down at me.

"I've had nightmares about bears since Dad's friend died. Nobody knew. Here I am, a grown woman, and I'm afraid of rivers and bears. What's wrong with me, Persephone?"

The cub rubbed against my face with her muzzle, leaving a wet trail. Did she really have berry breath, or was it my imagination?

"Nothing is wrong with you, Diana. Most people are afraid of bears," Persephone said, crouching down to scratch behind the cub's ears. "You just have to learn you can talk to people about your feelings. Did you ever tell your dad about your nightmares?"

"No," I said. I felt vulnerable, no longer a confident adult.

"Well, now you know you should," she said. "Let's go see the other bears."

As Persephone stood, the cub rubbed my face one more time with her wet black nose and ran back to her mother. I reluctantly rose and followed Persephone, hoping she could protect me.

"This is a good omen. Bears are sacred to Artemis," Persephone said as the bears calmly observed us as we moved closer. The largest nodded, while the others stood still. "Strong females with strong connections," Persephone said softly. "Diana, these are mothers, daughters, and grandmothers."

We stood without talking and watched the bears. I gasped and stepped back when the largest female stood on her hind legs and roared, pawing the air. Persephone held up her arms and began singing. The bear roared and Persephone stopped singing, then nodded as the bear roared again, softly this time.

The bear dropped down on all fours, her thick fur moving as she hit the ground with her front paws. Then she looked into my eyes and bowed her head, lowering the front of her body by bending her knees. She stood up, grunting softly as Persephone nodded once again.

"She's telling me why they're here," Persephone said, turning to look at me. "As I said a minute ago, to Artemis, bears are the most sacred animal. These have come together in a rare event. Grandmothers, mothers, and granddaughters are all here to greet you. Artemis couldn't be here now but sent these bears to honor you and give you courage as we start the quest."

The bear roared softly and Persephone translated, "She said the power of our grandmothers and mothers will guide us."

"Thank you," I said, looking the large bear in the eyes. But I didn't move closer.

Apparently, that's all I needed to say, because she bellowed one more time and turned to walk away. The rest of the group moved aside as she passed, then followed behind in a line. The last two bears, the cub and her mother, remained to look at us. Persephone held my hand as the mother bear turned, her little cub following behind.

We stood silently as they walked away. "You love your mother very much, don't you?" I asked, thinking about the bear's message.

"Yes," Persephone. "My mother and I suffer when we're apart, but I love Hades and want to be with him. You mourn the loss of your mother, I know. I can feel your grief." Persephone turned kind green eyes on me, and I nodded. "You'll live with this hole in your heart until you fill it with joy by recalling the memory of your mother."

"I can't remember anything about her," I whispered, gripping

Persephone's hand. "I can't even remember the sound of her voice."

"You will, in time," Persephone said. "You just have to open your heart and let the memories back in."

"I can't," I said.

She placed her hand on my head. "You'll find a way," she said gently. "But now it's time to go back to the chariot."

As soon as we were airborne, meadowlarks joined us with the familiar flapping of wings. I looked over the side, and the birds moved apart, seeming to know I wanted to see the line of bears progressing through the meadow. I watched until they entered the safety of the forest and were lost to my sight.

"That was really something," I said.

"The bears gathered because of you," Persephone said. "Nature knows we're working together now."

I didn't respond, not convinced forces were moving because of us.

"You'll see," Persephone said.

***

We flew throughout the afternoon and, late in the day, reached the foothills of the Absaroka Mountains. "My mother planted meadows of special grass all over the planet. Look below and you'll see the meadow where we'll land." The horses called loudly. "They can spot my mother's grass from up here," Persephone said with a laugh. "Hold on."

By now, I was used to the small jolt as the chariot hit the ground. The horses trotted briskly in the meadow, stopping at the edge of the clearing.

"We'll make camp just inside the cover of these trees," Persephone said. She jumped down and began to unhitch the horses. "I'll set up our campsite while you take the horses to find water. They won't leave if you direct them to stay in the meadow. And, look, Golden's wound is healing nicely."

"Okay," I replied.

Taking care of horses in the mountains was a familiar routine, so I walked with the mares to edge of the trees, spotting a small creek running out of the forest. I led Golden and Glenda to the creek so they could drink, and then back into the meadow. "Stay here for the night," I said, and they nickered in reply before lowering their heads to eagerly grab bunches of Demeter's mountain meadow grass.

I returned to the creek and crouched to cradle water in my palms, gratefully slurping from my cupped hands. Walking a short distance along the edge of the forest, I stopped to look over the meadow, listening to the singing of birds in the trees. A movement to the right caught my eye, and I turned my head to see a magnificent female elk walk out of the forest only a few feet away. She entered the meadow and turned to look at me, pausing with her head held high.

I saw the intelligence in her eyes. After a short pause, she moved toward me. I was unafraid because of the dynamic, positive energy flowing from her. She halted in front of me and raised her head to sniff the air.

When I extended my hand, she startled me by gracefully bowing, and I touched her forehead. Her hair was soft and her head warm. Long black eyelashes curled above her deep brown eyes, and she nuzzled her nose against my shoulder, just as our horses did on the ranch. Heat emanated from my necklace.

Without warning, I was running like the wind, my feet pounding on a trail next to a swift river. The same thing had happened when I was in the cave with Hades and he touched my necklace. *Where am I? In a dream?*

Looking down, I saw my feet encased in beaded moccasins; a deerskin dress flapped against my legs as I ran. That felt real. I heard thuds as my feet landed and I saw small puffs of dust fly up from the trail. My long braids thumped against my back, matching the rhythm of my heart. I looked across the river to see a female elk leading a small herd, keeping pace with me as sunlight glinted off the water between us. Laughing, I looked forward as it all evaporated and I once again stood in the meadow, my hand on the forehead of the elk in front of me.

Raising her head, she stepped back and bowed to the ground as if blessing my journey and turned to walk into the forest. When she reached the edge of the clearing, she looked back at me before entering the cover of the trees.

Still caught up in the power of the magnificent animal, I jumped when I felt a hand on my shoulder.

Persephone stood beside me with a solemn look on her face. "The elk made herself known to you," she said. "That's another good omen for our journey."

"She let me touch her," I said.

"I saw that."

"I didn't realize what Willy meant when he said the elk was my animal. I still don't completely understand."

"This is an important moment for you," Persephone said. "You'll understand more as time goes by."

Standing quietly side by side, we watched the horses grazing in the meadow. "Let's go back to camp and get some salve for Golden's wound. Then we can eat," Persephone said, breaking the companionable silence.

I wasn't ready to tell Persephone how I'd been transported to a riverbank, running with the elk, so I took one last look at the meadow and followed her a short distance into the trees where she'd set up our campsite. A small tent stood apart from a ring of rocks. The fire ring looked like it was used for years, but the trees surrounding the campsite were healthy and strong. Indigo perched on a rock near the tent.

"People camped here before, but they properly cleaned up the site and left only the ring of rocks for our fire," Persephone said approvingly. "They know the rules of the forest."

"Pack out whatever you pack in," I said, repeating what Willy'd taught me.

Persephone had already pulled the chariot to the edge of our campsite and unpacked the gear. "The chariot is so light that I can move it on my own," she said. "I'll get the salve and we'll take care of Golden."

We walked back to the meadow and examined Golden's right haunch. I was relieved to see the wound seemed clean.

"It's only superficial. The bullet grazed her and didn't penetrate the muscle," Persephone said while she gently rubbed salve onto wound. "She'll heal quickly."

Golden didn't seem to be in much pain. The mare looked back, flicked her tail, and then continued pulling bites of meadow grass while Persephone rubbed her back.

"Tomorrow, we will fly to the top of Younts Peak and fill our flasks with *Aqua Pura* from the source of the Yellowstone River," Persephone said. She pointed across the meadow to a tall, rugged mountain. "That's where we will be going." As we watched, the sun moved behind the tall peak, turning the sky from blue to purple and red, and then it was gone. Darkness came quickly in the mountains.

Back at the campsite, Persephone stacked a few dead pine twigs in the center of the campfire pit. She held her hands over the twigs and a green glow emanated from her hands. I gasped when the twigs caught fire and burned brightly, even though there were no logs or branches in the fire ring.

Persephone laughed. "We don't need to add wood. My fire will keep burning as long as we need it. There are some advantages to camping with a goddess," she said.

We sat on logs around the campfire and drank tea made from the creek water and heated on the campfire in the metal pot Persephone placed on a rock at the edge of the flame. Nibbling on honey cakes that I shared with Indigo, I contentedly watched the green flames in the campfire. I was used to this evening ritual. When I camped with Dad and Willy, long days on horseback ended like this, often in companionable silence, broken only by the snap of the campfire and Willy's soft voice as he told stories handed down from his ancestors.

Willy had taught me the ways of the forest on our trips in the mountains. I learned how to spot animal trails in the woods and walk carefully on pine needles so as not to make a sound. He showed me how to identify animal tracks and droppings and distinguish the markings of bears on pine trees in the forest. I learned to recognize the calls of magpies, the song of Mountain Bluebirds, and the clear cry of Red-tailed Hawks.

My favorite game was a form of hide and seek. Willy would walk with me into the forest and then leave me alone. My job was to find my way out and sneak up on him so quietly that he couldn't hear me. After years of playing this game in the mountains, last summer had been the first time I finally caught him by surprise, so keen was his hearing. He could detect my silent footfalls even when I walked on a forest floor covered with needles. We switched roles, and I hid. Of course, it didn't take him long to find me.

I learned to recognize the sounds of animals in the forest, the soft rustling of creatures in the underbrush, and the tell-tale snap of a twig when a deer was nearby. Once, we found a fawn hiding at the edge of the meadow, its mother nowhere in sight. Willy said to leave the baby deer alone so the doe would come back and find it without being scared by the scent of humans.

"Willy taught me how to track animals," I said to Persephone, breaking the silence. Indigo tucked her head under her wing and dozed while she perched on a rock near me.

"He's a wise man," Persephone said. She yawned, and added, "Well, we should sleep now so we can get up before sunrise. As soon as the sun comes up, I want to be on our way. We have a long day of traveling and I want to start early." She stood and moved to the fire, leaned over it, and blew one swift breath, as if it were a candle. When the fire immediately stopped burning, I laughed.

Darkness enveloped the campsite momentarily until a green light lit the area. Persephone held a green gem in her hand, illuminating our way to the tent.

Once we were inside, Indigo flew to a corner, nestling close to the side of the tent. Soft blankets formed our beds on the ground, and I followed Persephone's example as she took off her boots and crawled inside one set.

"Bamboo?" I asked, stroking the soft covering.

"My mother's specialty," Persephone said, chuckling as her green light dimmed.

I fell asleep with a smile on my face.

***

I must have slept soundly because the birds woke me up and I was

68

refreshed. The predawn light was strong enough for me to see that Persephone was no longer in the tent. Quickly pulling on my boots, I stepped out as she came walking back from the direction of the creek. I headed there to wash my face with cold water before we ate breakfast. Then we broke camp, clearing all traces of our presence except for the fire ring, leaving that intact for the next campers.

Working together, we stored the gear and pulled the chariot to the edge of the forest where Golden and Glenda waited. While Persephone hitched up the horses, I looked at Golden's wound, pleased to see that it was already scabbed over and healing without any redness or swelling.

The horses trotted across the meadow and became airborne just as the sun came over the horizon. A flock of Mountain Bluebirds surrounded us, and Persephone laughed. "They want to take over for the meadowlarks."

I'd seen plenty of Mountain Bluebirds before, but never in a flock. The morning sun highlighted the brilliant blue of the females' wing tips and backs, and the all-blue males. As she flew out of the chariot to join them, Indigo trilled, her wings beating quickly.

"You're looking at the highest peak in the Teton Wilderness," Persephone said as the sun warmed the chariot.

I looked over the edge to see a green mountain slope. Ahead, a large snowbank wrapped around the base of a granite cliff.

"We're going to land at the edge of that snowbank," Persephone said, turning the chariot and directing the horses to the ground. The bluebirds flew off to the right, and Indigo flew into the chariot. "This is just our first stop of the day."

We landed, and the horses trotted to a stop, the brisk morning air cooling my face. Indigo and I followed Persephone out of the chariot. She turned and lifted the padded seat to reach into the compartments, handing me the pouch containing my flasks. I removed the gift from Demeter, leaving the flask of *Aqua Fortis*. I looked at the image of the elk on the front of the bronze flask, feeling again as if she were looking at me. Rubbing the smooth surface, I stared at the details in the scene. Pine trees were etched behind the elk, who was clearly a female because she had no antlers. Her long legs tapered to dainty hooves, and her square muzzle faced me as she munched on mountain meadow grass.

"Let's fill our flasks," Persephone said. "You are about to drink *Aqua Pura* from the source of the Yellowstone River. Did you know the Yellowstone has no dams? It is the longest undammed river in the lower forty-eight states." Persephone turned and walked toward the snowbank, and Indigo followed. "We're going to have to walk on this snowbank until we reach the lake at the bottom of the glacier. This is where the Yellowstone River begins."

I followed Persephone as she moved onto the snowbank, glad I was wearing my bamboo boots, which were warmer than my cowboy boots. We walked a short distance on the snow until we reached a rocky outcropping. Stepping up on the rocks behind Persephone, I gasped. A small glacial lake nestled at the base of a large bank of snow. I heard water trickling as it flowed from the glacier into the lake. The sun crested the rock of the mountaintop and lit up the lake, which reflected the clouds floating in the sky. A cold breeze brushed across my face, and the scent of ozone crackled in the air.

I'd viewed many mountain lakes like this in the Wind River Mountains above Sinks Canyon, but this one was special. Its smooth surface reflected the blue sky and clouds perfectly, and the cold air moved around us as the sun warmed my head. Indigo flew out over the water but returned quickly when the sharp cry of a Bald Eagle filled the air. Persephone leaned down, unscrewing the lid to her flask.

"Fill your flask and drink," Persephone said.

I removed the cap, kneeling on the rock to place the flask in the water. Indigo landed next to me, chirping. My hand quickly grew cold while I held the flask underwater to fill it. I rose with Persephone and we drank together, our heads tipping back to let the clear water flow down our throats. We watched as Indigo hopped closer to the water, dipping her beak in the lake. She sipped and titled her head back, drinking in the fashion of birds.

I was exhilarated, standing on top of the world in the morning sun drinking *Aqua Pura* from the source of the Yellowstone River. I lowered my flask to see Persephone watching me solemnly.

"Persephone, Willy told me that his mother's people, the River Crow, actually had another name for the Yellowstone River. Do you know what they called it?" I said.

"Yes," Persephone said, "I do. What did Willy tell you?"

"He told me that they called it the Elk River," I said. "Now I know why we came here for *Aqua Pura*. I didn't think about that until just now."

Persephone smiled and nodded. "The elk is your animal, Diana, and water from the source of this river will bring you great strength of spirit. You have a destiny to fulfill. The elk teeth will protect you, and *Aqua Pura* from the source of the Yellowstone River will sustain your spirit. Do you understand?"

I could only nod as the power of the moment overwhelmed me. "I am glad we're here together," I said, finally able to speak. Indigo flew to my shoulder and twittered. "I'm glad you're here, too, Indigo."

The elk teeth on my necklace grew warm. "Willy told me the story of these elk teeth," I said, reaching up to pull the necklace from under my shirt.

"He did?" Persephone asked.

"Yes. Let's sit down so I can tell you," I said. We moved to a dry section of the rock. Indigo flew away from me to perch on Persephone's shoulder. Although it was dry, the rough surface of the rock was cold, and I pulled my knees up to my chin, warmed by the sun and the heat of my necklace.

"He told me this story last year when my dad, Willy, and I were in the Wind Rivers on a pack trip at the end of the summer. Every night when we camped, he told stories about his people, the Eastern Shoshone. One night, he talked about his mother's people, the River Crow. My dad had gone to bed early because he was tired, so it was just Willy and me sitting around the campfire."

"I will tell you the story of your elk tooth necklace," Willy said. He'd looked into my eyes before returning his gaze to the campfire. The sharp angles of his face were highlighted by the light from the blaze, and his soft voice cocooned us in a verbal tent.

"My full name is Running Elk Moon," Willy said.

I was transported back in time as I listened.

"The night before Running Elk Moon was born, an elk appeared in her mother's dreams, so she was named Elk Moon. The elk was her animal from birth, but she was always running, running, running as a young girl. That is how she earned her name, Princess Running Elk Moon.

Her father was chief of the River Crow. They lived on the plains next to the Elk River, which the white man later called the Yellowstone. They lived off the land, hunting deer, elk, and buffalo and picking roots and berries.

"In winter, they camped in the meadow where the plains ended and the mountain foothills began. Green meadows changed to slopes covered in Ponderosa Pine, a giant of a tree, providing cover for countless grasses and shade plants. The pine needle-covered forest floor was quiet, hiding the sounds of her feet as she ran through the trees. In the spring, dappled sunlight frosted small woodland flowers, and occasionally stands of green grasses sprouted defiantly from the sandy soil. Strong, striped snake grass blazed forth from the gravel in front of tall boulders among the trees.

"Out on the plains was the Elk River. At times, the river was a turquoise flow because it carried so many minerals from the snowpack high in the mountains where birds breathed in the cold scent of damp granite.

"Late one spring, as she ran on the grassy banks of the river, a woman came along in a covered wagon like the white men used. Running Elk

Moon did not recognize the woman, but she was brown-skinned, so Running Elk Moon thought she could trust the woman when she stopped to speak. She knew the language of the River Crow, so Running Elk Moon had no fear when the stranger asked for help getting water from the river.

"She jumped out of her wagon and went to the back, gesturing to indicate Running Elk Moon should follow. When Running Elk Moon walked to the back of the wagon, the woman grabbed her, throwing her shawl over Running Elk Moon's head. She struggled to escape, but another person helped tie her up with rope. When she was helplessly tied up, they pulled the shawl off her head and hauled her into the wagon. Several other children were already there, and she knew she was in danger.

"They tied her to the inside of the wagon. 'Be quiet or we will kill you,' the woman said. She saw the other adult, who was also Crow, but not a member of her village.

"Terrified, she remained quiet as they turned the wagon around and drove the other way, following the banks of the river. As was her custom, Running Elk Moon had been running, running, running on the riverbank. Now she was away from her village, and no one saw them take her away.

"They drove all day and camped that night. They kept the children tied up in the wagon, only letting them out one by one for food and water. They traveled the next day and finally came to a white man's fort, where Running Elk Moon found out that some white men paid the woman to capture River Crow children. Running Elk Moon spent the next four years there, in a place called a boarding school.

"All of the girls slept in one room on stiff wooden beds. She cried every night for her mother. They beat her when she spoke her own language. The white people took away her doeskin dress and moccasins. Instead of her soft dress brushing her skin, she was forced to wear stiff clothing that covered her arms and buttoned up to her neck.

"Everything was hard about the white man; the sticks they used to beat the children and the shoes they were forced to wear. Running Elk Moon could no longer feel the earth beneath her feet, only the hard bottom of the shoes. And, worst of all, they would not let her run. Instead, she went to school each day to learn the white man's language. The girls had to sew and work in the garden.

"Running Elk Moon wondered why the white men and women were so angry. Why did they hate her and steal her words? Why must she pray to their white god instead of to the sky, sun, and wind? Why did they eat meat without blessing the lives of the animals they ate?

"Those were painful years. She stopped crying at night but did not let them destroy the joy in her heart. Every night in her dreams, she ran with the elk next to the river by the light of the full moon. She did not let the white man break her spirit. Even though she was forced to learn English, she did not forget the language of her people. Every time she learned a new word in English, she repeated the word in her head in the language of her people, the River Crow.

"One day they said she was too old to stay at the boarding school and they sent her back to her people. The River Crow no longer lived on the banks of the Elk River in winter but were instead confined to the reservation. They could no longer roam next to the river in the summer and could not find food. Finally, they depended on white men to give them food at the fort. The whites withheld the food unless parents sent their children to the boarding school.

"She was by now old enough to find a husband and married a strong warrior named Many Horses. He killed an elk before their wedding and, in the tradition of their people, gave her a necklace with the ivory teeth from the elk. Soon, they had a daughter and named her Little Elk Moon. After the baby was born, Running Elk Moon dreamed that a warrior queen with a bow and arrow came to her and said she must give the elk tooth necklace to her daughter when she became a woman. It is the River Crow tradition that a woman's husband gives her an elk tooth necklace, but Running Elk Moon knew she must trust the wisdom of her dream and pass the necklace on to her daughter."

***

"Diana, let's finish this story later today. Right now we should get back in the air." Persephone interrupted me as I told the story of Running Elk Moon. "We'll be in the chariot all day and you can finish telling me then."

"Okay," I said. "This boulder isn't so soft, anyhow."

We filled our flasks again. Indigo flew ahead as we retraced our steps in the snow to climb back in the chariot. Placing the Elk River *Aqua Pura* flask back in the pouch, I settled in for take-off. Indigo joined me as Persephone gathered the reins in her hands. The horses moved quickly through the meadow and lifted us into the air. Noisy gabbles accompanied the Western Meadowlarks that jostled for space on each side. Indigo joined the meadowlarks, flapping her wings to keep up with the larger birds.

I'd flown over mountains in an airplane years before in fifth grade when I flew with my dad out of the small Riverton airport, twenty-three miles from Lander. As we traveled in the turbo prop plane, we could clearly see the mountains on the way to and around Denver. But this was nothing like that bumpy plane ride. This was glorious. The chariot flew low over the mountains, so low that I could see the treetops and then herds of elk grazing above the tree line. In fact, the elk looked up without fear as we passed above, and I gazed down, watching them lower their heads and resume grazing.

"They have no fear because they know it's you, "Persephone said, as if she understood my thoughts.

The horses snorted and the meadowlarks flew away from the chariot, replaced by an entire flock of Mountain Bluebirds, the sun shining brightly on their brilliant blue wings.

"We've entered Idaho airspace," Persephone said, and the chariot flew on.

CHAPTER SEVEN
POSEIDON ON PLASTIC

Mountain Bluebirds sang as they replaced the Wyoming meadowlarks. Seeing an entire flock of brilliant blue birds was spectacular. They were small but determined to keep up. Our little bluebird darted out and joined the flock, turning her head to look my way before tweeting at the bluebird next to her.

"Indigo seems happy to see the bluebird flock," I said

"They'll be with us while we fly over Idaho," Persephone said. "We're headed directly west for the coast of Oregon."

I must have dozed, because the next thing I knew, excited bird calls surrounded the chariot as the bluebirds flew to the left and right. A flock of birds with bright red heads, yellow chests, and black wings and tails flanked us.

"Western Meadowlarks are the Oregon state bird," Persephone said, "but these Western Tanagers beat them to the chariot, so they'll escort us through Oregon air space."

"I thought we were over Idaho," I said, rubbing my eyes and yawning. I looked over to see Indigo dozing in the corner of the seat, but she lifted her head as I spoke.

"*Aqua Pura* is powerful," Persephone said, turning to look at me. "Your first time drinking that gave you a burst of energy, and then you fell asleep. Indigo joined you in a nap. We'll reach the coast this afternoon and eat lunch while we fly."

I moved off the cushioned seat while Indigo fluttered to Persephone's shoulder. Lifting the seat cover, I rummaged through our supplies and pulled out a package of honey cakes, remembering Demeter's bees as I smelled the honey. I handed a honey cake to Persephone and placed a portion on the floor for Indigo. We ate in silence as I looked out over the broad plain ahead. I liked the way we traveled without talking.

My neck grew warm, and I reached up to touch my necklace. It pulsed with energy, making me think of Running Elk Moon, the first person to wear these elk teeth. The vibrations against my neck were warm and comforting, a soothing protective sensation.

"You're a good traveling companion," Persephone said. "We're out of the mountains and will be over the high plains of Oregon for a while, so it's a good time for you to tell me more about your necklace."

"I was just thinking about that," I said. I finished my honey cake and put the milk protein wrappers back inside the storage bin. Then I joined Persephone again at the front of the chariot. "I'll tell the story just the way Willy told it to me."

"I love Willy's stories," Persephone said.

"I told you that Running Elk Moon had a dream about a warrior queen," I said and continued the story as Willy'd told it to me.

"When Running Elk Moon told her husband about the dream, he nodded as if he knew. 'I left this reservation and returned to the Elk River to hunt,' he said. 'I knew I must find an elk in the lands where we grew up. I thanked the animal for giving her life so we could eat. I returned and shared the meat with our people, but I kept the elk teeth for your necklace.'

"As their daughter grew, Running Elk Moon continued to run, but now she ran on the banks of the Bighorn River on the Crow Reservation. She was comforted by the fact that the Bighorn flowed into the Elk River.

"One year after their daughter was born, she ran in the early morning on the banks of the Bighorn. Ahead, a figure stood in the grass, so she slowed to a walk. Running Elk Moon had no fear because she recognized the woman. Tall and slender, the woman carried a bow and arrow. Two large dogs stood by her side.

"'You're the warrior queen from my dream,'" Running Elk Moon said, stopping in front of her.

"'Yes, I am. I have important news for you.'"

Running Elk Moon could tell the woman was not of this world because she was taller than any other woman or man, and radiated power.

"'You are first in a line of women who must protect the elk tooth necklace,'" she said. "'Pass it on to your daughter, Little Elk, and she'll pass it on to her daughter, who will be named Swift Elk Moon. She must leave your reservation and find a husband on the Wind River Reservation in Wyoming. Your family will protect the necklace until it reaches its rightful owner in the future.'"

"Running Elk Moon agreed to do this, even though it saddened her that one of her descendants would leave the Crow people. The warrior queen reached out to touch the necklace. Searing joy spread through Running Elk Moon's body when the woman's hand covered her necklace, convincing her this woman was not an evil spirit. Nodding, the woman turned and walked away.

"As soon as Little Elk was old enough, Running Elk Moon took her daughter along, running at a pace the young girl could manage. When Little Elk became a woman, Running Elk Moon told her of the encounter with the warrior queen. Little Elk married, and when she gave birth to a daughter, she named her Swift Elk Moon. When Swift Elk Moon was a young woman, her mother gave her the necklace and said that she must leave the Crow people and travel to the Wind River Reservation in Wyoming to find a husband. Running Elk Moon said goodbye to Swift Elk Moon, knowing she must fulfill her duty by taking the necklace with her."

Persephone said, "So that's how the necklace ended up in Wyoming. But how did Willy get the necklace?"

"His mother, Swift Elk Moon, told him that the night before he was born, a warrior queen came to her in a dream," I said. "The tall warrior queen carried a bow and arrows and was accompanied by two large dogs, so she knew it was the woman from her grandmother's dreams. The warrior queen told Swift Elk Moon that she would have no daughters, only a son, and she must give him the elk tooth necklace."

"And that child was Willy," Persephone said.

"Yes," I said. "Now I understand that it was Artemis who planned this. She was the warrior queen who met Running Elk Moon on the Crow Reservation and came to Willy's mother, Swift Elk Moon, in a dream."

"You can also see the significance of the moon in this story," Persephone said. "Artemis is not only goddess of the hunt and protector of animals, but also goddess of the moon."

Goosebumps rose on my arms as I thought about the line of women who had protected my necklace so that Willy could pass it on to me. He had an important role in this legacy as well.

"I still don't know why Willy gave the necklace to me," I said.

"You'll find out," Persephone said. "We'll meet Artemis one day and you can ask her."

"Okay," I said. "I guess I'll have to wait and see."

The tanagers providing cover for our chariot chirruped excitedly, the sun glinting off their bright red heads. I looked below as the birds separated, revealing a broad expanse of trees.

"What's your favorite color?" Persephone asked.

"Blue," I replied.

"See?" Persephone said. "The color of water."

I looked down again to see the treetops giving way to a steep cliff and there it was, my first look at the ocean.

The Western Tanagers flew off to the right and left, and larger white birds with black legs and grey wings tipped with black edges moved in from behind.

"Meet the Black-legged Kittiwakes," Persephone said.

The chorus of their calls combined with the power of the ocean. I'd known it would be big, but hadn't anticipated the vastness of the Pacific Ocean as it opened up before us. Indigo moved from Persephone's shoulder to mine, looking around with interest.

At home, I experienced miles and miles of Wyoming prairie, smelling the tangy sagebrush that turned the prairie light green. I loved the softly weaving wheat grass interspersed with sage. The prairie was solid and unmoving, save for the ripple of soft rises on the horizon and the wind on the grass.

The ocean was a surprise. I'd seen thousands of acres of wilderness from Wind River mountaintops but hadn't expected the sense of power brought on by the easing and swelling of the vibrant blue expanse of the Pacific Ocean.

"You're feeling the power of Poseidon," Persephone said.

A huge number of dolphins broke through the waves just ahead of us. "Look," I cried.

Persephone laughed. "We have a new escort. There are over a hundred dolphins below us."

I gasped as Persephone directed the horses to fly closer to the waves. The kittiwakes moved from below the chariot, joining the birds on either side. When we were near enough, I heard the dolphins splashing through the waves, sending up spray as they surfaced and dove, their shiny grey bodies glistening in the sun. Leaping out of the water, they crested the waves, one after the other, swiftly moving ahead.

The kittiwakes kept pace on either side, while the dolphins bounded in and out of the ocean. I shouted into the wind as salt water sprayed my face. This was the same exuberance I'd experienced when galloping across the pasture on Daisy. Persephone seemed to be laughing, but I couldn't hear over the roar of the dolphins breaking through the water, leaping into the air and splashing back down again, only to resurface repeatedly. Speed, water, sunlight, and animals in motion converged in one glorious moment before the horses pulled the chariot higher in the sky, the kittiwakes maintaining their position at the sides of the chariot.

"Wow," I hollered, turning to look at Persephone. Her green eyes gleamed as we laughed together. "Do that again," I yelled.

"The dolphins are turning south, and we're headed west to see Poseidon before we fly to Eos at the edge of the world," she said. "Maybe they'll find us on the way home." She was right; the dolphins leaped while turning away from us.

I wondered what it would be like when we reached Oceanus, the river that circled the globe and was the source of water for all rivers, lakes, and streams on the planet.

"We'll meet Poseidon soon," Persephone said. "There he is now, in fact, in the distance."

I remained at the front of the chariot while Indigo gripped my shoulder with her little black feet. Ahead, a large area of white seemed to be undulating with the waves. As we flew closer, I could see it was no ordinary place. This island was vast, covering an extraordinary expanse of water. Large white birds rose and dived overhead, darting down and flying up again.

"You can thank humans for that island of plastic," Persephone said. "Poseidon contains it here in the north Pacific with the force of the ocean currents. People dump barges of trash, and the plastic floats before breaking apart."

I looked down, horrified by the amount of floating debris. As we reached the outer edges, I saw bottle ends and parts of toys. A doll's head bobbed in the waves as we flew over, its empty eye sockets gazing up in despair. I gasped as we passed over a plastic horse with a broken leg that looked just like the one I'd thrown away years ago.

"Poseidon," Persephone called, and the mares neighed a greeting.

The chariot slowed and hovered next to an enormous seashell throne. Leaning comfortably back was a giant blue figure, holding what looked like a pitchfork, and I realized this was Poseidon with his trident. His skin was a shifting blue color, at one moment deep blue like the summer sky, and the next, an aquamarine that I'd seen only in photographs of the Caribbean. When he stood to greet us, his color changed to the vibrant blue of early evening.

"Persephone," he bellowed. "My beautiful Queen of the Underworld." The diving birds called and the horses bowed their heads while continuing to keep us afloat in the air. "You've brought Diana with you," he said and then laughed loud and long. "Welcome to my island of trash. You will help save *Aqua Pura*. Long have we waited for you, Diana.

"Hello, Indigo. I've heard about you, little Mountain Bluebird."

Indigo flew away from me and perched on Poseidon's shoulder. He moved one massive blue hand up, holding out his index finger. Indigo hopped on, and he brushed her head with the forefinger of his other hand.

"I have a surprise for you, Indigo," he said. "You're going to fly with a Wandering Albatross from Australia. Here she comes now."

My eyes followed as he nodded toward a giant bird flying low above the waves. Her wingspan was easily twelve feet across. The trash island rocked gently as she landed next to Poseidon. He placed Indigo on the other bird's back and the albatross squawked once before awkwardly running along the trash and taking off again, her giant wings spread wide.

"They'll be back," Poseidon said, sensing my alarm. "I want to give Indigo a chance to fly with the big birds while she's out here on the ocean."

"Poseidon, we should help you with this trash," Persephone said. She landed the chariot on the floating garbage island. Glenda and Golden whinnied nervously when their hooves sunk deeply into the plastic. Poseidon swept his hand over the trash, and a pearlescent platform materialized. The horses walked onto the solid surface, clearly more at ease.

Poseidon looked at me and winked. "Shells are my thing," he said.

Persephone dropped the reins and stepped out of the chariot.

Before she reached Poseidon, he walked toward her, a blue tower above her dark hair. "My lovely niece," he said, causing the mares to whinny in response. Grabbing Persephone around the waist, he lifted her up, gently twirling around. She laughed and reached out to hug him, her dark hair a striking contrast against his blue skin. As he hugged her in return, I remembered that her father was Zeus, ruler of the sky, and Poseidon was his brother. Placing Persephone down, he turned toward me.

"Come out of the chariot," he said.

After I stepped onto the shell platform, I felt the full weight of Poseidon's blue gaze. I moved closer to Glenda, placing my right hand on her flank for comfort. The god of the ocean and all lakes, rivers, and streams looked deeply into my eyes as if he knew my fear of raging rivers and my love of calm mountain meadows. I remembered the time last summer when I'd ridden Daisy across a deep section of the Big Sandy River in the southern Wind River Mountains.

Our ranch was on the eastern side of the Continental Divide, where all the rivers flowed into tributaries that in turn fed the Mississippi River. Last summer, Dad had said we should take a trip to the other side of the Continental Divide, which was west of Lander at the top of the mountains near South Pass, Wyoming.

On that side, the rivers flowed into the Pacific Ocean, and Big Sandy River flowed into the Green River, which led to the Colorado River and the Pacific Ocean.

Dad had said I'd like the river near Squaretop Mountain in the Bridger Wilderness Area, so we'd packed our gear, loaded three riding horses and one pack horse in the horse trailer, and driven to the Big Sandy River trailhead on the other side of the Wind River Mountains.

One afternoon, I left camp and rode Daisy bareback down to the river where there was a deep, wide pool. The water was so clear, I saw trout swimming near the sandy bottom. I'd ridden across many mountain streams and rivers on horseback in the past, but had never seen a wide pool like this in a river. Surprised I wasn't experiencing my normal fear of rivers, I urged Daisy on with my heels, holding tight while the mare walked into the water and soon reached a point so deep that she had to swim.

My horse moved effortlessly in the water. I gripped with my legs, holding onto her white mane, letting her take the lead. Daisy was in charge now, and it was like floating in air while she swam across the river. Once she was near the opposite bank, Daisy was able to walk on the sandy bottom. Laughing, I held on tightly when we came out of the water, which a was a good thing because Daisy immediately stopped, and, just like a dog, shook her entire body from head to tail. I almost fell off, and I was wet up to my chest, but I didn't care.

Poseidon's laugh brought me back to the present. Nodding his large blue head, Poseidon said, "You know my rivers and streams well, Diana. Wyoming is a major source of *Aqua Pura*."

"I know," I said. Years ago, Willy had told me Wyoming was the source of four major river basins in America.

"I'm going to help you understand the miracle of water by allowing you to experience the water cycle," Poseidon said. "Don't be alarmed, but in your mind, you will now be a molecule of water."

Before I could even think about becoming alarmed, he stood tall on the plastic island, raised his blue arms in the air, and shouted, "Hold your breath."

I gulped in air. My legs turned to jelly the way they do when a nurse gives me a flu shot. I turned to liquid and dove down, down, down, joining millions of molecules of water. We circled deeper and deeper into the ocean. I was one molecule made up of two atoms of hydrogen and one of oxygen, chemically bonded. I was alone, but among many. The joy of voices raised in song filled my heart as I bonded with millions of water molecules to form one drop caught up in the ocean currents controlled by Poseidon.

The drops of water rose to the ocean's surface, and we transformed like a butterfly coming out of its cocoon. The sun's rays warmed us, and, along with my millions of bonded friends, we evaporated, still molecules, but now separated into a new form, floating to the sky as vapor. When we soared high above the blue ocean, Poseidon's laugh followed us. We giggled and danced, coming together again to form a cloud floating in the sky. As a vaporous cloud, we traveled on the wind, laughing, and bouncing off each other, but still vapor.

More and more water vapor joined our cloud as we floated in the air toward land. Once over land, we became so thick and dense that we began to precipitate and fall, coming together again as millions of molecules to form one drop of rain. We crashed to the ground, forming puddles that ran toward streams and rivers, singing a joyous song of movement and cohesion.

Native American girls ran next to us on the riverbanks, laughing in the sun. The sun captured me, and I rose to the sky in a frenzy of vapor, seeking other water vapor to form a cloud once again.

The cycle repeated endlessly. Sometimes, I fell to earth as snow. Other times, I joined millions of molecules falling over parched land in the long rain season on the Serengeti Plains of Africa. I hurtled into dry riverbeds that swelled to fill empty lake beds. I pummeled to earth with torrents of rain on the Mississippi River, racing toward the ocean while ancient people paddled canoes and wove baskets on the grassy banks of the river. I fell to earth and traveled to deep underground aquifers filled with water as old as time.

Finally, I evaporated one more time, flying on high clouds streaming out like mares' tails. I traveled inland and hovered above Wyoming in a dense winter cloud that dropped two feet of snow on Sweetwater Gap in the Wind River Range. Remaining snow throughout winter, I melted in the spring, racing with other drops in a stream that fed the Popo Agie River. Crashing over boulders into Sinks Canyon, I glimpsed myself as a girl standing on a rock at the edge of the river. *How can I be a drop of water, and, at the same time, see my human form standing on the rock next to the river?*

Before I could answer that question, my water drop form dove into Sinks Cavern and barreled into tiny crevices in the soft rock. I traveled in the dark on the journey through the underground lake, only to surface two hours later down the canyon by seeping through limestone rocks in a natural spring. I again joined the flow of the river out of Sinks Canyon, past our ranch, and into the broad plain of the Lander Valley.

"You're back with us, Diana," Poseidon said.

I became solid and sat with a thump on the island of plastic. My legs still felt like liquid as Persephone pulled me to my feet.

"Drink this," she said, holding out my bronze flask of *Aqua Pura*. "I took it out of your pouch in the chariot."

I leaned against her, focusing on the flask in my hand. The elk stopped grazing and looked up at me, and droplets of rain fell on her upturned nose. Shaking her head, she resumed eating while the rain dripped off her back. It seemed I'd been gone a long time, but apparently only a moment had passed.

"This is nuts," I said and took a drink of *Aqua Pura*, which tasted clean and smelled of ozone.

Poseidon laughed. "Now you know the miracle of water. Water is still pure in the mountains of Wyoming, but in the ocean, it's a different story," Poseidon said as a white pelican landed on his shoulder and began to preen. "Even the creatures in the deepest trenches of my ocean have become poisoned by plastic." He gestured toward the floating debris. "It takes great effort to use my ocean currents to contain this trash. I can't keep it all here, and fish in the bottom of the ocean are eating bits of plastic, thinking they see food."

"But what can I do?" I asked.

"We need you to help save *Aqua Pura*," he said.

Suddenly, two dolphins surfaced next to the island, chattering loudly. They rose higher out of the water, seeming to stand upright as they moved back, continuing to make a clicking noise, like I'd seen in movies and on television.

Poseidon turned immediately and listened intently. Then he nodded and looked at us. "I need your help with the leak below an oil platform in the Gulf of Mexico," he said. "I can't take care of it because I have to stay here and control this plastic. I thought it was a slow leak, but now my dolphin scouts tell me the pressure from natural gas is growing as they pump more oil, and the rig could explode in a few days. I wanted to visit with you longer, but you'll need to leave right away to ask Eos for the use of her horses before going to the Gulf."

"Maybe we should help you control this trash," Persephone said, even as she moved toward the chariot.

"Getting to that oil platform is more important right now," Poseidon said gravely. "The dolphins said the rig might blow sooner because of the pressure. I'll need the king of my dolphins and his fastest warriors to help you prevent a disaster. While you ask Eos for the use of her horses, Lampos and Phaeton, I'll assemble the dolphins and sea birds. They'll meet you in the Gulf of Mexico just south of the oil platform. You must hurry. Thousands of gallons of oil have already leaked into the ocean and gas is moving up the pumping pipe." Poseidon paused and shook his great blue head. "You must quickly reach Eos and borrow her horses. And that won't be an easy task."

"We'll leave right now and fly all night to Oceanus," Persephone said. "I'll plan on meeting your dolphins in the Gulf of Mexico tomorrow."

"Go quickly," Poseidon said. "They tell me the rig has started leaking oil at an alarming rate, and we know the gas will cause an explosion. Goodbye, Diana. We'll visit for a longer time on another day. I want to hear about Daisy. I created horses, you know."

"Thank you, Poseidon," I said, not sure whether I thanked him for horses, or water, or for containing the island of plastic. Persephone jumped back in the chariot, and I followed her.

"Wait. Where's Indigo? We can't leave without her," I said. As Glenda and Golden trotted on the seashell platform, it increased in length ahead of us. I turned as a shrill cry came from above. Flying in on the back of the great Wandering Albatross from Australia, Indigo sang out a greeting.

As the albatross flew over the chariot, she tilted her body to the right, and Indigo flew from her back into the chariot, landing with a plop on the padded seat. With a sharp cry, the albatross flew to Poseidon, perching on the back of his shell throne. Indigo regained her footing as we rose into the sky.

"To Oceanus," Persephone instructed, and the mares whinnied and flew higher into the air, heading south.

I looked back at Poseidon. He raised his trident above his head, his voice carrying over the waves. "Go safely, Diana. Take care."

"I will," I shouted before moving to the center of the seat and facing the front.

Persephone's hair streamed back in the ocean wind. She broke into a clear, high song,sustaining one pure note until the kittiwakes returned, surrounding us. Indigo hopped over to huddle next to me as we raced above the ocean.

CHAPTER EIGHT
THE BLUEBIRD REPORT
BIRDS OF OLD

I must have dozed off when Diana finished her story about Running Elk Moon because I woke up to the sound of excited chirping as the Western Tanagers of Oregon flew off to the right and left in front us. For a brief moment, the only sound was the wind. I hopped up on the seat to look around, but I still couldn't see over the edge, so I perched on Diana's shoulder.

There. Now I could see. The color blue stretched before us, and I realized this was the ocean. Excited calls filled the air and larger birds flew in to surround the chariot. White with black legs and grey wings tipped with black edges, these birds didn't bother to fill in the space underneath. There wasn't likely to be anyone to see us from there.

"Black-legged Kittiwakes," Persephone reminded me.

I barely registered her words, so great was the power of the water below us. The ocean was blue, a dark blue expanse of moving waves, like grass blowing in the wind across the meadow. Calling to one another as they flew, the kittiwakes jostled for position, finally settling in on both sides.

One bird turned and squawked at me. "Welcome to the ocean, little bluebird. Behold the greatest force on the planet: the power of water."

I cheeped in response and looked ahead, gripping Diana's clothing for security. Never had I seen such breadth of water, rivaling the sky as it hugged the edges of the planet. As far as I could see, there was nothing but blue, with an occasional white fluff of sea foam as it bubbled upon itself. Hypnotic, the giant waves rolled across the ocean, announcing their majesty with every move.

"You're feeling the power of Poseidon," Persephone said. "There he is in the distance."

Diana stood to join Persephone at the front of the chariot, and I held on as she moved. Ahead, a large area of white rolled with the waves while sea birds rose and dived overhead, darting down to the island and flying up again. Then I saw Poseidon, sitting on a huge pearlescent, shell-shaped throne.

He was bluer than my father. Now I knew where the color of the sky came from. The sky at dawn, the sky at sunset, the sky when it's turquoise near the horizon and clear blue above. Did Poseidon reflect the sky or did the sky reflect him? Did Poseidon infuse clear water, turning it blue when viewed from above or did he gain his color from water? My father was nothing compared to the majestic blue of Poseidon. His voice boomed across the waves as we flew closer.

"Welcome to my island of trash. Artemis told me you will help save *Aqua Pura*. Long have we waited for you, Diana," he said. "And you brought Indigo. I've heard about you from Artemis, little Mountain Bluebird."

I flew away from Diana and perched on his shoulder. Reaching up a great blue hand, he held out his index finger and I hopped on. He touched my head with his other hand as I looked into his eyes, where the vastness of the sky and ocean was reflected, stretching across time.

"I have a surprise for you, Indigo," he said. "You're going to take a ride with a Wandering Albatross from Australia. Here she comes now."

I looked up to see a giant bird coasting toward us. The island rocked as she landed next to Poseidon. "You'll be back, Indigo. I want to give you a chance to fly with the big birds of old." He placed me on her back and she squawked before running along the island of trash and taking off again, her giant wings spread wide.

I gripped her feathers tightly, hanging on from my perch between her wings. Now I knew what my mother meant when she said we were descended from dinosaurs, for this was indeed a bird from the great line of dinosaurs that flew over the oceans long before humans came into existence.

"You have the heart of a dinosaur, little bluebird. I feel it in the grip of your feet," the Wandering Albatross said. Flying low across the water, she didn't even flap her wings to stay aloft. The wind tugged at my head feathers and I ducked lower, snuggling into safety between her wings.

"My name is Indigo," I said. Mother had taught me to politely introduce myself to other birds. "What's your name, great albatross? You're bigger than a Bald Eagle."

"I am Wanda, the Wandering Albatross," she said. "I come from down under near Australia. I flew here at Poseidon's command. An army of albatrosses is flying north to help you on your quest. You are indeed in great company, Indigo, if you travel with Persephone and Diana."

"I'm only a little bluebird," I replied. "But I'll do what I can." I puffed up in pride, but quickly sank down again when the wind threatened to pull me off Wanda's back. "How big are you?"

"My wingspan is twelve feet across," she said. "I'm twice the size of a tall human and twice the size of a Bald Eagle. I can fly over six hundred miles per day, scouring the ocean for food."

"Do you eat bluebirds?" I asked in alarm. I knew my wingspan was only six inches, and my father's was eight.

"No, we eat squid, octopus, fish, and whatever else we can find in the ocean," she replied. "But a great tragedy has befallen our entire albatross species."

"What? How could anything harm a bird of your size?"

"Albatross chicks are dying because their parents feed them plastic."

"You mean like the stuff on Poseidon's island?"

"Yes. That's not his island, it's a great garbage patch in the Pacific. He uses the currents of the ocean to corral the plastic, but he can't gather it all. Some sinks to the bottom of the ocean in small particles, reaching the deepest canyons in the sea. Other plastic washes up on the beaches of the world, and my species collects it to feed their young, thinking they've found fish and squid," she replied. "We've tried to educate them, but not all the birds listen. The babies then die a slow death by starvation because the plastic in their little bellies cannot be digested. The parents think they are helping their hatchlings. Even I made that mistake."

"You fed plastic to your hatchling?" I asked.

"I didn't know what I was doing," Wanda said softly. "My baby died a slow, torturous death."

"How sad," I said. I thought of my mother working so hard to feed the new hatchlings in the meadow above Sinks Canyon.

"The agony of watching my poor feathered baby die of starvation was unbearable. The more food I brought from the ocean, the thinner and weaker she became," Wanda said. "My baby kept saying, 'It hurts, Mommy, it hurts.' And I couldn't help her."

Wanda continued her tale as we flew over the waves. "I increased the amount of food I brought each day, but soon she couldn't even lift her small head. Her belly was big, but she was dying of starvation as I unknowingly gave her plastic instead of real food," Wanda said. "My baby closed her eyes and eventually stopped breathing. I stayed with her body for weeks. When I flew off to find food for myself, I returned to see the seagulls had ripped open her belly. It was full of undigested food. I filled my beak with the stuff and raced to find Poseidon.

"'What is this? What fish lives in the ocean but does not help babies live?' I asked him.

"'Look around,' he said, sweeping his arm in a broad gesture. I followed his hand with my eyes and saw that his throne rested on a giant, undulating patch.

"'This is plastic,' he said. 'You've been feeding your baby false food. Plastic will not help birds grow.'

"I wept when I realized I had unknowingly killed my own child," Wanda said to me.

"I'm so sorry, Wanda," I said, not knowing what else to say.

"Thank you, Indigo. I hope you never feel the pain of losing a hatchling," she said. "When Poseidon asked me to join his army, I agreed immediately. I vowed to stay and help him."

"Where did the plastic come from?" I asked. "Who planted it in the ocean?"

"Humans," Wanda said. "They use plastic for everything and then throw it away. Other humans load it on large barges and tow it out to sea, dumping it into the ocean."

"That's horrible," I said. "Why would they do that?"

"They don't want to soil their own nests and they think the ocean is large enough to hold their trash. But it's not. As more and more humans have hatchlings, they use more and more plastic and throw away more and more trash. Poseidon is overwhelmed with plastic and that's why he needs Diana's help to save *Aqua Pura*, the clean water on our planet," Wanda said.

"Let's talk of happier things. Look ahead at the blue ocean," she said, diverting my attention. "I fly above the waves, catching the power of the wind. I don't even have to flap my wings much to stay aloft. That's how I can fly for hundreds of miles each day in search of food."

"I eat grasshoppers and crickets," I said.

"We're both descended from the greatest bird of all time," Wanda said. "Twenty-five million years ago, the largest sea bird of all had a twenty-one-foot wingspan. That is almost twice my size. You, too, have the heart of a dinosaur, even though we eat different food."

"My mother taught us that in the nest," I said. "But she didn't know about this big bird you describe."

"All good mothers teach hatchlings that they possess the heart of a dinosaur. We're all descended from the birds of old. You must have a good mother," Wanda said.

"She is a good mother," I said. "She'd be proud to know I'm flying with you over the ocean."

"Why don't you do that now on your own?" Wanda said. "I'll slow down, and you can hop off and catch the air current."

I let go and flew, struggling at first to ride the wind. I flapped and flapped, but soon found that if I simply extended my wings, I could soar over the waves behind Wanda with only an occasional flap. She slowed her flight, allowing me to move alongside.

"Since you're flying on your own now, I'm going to dive in the water and catch some squid for you to taste," Wanda said.

"Wait. I only eat insects," I shouted, but it was too late. Wanda dove into the ocean and briefly disappeared. I continued flying but wondered what would happen if she didn't surface again. Could I make it back to Poseidon's trash barge? What if she never came back, and I fell into the ocean? All at once, this huge expanse of beautiful blue seemed dangerous. The sun disappeared behind a cloud and the ocean turned dark blue, the waves no longer friendly. Just when I was about to turn around to find Diana and Persephone, Wanda surfaced, a large creature in her mouth.

She floated on the water, talking around her catch. "Come down here and I'll give you a piece of squid!"

Her body moved up and down with the waves, but it looked calm enough for me to fly next to her.

I hovered in the air next to her beak just as she gulped most of the squid creature. One little part stayed outside of her beak. I pecked at that section and tasted my first squid. "It's salty," I said, and finished swallowing so I could talk. "It squeaked when I grabbed it!"

Wanda laughed. "That's the texture of squid. Jump back on my back and we'll go back to the island."

I landed on her back, relieved to grip the feathers once again at the base of her neck.

"Hold on," she said. With those two words, she began to run along the surface of the waves until she gained enough speed to spread her wings and become airborne.

The sun came out again and the ocean returned to a glorious blue.

"Plastic is killing more than just birds," Wanda said, returning to our earlier conversation.

"That's terrible," I said.

"Whales and dolphins also mistake plastic bags for food. I saw a dead whale the other day as it floated up to the garbage patch. Poseidon told me it was filled with plastic bags because it kept eating them, but never filled up with food," she said. "When I asked how he knew that, he pointed to the plastic bag hanging out of the whale's dead mouth. He pulled it out, and more bags came out with it."

"That's horrible," I said. "What's a whale?"

Wanda laughed. "A very large animal, bigger than a tree. But right now, I need to get you back to Poseidon."

As we flew back to the garbage patch, I was astonished by the ease with which she soared over the waves. As we came close to the floating plastic island, she flew at an angle over the chariot, and I hopped off, landing on the seat next to Diana.

"I will see you again, Indigo," Wanda said, flying out over the ocean once more.

"Goodbye, Indigo," Poseidon shouted.

When I perched on Diana's shoulder to see him, the chariot began to move and we raced into the air, heading south.

CHAPTER NINE
EOS OF OCEANUS

A sense of urgency possessed our flight and the mares gained speed as the ocean rushed by below. Indigo hopped from my shoulder to the seat, and I risked a glance over the side. Soon, the birds stopped flying under the chariot and moved to the sides, becoming a protective escort more than screening us from anything below. Indigo moved close to me, huddling against the warmth of my leg.

"You must ask Eos to let us use her horses," Persephone said after we flew for some time. "She does not loan them out freely because they're so powerful."

I moved Indigo to the corner of the seat and joined Persephone. "Why can't you ask her?"

"This is your task, not mine," Persephone said.

"I didn't ask for it," I said.

"Nonetheless, it's yours to complete. Eos will challenge your request to use the horses, so speak with conviction, Diana."

"What can I say to her?"

"You'll know when the time comes," Persephone said, looking seriously into my eyes.

Watching Glenda and Golden pull the chariot through the air, I wondered about the immortal horses of Eos. Would she even let us use them? What color would they be? What do immortal horses eat?

"We have a long journey through the night," Persephone said, derailing my thoughts.

She wasn't kidding. We ate dinner in the chariot, drinking *Aqua Pura* from our flasks. The horses flew on through the night, and I slept again, waking while it was still dark. Indigo's soft feathers warmed my face as she slept next to my cheek. I sat up, careful not to knock her off the seat cushion.

"The sun is about to rise," Persephone said.

As I scanned the horizon, pink flooded the sky, and the smell of ozone filled the air. The powerful wind pushed me back and caused Persephone's hair to fly out behind her. The spray of saltwater burned my eyes.

The stars dimmed as dawn advanced. I heard Eos before I saw her. A high, powerful hum filled the air, followed by a soprano voice singing with such clarity that I didn't know whether the tears in my eyes were from the saltwater spray or the deep joy in my heart. Persephone pulled on the reins, and the horses spread their wings wide to keep us suspended in the air as we watched Eos bring light to the sky.

The singing stopped. A pearlescent chariot flew above the curve of the Earth. Standing tall and strong inside it was a slender figure with white wings. As it moved closer, I could see her hair, the color of new spring grass, streaming behind in the wind. Her violet skin contrasted vividly with her white wings and green hair. She drove with ease as the sun moved above the line where the ocean meets sky, coloring the clouds with yellow tendrils. After pulling the sun over the horizon, the chariot broke free and sped toward us, accompanied by a strong wind.

Eos stopped in front of us, her blue eyes challenging and honest. She folded her wings, and the feathers shimmered in the morning sun as my eyes were drawn away from the goddess of the dawn toward the magnificent horses snorting and pawing the air.

Lampos and Phaeton were a perfectly matched pair, from their chestnut bodies and shiny black manes and tails to their polished black hooves.

"They're bays," I said to Persephone.

"They're fast and strong, like Thoroughbreds, to aid Eos as she brings forth the dawn and sweeps away the night sky," Persephone said.

I recognized Thoroughbred lines in the graceful curve of their long necks and powerful haunches. Built for speed, they possessed strong shoulders, broad chests, and muscular flanks. Their long flowing tails shimmered like black silk as they moved.

"Good morning," Eos said. She sounded pleasant enough to my ears. "Follow me to my island."

Lampos and Phaeton turned to the right and flew toward a speck on the horizon. We followed behind, with Glenda and Golden straining to keep up with the powerful immortal horses.

Eos landed on a bluff high above the waves crashing against the rocky shore of the island, and we set down beside her. Bounding to the ground, Eos moved to the front of her horses, standing calmly as we jumped out of our chariot.

A joyous singing filled the air as a flock of birds flew across the island toward the bluff.

"Meet the Birds of Dawn," Eos exclaimed, gesturing toward the flock with a slender arm and unfurling her wings.

The birds fluttered around her head. Bright, beautiful, iridescent, with wings of the ever-changing colors of the dawn, they flew to Indigo where she perched on the chariot. They seemed to sing in unison as they turned to fly away. Before following, Indigo looked back. I was alarmed, but Persephone waved.

"They'll be back," Eos said. "They want to show her the River Oceanus, the source of all rivers, lakes, streams, and aquifers." Turning back to the horses, she gestured toward the one on the right. "This is Lampos."

I relaxed at her words, knowing Indigo would return as she had after flying off with the albatross earlier. I focused on the horse next to Eos.

"Come closer," she said.

I could tell by looking into his eyes that Lampos was a wise, thoughtful, and experienced horse. Bobbing his head up and down, he looked directly at me and neighed. I moved closer and rubbed his neck, unafraid, even though he towered over me.

I stepped back to look at Phaeton, but one look in his eyes convinced me that this was a horse that could not be controlled. He had a wild look, making me feel he did not fully connect with humans. Of course, after all, he was immortal. I knew we could count on Lampos, but not on Phaeton.

"His heart is a tortured wind that makes him crazed," Willy would have said.

I'd experienced animals like this. Bayside, the horse Grandpa bought at auction when he bought Buckskin, could not be bridled or ridden, but she accepted a halter and pack saddle. We kept Bayside to carry gear into the mountains, and she was surefooted and confident on the trails, easily following the horses in front of her. But the minute she was alone in the barn with a human, she became combative, and her wild eyes rolled up. Willy said that someone must have abused her in the past.

Phaeton was wild like Bayside, and clearly must be treated with care. He looked at me sideways, his ears flat against his head. I stepped back.

"Phaeton," Eos said sharply.

The horse blew through his nose, pawed the ground with his right front leg and calmed down, leaning against his brother. I could never trust Phaeton. He was too wild. However, as long as he was with Lampos, I knew he would comply with my commands.

I looked at Persephone, and then turned to Eos. "We would like to borrow your horses for an important quest," I said.

"I am aware of your quest," Eos said. "Tell me why I should loan my immortal beasts to you, a mere human." Eos was easily eight feet tall. As she confronted me, her wings unfurled. Our mares nickered nervously and stepped back.

Persephone placed her hand in the small of my back, gently nudging me forward. Uncertain how to begin, I glanced back at Persephone, but she said nothing. Eos folded up her wings and the air grew cold, like a winter dawn with snow sparkling in the early rays.

As Eos stood tall and powerful in front of me, I thought of Poseidon, containing the island of trash with his ocean currents. I thought of my grandmother Helen, fighting to keep the ranch from developers. I thought of Rachel Carson, bravely standing up to chemical companies and exposing the truth of their toxic sprays. I thought of Willy, who taught me the ways of the mountains. Finally, I thought of the clear, clean waters of the Popie Agie flowing out of the Wind River Mountains into Sinks Canyon.

I knew what to say.

"I am Diana, the girl who will help save *Aqua Pura*." My voice was soft at first but gained strength as I spoke. "The River Oceanus is the source of pure water on the planet, and in other parts of the globe, humans are polluting water and using it up at an alarming rate. Right now, we have to prevent a disaster at an oil rig in the Gulf of Mexico, and for that, we need your beautiful horses."

Eos looked at me boldly. "Again, tell me why a girl should have the use of my horses."

I straightened my shoulders and faced Eos with pride. "I am the girl who comes from the west where water flows pure and strong. I have lost my mother, but I will not lose the battle to save our planet. Humans are responsible for destroying clean water, and I must lead us away from that dangerous path." I finished with confidence, knowing I meant what I said. I would fight to save the water that had taken my mother.

"We must protect the ocean because, ultimately, it is the source of Oceanus, the river that circles the world and provides water to the aquifers, springs, lakes, and rivers. We cannot win the battle without your horses," I concluded. Heat emanated from the elk tooth necklace hidden under my vest. My fear evaporated and I returned the forceful gaze of Eos, goddess of the dawn.

"I know the grizzly and the elk have come to you, Diana, and that you wear the elk tooth necklace for protection. It gives you strong medicine from Willy's people. Now I know you are ready to fight for *Aqua Pura*," she said. "Even though you are untested in battle, you bravely faced me. Not many humans would do that." Eos smiled, and her green hair turned vibrant red. "Very well, Diana. You come from the west in the time of great need." She nodded. "I name you Diana of the Wind Rivers. Lampos and Phaeton are yours to use on this quest, but you must respect them and return them to me."

Lampos whinnied and bobbed his head while Phaeton blew loudly through his nose and pawed the air.

"Thank you, Eos," I said. "We will return them to you." I turned toward Persephone, who began to unhitch Golden and Glenda from our chariot. We quickly connected Phaeton and Lampos, leaving the palominos with Eos.

"I'll feed them and return them to Demeter," Eos said. "I want to check on the status of the Ogallala Aquifer. I hear that humans want to build a pipeline under the Ogallala to convey oil from Canada. Why do they want to destroy the planet just for oil?" She scowled.

At that moment, Indigo returned with the Birds of Dawn, who sang in unison as she landed in the chariot. I climbed aboard after Persephone, who gathered the reins in her hands, and, at her urging, Lampos and Phaeton trotted a short distance toward the edge of the cliff, quickly becoming airborne. I looked back to see Eos waving from the bluff, her wings unfurled and her hair streaming in the wind. The sound of her high, clear voice singing a wordless tune followed us over the ocean.

CHAPTER TEN
THE BLUEBIRD REPORT
THE BIRDS OF DAWN

Eos stopped before reaching our chariot, her blue eyes challenging and honest. She had wings! Wings like I have never seen, white and magnificent. She folded them gracefully at her side, but the tops rose above her shoulders, shimmering in the morning sun.

Her horses were bigger than Glenda and Golden, even bigger than Hades' black horses. They pawed the air, wings suspended to keep the chariot aloft.

"They're bays," I heard Diana say, but Persephone's reply was lost to me as I admired the splendid wings of Eos.

"Follow me to my island," she said.

Turning her chariot to the right, she urged her horses toward a speck on the horizon. I was pushed back against Persephone as Glenda and Golden took off, straining to keep up with the bays. Eos landed her chariot on a bluff high above waves that crashed against the rocky shore below and we landed next to her.

I stayed put when Persephone and Diana jumped out of our chariot. As they walked up to Eos, a high chorus of bird voices filled the air, and a flock of birds flew across the island toward the bluff.

"Meet the Birds of Dawn," Eos exclaimed, gesturing toward the flock with a slender arm while unfurling her wings.

The birds flew around her head, chirping in unison. "Come with us, Indigo," they cried.

Bright, beautiful, iridescent, with wings of the ever-changing colors of the dawn, they flew to me where I perched on the chariot. Mesmerized by their movement, I was lured by their voices.

"Come with us," they said again. "Eos will talk for a while. She always does."

I followed their exuberant flight as they took off, but first glanced back to see that Diana and Persephone stood before Eos, who towered above them both. Persephone turned to wave.

"It's okay. She knows you're with us," the Birds of Dawn chorused.

Flying low over the waves, I followed, leaving Diana and Persephone behind. At first, I was worried, but the farther we traveled, the greater my joy, and my worries disappeared as I raced after the iridescent birds.

"We're taking you to the source of all water," they sang. "You must see the River Oceanus, the source of aquifers, rivers, lakes, and streams."

By now, I was used to the way they talked. As we flew, they told me about their lives. "Each morning, we accompany Eos as she brings dawn to the horizon," they said. Curiously, their multiple voices blended perfectly as one. I wondered how they could fly and speak in such harmony.

"We build our nests on the cliffs of the island where Eos stables her immortal horses, Phaeton and Lampos. At night, some of us have the job of soothing the horses to sleep with our singing. Even though the horses are immortal, they do need sleep. Each spring, the nesting pairs of birds build a nest and lay six eggs at dusk. At dawn on the twentieth day, the eggs hatch."

"Can you slow down a little?" I asked. "I'm not used to flying over the ocean."

The birds slowed a bit and continued their chorus-talk. "Females and males take turns keeping the eggs warm while the other bird catches fish for its mate. On hatching day, a squadron hovers over the nest, singing the song of the new day, awakening the magic in our species. The special song must come at the exact moment of hatching. On occasion, one egg is late to hatch and that bird misses the song of the new day, forever changing its destiny. Nonetheless, the late hatchling is raised with love and care, unaware it missed the song that makes it a true bird of dawn. This bird then lives out its life in the stables, soothing the horses to sleep at night."

"So the little bird that misses the song doesn't cry?" I asked.

"No," they chorused. "Some of these birds have especially clear voices, and Eos selects them to become her house birds. They accompany her to bed at night, sleeping only after lulling her to sleep. These birds have a good life, even if they don't fly with us. Everything in nature has a purpose, even hatchlings who are too late for the song of the new day."

At this point, the entire flock broke into a harmonious and joyful song, trilling as we flew over the waves, their up and down notes matching our up and down flight. Then they continued their story.

"The hatchlings must hear the song of the new day immediately upon breaking free of their shells. Each spring, we form birthing squadrons. Kept busy on the cliffs overlooking the ocean, we race from nest to nest in response to the special series of notes sent out by the nesting birds when the eggs are ready to hatch. Imprinting on this song is like the imprinting all birds experience upon seeing their parents for the first time," they said.

"That happened to me," I said.

"Good point, Indigo. The new hatchlings imprint on the flock through this song and remain as one their entire lives, rarely singing alone. Just like it is said that the British monarchy will fail if the ravens leave the Tower of London, so it is said that if the Birds of Dawn leave Oceanus, Eos will cease to bring light to the sky. The ravens of the Tower of London modeled themselves after us," they explained, and then continued. "The other hatchlings grow swiftly and after twenty-one days, they fly for the first time."

"Just like I did," I said.

"Right, Indigo," they chorused. "For three months after their fledgling flight, the young birds undergo intense training to become Birds of Dawn. We teach them to sing in unison as they gain in size and strength. During this time, the parents work tirelessly to bring fresh fish and squid."

"I've tasted squid," I said. "My friend, Wanda the Wandering Albatross, gave me some."

"Did you like it?" they asked.

"It squeaked when I bit into it," I said. "But it was already dead. The squeak came from the texture."

Suddenly a large column of water burst into the air ahead of us.

"It's a whale," announced the Birds of Dawn.

We moved on, so I had little time to admire the new creature as we flew over its immense body, visible just below the waves. I turned to look back at the whale as the Birds of Dawn resumed their story.

"After three months of eating and instruction in choral singing, the new recruits begin the next stage of their training. We fly with them for short periods of time over the ocean, extending the distance a bit longer each day. After a month of strength training, the young birds are ready for the first coating of their wings with spray from the River Oceanus. The training squadron carefully supervises this because flying over the river is dangerous, and not all the young fledglings survive."

"Oh, no," I said.

"The first coating of their wings gives the young birds the strength they need to fly with the swift immortal horses, which is an arduous task. We all fly back several times a month to gain renewal and energy from the River Oceanus. Finally, at six months of age, the youngsters are ready for the last stage of preparation to become a true bird of the dawn."

"What is that?"

"Each bird must fly alone," they said.

"Alone?" I repeated. "Why alone?"

"Being alone is a true test of the new bird's voice," the flock replied.

"That must be hard," I said.

"Yes," they said. "Each bird in training leaves the cliffs at dawn one week before the winter solstice when the Halcyon Birds of the world are nesting on the ocean."

"Wait," I said. "Birds nest on the ocean? How can that be?"

"Poseidon calms the ocean one week before and one week after the winter solstice. The Halcyon Bird builds a nest on the ocean and incubates the eggs for fourteen days, seven days before and seven days after the winter solstice. It is during this time that our young must make a solo flight and sleep overnight in the nest of a Halcyon Bird."

"That bird lets them in the nest?" I asked. "Bluebirds don't let any other birds in our nests."

"The young Birds of Dawn fly solo at this time and sing a song alone in the final stage of training," they explained. "This is the true test of its ability to live as one with the flock. If it can charm the Halcyon Bird, it can sing with the Birds of Dawn. The youngsters experience the three stages of training: imprinting on the song of the new day, coating their wings with spray from the River Oceanus, and flying alone to charm the Halcyon Birds of old. If the young trainee returns, he or she is now an official bird of dawn and can accompany Eos the next day as she takes away the night sky with the vibrant rays of the sun." The Birds of Dawn ended their story, filling the air between our wings and the ocean with a brilliant high note.

"But what happens if a fledgling cannot charm the Halcyon Bird? Does it die?" I asked.

"No. If the young bird doesn't return, we send a rescue squadron to guide it back to the island. These birds will join the stable birds and comfort the horses at night."

Relieved the youngsters did not die alone on the ocean, I flew after them, moving faster than ever, free and wild in the first rays of dawn shooting over pure sparkling water at the edge of the world. The smell of ozone in my beak was followed by the scent of rainwater as the Birds of Dawn slowed their flight. When I caught up, the spray of fresh water mixing with salt stung my eyes. I adjusted my speed to join the flock as it hovered over a river of water cutting through the waves.

Below, bright blue flowed against the darker blue of the ocean. Sweet freshwater spray dancing in the air fractured into rainbows in the morning sun. The Birds of Dawn laughed while diving in and out of the spray.

"Don't fly too close to the river," they shouted. "Just let the spray coat your wings."

At first, I coasted above and watched, but as they swirled in flight in the spray of Oceanus, I lost my fear and joined them, sunlight warming my wings after the pure cold water splashed on my feathers.

Last winter, when my flock migrated to New Mexico, my mother had introduced me to the wonders of a fountain when she took me to a backyard rock garden. We splashed and played in the dancing water and the warm desert sun baked us dry. This fresh spray of water at the edge of the world, with the laughter of the Birds of Dawn filling the air, was far better than my first fountain experience.

Cold wetness coated my wings and they tingled. I looked to my right and saw the side of my body and my entire wing were Mountain Bluebird blue.

"What color am I?" I shouted.

"You're cerulean blue," the flock chorused.

"All over?"

"Yes. The spray from Oceanus fulfills your deepest yearning."

"I've always wanted to be blue like my father, and now I am," I cried, diving closer to the river's surface. "In my species, only males are cerulean blue!"

"Come back, Indigo," the Birds of Dawn called. "If you fall in, you will not come out of the River Oceanus."

Suddenly, the birds flew up and away from the river of water flowing through the ocean. "Time to leave," they cried. "Persephone is waiting."

I wanted to stay forever, spinning and diving in the ozone-scented sunlight.

"Indigo, we have to go. Fly with us now," they commanded.

Coming to my senses, I dragged myself away from the rainbow spray and flew to join the Birds of Dawn. Hovering in the air, they waited for me before taking off across the ocean. The joy of dancing in the spray remained with me as the sun dried my wings on the flight back to Persephone. When we reached the cliff on the island, I looked at my wing and saw the spray from the River Oceanus had dried, and my feathers were no longer cerulean blue.

"It's gone," I said. "My wing is back to grey with blue tips."

"You'll find your blue someday, Indigo," the Birds of Dawn chorused. "Until we meet again, take care of yourself."

"Goodbye," I said, landing in the chariot. Persephone was already on board, and Diana climbed in to join me. As the horses trotted along the cliff's edge, I wondered what the birds meant by telling me I'd find my blue someday. Before I could ask, Phaeton and Lampos pulled us away from the island and into the sky, leaving the birdsong behind.

CHAPTER ELEVEN
QUEEN PERSEPHONE

As we left Oceanus, Persephone's clear voice filled the air above the waves. A flock of white birds converged on the chariot in response to her call and kept pace with the powerful flight of Lampos and Phaeton. Persephone's face was determined as she controlled the immortal horses, who at first tossed their heads in defiance, but quickly calmed down as they recognized the strength of her hands on the reins.

"Stand with me, Diana," Persephone said. "Come see the Snow Petrels and our new horses."

I joined her, eager to watch the flight of the horses. Persephone held the reins firmly and smiled at me.

"You must be able to command Lampos and Phaeton," she said. "Lampos will listen and Phaeton follows his brother. I want you to take the reins."

I briefly hesitated, and then grasped the reins, knowing the horses must not feel my fear. For one moment, Persephone held on with me, and then she released control to my hands.

A jolt of energy came through the reins from these animals. Controlling their flight was different from petting their foreheads, and when the horses realized I held the reins, they tossed their heads and whinnied, rocking the chariot.

"Fly to the Gulf of Mexico," I commanded, and the horses obeyed by increasing their speed. Triumphant joy surged through my veins and I laughed into the wind. The waves below rushed by; around us, the Snow Petrels increased their pace.

As the day wore on, the horses flew without fatigue, carrying us toward the Gulf. Persephone and I alternately controlled the reins, and in the late afternoon, I sat on the padded seat, eating honey cakes.

"Drink some *Aqua Pura*," Persephone said.

Drinking from the bronze flask I'd filled at the source of the Yellowstone River, I was fortified by the clean mountain water. Pulsing with energy, the elk tooth necklace warmed my skin, and confidence surged through my body.

The sun was setting and the moon rising by the time we neared the platform, its tall derrick outlined against the sky, surrounded by black water. As we drew closer, I saw men and women running on the deck, lowering boats into the ocean. The flock surrounding the chariot flew away.

"It's unusual for petrels to fly this far north. They're leaving now because they know this rig is going to explode," Persephone said. "We have to pull the derrick down and plug the leak before that happens."

But before we got there, a loud explosion rocked the structure, sending flames into the sky. At Persephone's urging, Lampos and Phaeton carried the chariot toward the fiery platform where people jumped from the deck into the black water below.

I gasped, thinking they would drown, but dolphins surfaced next to the jumpers, who had the sense to grab onto their dorsal fins. Once the humans latched on, the dolphins carried them away from the fire. Several Coast Guard cutters raced across the Gulf. Each boat stopped while the crew on board threw lifelines to the swimmers, who let go of the dolphins and grabbed the circular lifebuoys. I was grateful Poseidon had sent the dolphins to rescue the workers.

"Won't the Coast Guard guys see us?" I shouted to Persephone.

"They're focused on rescuing the people in the water, so I don't think they will. Plus, the smoke all around will hide us," she said.

The chariot slowed as it reached the burning derrick. Through the smoke, I looked down as we hovered above a slick sheen of oil glimmering in the setting sun while a sickening smell of burning oil flooded the air. We remained suspended above the slowly moving oil-covered waves, which began to rise and take form in front of the chariot.

"What is that?" I shouted to Persephone. At least I thought I shouted, but my voice came out in a whisper. My stomach churned as I watched the thing grow until it shimmered in front of us.

"I am the daughter of Demeter and Zeus," Persephone cried in a booming voice, raising her arms in the air, seeming to grow taller. The emerald in the circlet of gold on her head glowed brilliantly. Lightning cracked and a radiant green light surrounded her, sending a green beam into the sky. "I am Persephone, Queen of the Underworld, and I command you to stop polluting these waters!" Her voice reverberated in the air. "You will return underground where you belong." She extended her arms higher. Gone was the mischievous companion I'd known on our journey. In her place stood a magnificent young queen, sending forth powerful rays of light from the emerald on her crown.

I wasn't afraid, just filled with immense pride as Queen Persephone revealed her true power. When her voice faded, an evil, mocking laugh filled the void.

"You poor, misguided creature," said a deep voice from the sheen of oil. "Nothing can destroy me." The slick grew taller and towered over the chariot.

The wall had no mouth or eyes, but the voice came from an area near the top, which rippled as it spoke.

Persephone laughed, sending an onslaught of green energy toward the slick, and directed me to shoot arrows through the towering form. In the ocean below, the last of the workers jumped from the platform, carried away by dolphins. I took out my bow and sent my arrows flying, creating holes where they pierced the oil wall. Birds screeched and flew as they do in a feeding frenzy, and then raced through the holes created by my arrows.

A bolt of blue caught my eye as I notched another arrow. Indigo was flying out of the chariot. I called her name, but she ignored my cry. Joining the other birds, she flew through the towering creature and pierced it with her tiny beak. Then she disappeared into the blackness.

"Indigo, no," I screamed, and released my arrow above the place where she'd disappeared.

Weighed down by oil, some birds spiraled into the sea, while others kept diving, causing the holes to grow larger. I continued firing arrows. A plopping sound from behind diverted my attention, and I turned to see Indigo on the seat of the chariot, covered in oil. I was relieved to see her fluttering her wings to shake it off because I had no time to help her.

Persephone continued to pulse green light toward the slick, and I shot arrows as soon as they returned to my quiver. Just when it began to slump, as if our barrage of arrows and green light weakened it, the monster stood higher and roared. As Persephone directed the beams toward the creature, it seemed to draw her energy into its mouthless, rippling, faceless head.

I launched arrows through the body of the beast, but the holes I created sealed up again. Persephone pulled on the reins to move the chariot back, but the creature's hold on her beam of light pulled us closer. Soon it towered higher and reached out with a mass of oil, covering Persephone in slick darkness. A few drops splashed on my face, but the black goo entirely covered Persephone.

Her green light faded, and the slick formed a giant hand, shiny and blue-black. It was right next to me, but although I reached out, I couldn't stop it from pulling Persephone over the edge of the chariot and into the ocean. The horses whinnied as I looked down to see Persephone's face in the waves, determined and resolute.

"Protect the ocean, Diana," she yelled. The creature's black fist emerged from the water, covering the last beam of green light. She disappeared under the waves, and a triumphant laugh emerged from the beast.

"Persephone," I cried, tears mixing with the oil on my face.

Without hesitation, I leaped from the chariot onto Lampos's strong back, landing right behind his wings. I unhitched him, leaving the crazed

Phaeton behind. "Dive after Persephone," I yelled at Lampos, grabbing his mane, and gripping with my knees. I gulped air just as he dove into the water.

The waves slammed over my head, and I remembered with crystal clarity the awful moment all those years ago when my mom had drowned. I closed my eyes and surrendered to the downward pull of the ocean while the memories of that day rendered me helpless. Feeling my hands lose their grip on Lampos's mane, I was lost in the events of years ago ....

My parents and I were whitewater rafting on the Hoback River in Hoback Canyon near Jackson Hole. The water was high due to spring runoff, but we laughed while the rapids surged around the raft. Even our guide smiled until we swirled around a boulder and my mom was tossed overboard. "Save Diana," Mom yelled to my dad as the churning white river pulled her downstream ahead of us.

Dad and I watched helplessly as Mom was pulled under, despite her life vest, only to resurface again. This time, her eyes remained closed as she twirled like a plastic toy in the swift eddy. Dad cried out in anguish when her head slammed against a boulder. She went under again, and I covered my eyes with my five-year-old hands, unable to watch.

Now I tasted saltwater, sinking in the ocean as I relived that terrible time. While growing up, I had no memory of that day, even though I'd been there. Your mom drowned, people told me, but I couldn't remember the event. I had no memory of my mom. Not her voice, not her smell, not her face, not the touch of her hands.

I sank deeper in the ocean. Mom's smiling face appeared before me, beckoning me to follow. I only recognized her from the photo on the nightstand next to my bed. I closed my eyes, forgetting even Persephone and Indigo.

As I gave in to that memory, hands lifted me up, pulling me to the surface. The cold air touched my face and I coughed, inhaling a rotten taste.

"You can do this, Diana," Mom said. "You have the strength, and you know what to do."

I opened my eyes to see her next to me in the ocean. "Mom! I couldn't remember your face or your voice, but now I know it's you." Somehow, my mom was holding us both up in the slick ocean waves.

"Yes, it's me, Diana." Mom smiled and I recognized her features in a rush of love. "But I can't stay. You must do this yourself."

"Don't leave me again," I said, throwing my arms around her, hugging her. I wrapped my legs around Mom and felt a strong fish body under the water.

"I'm a mermaid now," Mom said.

She backed up, extending her arms, but continued to effortlessly support me in the water. "I swim with the other mermaids and the king of the merfish, Triton. Souls who drown can choose to stay in the water, so this is my home now," Mom said. "You must take Persephone back to the surface and defeat the oil slick."

I shook my head. "I can't go under the water. You disappeared there and never came back."

"Persephone needs you," she said. "Take a deep breath and dive down to find her." She pushed me away and waited. "You can do this, Diana."

Treading water next to Mom in the oily ocean, I cried. "I can't!" Lampos whinnied, reminding me he was waiting behind me.

"Yes, you can," Mom said. "You are Diana of the Wind Rivers and Persephone needs your help."

Gulping in air, I dove under water, expecting to see nothing, but a few feet below, Persephone floated on her back with her arms out, eyes closed. I kicked hard with my legs and swam toward her. Grabbing her arm, I pulled her to the surface, gasping as I broke through the oily waves.

"You're in charge now," Mom said. "Now get back in the chariot. The horses are right here."

I turned to see Lampos in the water behind me. A short distance away, Phaeton hovered just above the waves, holding the chariot aloft with a flutter of his wings. I grabbed Lampos's mane, climbed on his back, and leaned down to pull Persephone up. The horse remained steady in the water, waiting until I secured her in front of me.

Slick with oil, I struggled to hold Persephone and stay on Lampos as he flew out of the water and hovered next to the chariot. Gripping the edge, I pushed Persephone in and dragged myself in before turning to look down at Mom as she floated below.

"I've always been with you," Mom said. "Now you must let yourself experience the memories of our time together in your childhood. The other merfolk and I will plug the oil leak with seaweed, but you have to conquer the beast. It has grown and gained form, eager to be above ground. You must do that, Diana, while we work at the bottom of the ocean."

"Don't leave me! I just found you," I cried.

"You can finish this, Diana. I'll always be with you. You'll feel me in the breeze on your face in spring. I'll be the butterfly in the garden your grandmother planted. I'll be the sparkle on the snow when you ski down the frozen Sweetwater River in winter. All you have to do is search your memory and open your heart." She smiled, and, with a flip of her blue-green mermaid tail, she was gone.

Still upright, the oil slick moved toward the platform, but I had to help Persephone first.

I turned to see her lifting a weak arm over her forehead. Next to her was Indigo, her head tucked under one oily wing.

"*Aqua Fortis*," I said to myself, and reached under the chariot seat to grab my bamboo pouch and my rope. I reached in and pulled out the silver flask decorated with the pounded fish-scale design. It seemed so long ago that Hades had given me this water.

I propped Persephone in my arms. After unscrewing the cap, I put the silver rim of the flask spout to her lips and poured a small amount in her mouth. She sputtered and swallowed a few sips. She moaned again and opened dazed eyes. I gave her more of the precious water and watched as her eyes cleared.

"I'm okay," Persephone whispered. She tried to sit up but fell back.

"Lie still. I have to finish here and then I'll get you back to Hades," I said. Without hesitation, I took a long drink of *Aqua Fortis*. Energy surged through my muscles, restoring my confidence. I picked up Persephone and placed her on the chariot seat.

"What happened with that oil slick? How did it overpower you?" I wondered aloud.

"It gained strength from the energy of photosynthesis," she said. "I felt it draining my plant power. I became weaker as it became stronger."

"You stay here, and I'll get you back to Hades," I said. "I have to check on Indigo first."

Gently lifting the small bird, I held her little head between two fingers and forced her beak open before dripping *Aqua Fortis* in her mouth. She shook her head and fluttered her wings, opening her eyes and blinking.

"You'll be okay, Indigo," I said. "You're a brave little bluebird."

I pulled Persephone's wet cloak from behind her and bunched it up under her head, smoothing her brow gently. "You stay here. Phaeton will protect you." Ignoring Persephone's feeble murmur, I reached for the rope and my bow and arrows. Slinging them over my shoulder, I leaped on Lampos and turned to his brother.

"Phaeton, you have to take Persephone and Indigo away from the platform and wait. Lampos and I will return." Phaeton rolled his eyes and pawed the air with his front legs.

I gripped Lampos's rib cage with my knees. Then I leaned over and grabbed Phaeton's bridle, pulling his nose close to mine. "You listen to me, you ornery horse! For once in your life, this is not about you. Pull yourself together. I am Diana of the Wind Rivers and I command you to help me." I glared at him, desperately searching for understanding in the wildness of his immortal eyes. My determination must have gotten through to him, because Phaeton stopped prancing in the air and his eyes calmed.

Lampos whinnied at his brother and Phaeton nodded. I released his bridle and repeated, "Take Persephone and Indigo to safety and come back when I am finished." He bobbed his head again and flew away, pulling the chariot behind.

I secured my hands in Lampos's mane and clamped his body with my legs and knees, just as I did when galloping on Daisy over the fields on the ranch.

"Lampos, take me into the air so I can shoot from on high and bring this creature down," I said to the great horse, feeling his wings unfurl in front of my legs. Lampos surged up, and we flew toward battle.

CHAPTER TWELVE
THE BLUEBIRD REPORT
THE BIG DIVE

When I signed on to help Diana, I never expected to see the ocean, never expected to fight in a battle, and certainly never expected to see Persephone change from a kind, sweet goddess into a fierce warrior queen. Now here I was, huddled next to Persephone in the chariot. The last thing I remember is diving into the oil slick, breaking through to the other side, and flying desperately back to the chariot. I landed on the cushioned seat and tried to shake off the oil before closing my eyes. I woke up to find Diana pouring liquid in my beak.

Sputtering, I watched her grab her rope and the bow and arrows before taking off on Lampos. As I hopped on Persephone, Phaeton carried the chariot away from the battle, but stopped close enough for me to see the action. He extended and fluttered his wings, keeping us afloat in the air.

Diana and Lampos flew toward the oil beast. "I am Diana of the Wind Rivers and you will not pollute these waters," she shouted, her voice thundering across the ocean. She coiled her bamboo and spiderweb rope, twirling it over her head, just like I'd seen her do when Demeter gave it to her on the island in the Platte River. It was hard to believe that had been only a few days ago.

The oil slick laughed, just as it did when Persephone called out her challenge earlier. "You silly girl. You have no power over me."

It lunged toward Diana, but Lampos veered to the right, eluding the reach of the giant slick.

She twirled the rope around and around over her head, preparing to lasso the beast. The bamboo rope flew gracefully over the oil slick, falling around the top. Just as the creature reached up with a newly-formed hand to pull off the rope, she yanked on it. The rope encircled the top of the slick, while Lampos flew around and around, circumnavigating the monster, then flew a short distance away and remained there, holding the rope tight.

While the oil slick twisted and pulled the rope in a frenzy, Lampos held his place in the sky. Diana pulled her bow from her shoulder and loosed arrows in rapid succession. As each one struck, it created a hole, revealing the sky on the opposite side. Every time she sent an arrow, it circled around, returning to the quiver, and I mentally blessed the homing pigeon feathers Artemis had used.

While Diana continued to fly and shoot, the sea birds followed the arrows, using their wings to widen the holes. Soon the slick was riddled with holes. Tendrils of oil reached out from the side, attempting to again form a wall. Just when I thought the creature was defeated, some of the openings grew together and it stood tall. Diana continued piercing the beast with arrows, and the sea birds kept flying. Some were overcome by oil and gave one last dive before falling into the ocean.

Even from a distance, I could see that the feathers on Diana's arrows had become oil-soaked and limp, and one did not have the strength to fly back to the quiver. As it fell into the ocean, Diana let the other arrows fly. The shaft of each was slippery with black ooze, and I could tell it was harder and harder for her to secure arrows in the bow.

I spread my wings, rejuvenated by whatever Diana had given me to drink, and eager to help her in battle. Before taking flight, I spotted a giant albatross swooping through the sky with the other birds. "Wanda," I cried, recognizing my friend.

Wanda dipped her wing at me. "Indigo," she shouted. "This one is for you!" She dove, breaking through the slick with her sharp beak while the wide spread of her wings created a giant tear.

An entire squadron of albatrosses followed her, piercing the oil creature with their beaks, and widening the holes with their wings. Time after time, they flew through, enlarging the openings with their twenty-foot wingspans.

With each pass, their wings became coated with more oil, until several of the birds fell into the ocean, too weighed down to keep flying.

"Wanda," I yelled. "Stop! You'll fall into the ocean." She ignored me and flew up to take another pass through the greasy sheen.

"Stop," I shouted again.

This time she turned and looked at me, her beautiful white feathers coated in black ooze. Diving again, she kept her gaze on me as she deliberately swooped into the wall. She flew up and over another time, but as she came back around, the weight on her wings dragged her down, and she dove headfirst into the ocean with barely a splash. The blackened water parted as her tail feathers disappeared under the surface. The dirty water smoothed where she had been. She did not resurface.

"No," I cried and flew toward the slick, pounding through with my beak, feeling the blackness coat my blue wing feathers and tail. Around me, gulls and albatrosses of all sizes dove into the slick, many falling into the ocean.

I zoomed through to the other side and swooped up and over the beast, preparing to make another pass. As I flew, I wondered how this thing could survive the onslaught of birds when it was riddled with holes. Then it towered over Diana and Lampos.

I jetted higher, shaking my wings to rid them of oil. Some drops fell away, which helped. I knew there was little time left before Diana was overpowered. I flew higher in the sky to gain momentum, and dove down at an angle, headed straight for the mouth of the beast, —or at least what I thought might be its mouth.

It roared, and I dove directly into the orifice created as it did so. Just as I flew in, the creature snapped its mouth shut, clamping down on my tail.

"Indigo, come back," Diana yelled as I felt my body separate from my beautiful blue tail feathers, the only completely cerulean feathers on my body. Searing pain ignited my back.

I came out on the other side of the monster, holding my breath before I fell into the ocean. I tried pushing through the murky water with my wings, but I was not a water bird and struggled to see, while the saltwater and oil burned my eyes.

Without all my tail feathers, I couldn't push myself through the water, and my tiny feet were worthless as paddles. I tried using my wings but grew weaker. With one last upward thrust, I attempted to reach the surface. When I thought I could hold my breath no longer, a huge pair of webbed feet materialized from above and grabbed hold of my body, carrying me along as we burst through the waves.

CHAPTER THIRTEEN
RETURN TO SINKS CAVERN

"Indigo, come back," I yelled. "Not your blue tail feathers!"

With an evil laugh, the monster spit out multiple blue feathers after clamping down on Indigo. Then it made a coughing, sputtering, choking sound. I zinged my last arrow above where Indigo had disappeared and then I fell limply against Lampos's neck, expecting the slick to rise again. But, to my surprise, it collapsed, and did not rise from the water. Lampos whinnied in victory, but all I could do was lean against his greasy neck as I pulled the bamboo rope out of the water, sobbing over the loss of Indigo.

He flew back to where Phaeton held the chariot aloft, and I barely had the strength to hitch Lampos to the chariot next to his brother. For once, Phaeton remained calm while I worked, whinnying nervously when I crawled along his brother's back and into the chariot.

"Let's fly up and look for Indigo," I said.

As I grabbed the reins, a large oil-covered bird flew to the chariot, dropping a limp form onto the seat next to Persephone. Then she flew off with a squawk.

"Indigo! You brought her back! Thank you," I shouted to the large bird as she flew away. I looked back to see that Indigo was safely on the seat next to Persephone, her little body sprawled next to the now-quiet queen. Indigo chirped with her eyes closed. "Oh, no," I whispered. "You lost most of your tail feathers." Only two of her precious blue feathers remained. Knowing this was no time to stop, I faced the front of the chariot, lifting my hands to hold the reins firmly.

"Take us to Hades," I shouted to the immortal horses of the dawn, knowing they would take me to Hades and the *Aqua Vitae* only he could use to revive Persephone. As the horses flew up and north over the ocean, I glanced down to see the last of the exhausted men and women clinging to the fins of dolphins that carried them to safety, supporting them in the water while crew members from the Coast Guard cutters pulled them on board.

I was dirty, wet, and covered in oil, but I squared my shoulders and held the reins, controlling the horses while Persephone and Indigo rested safely on the padded bench, their eyes closed. The emerald nestled in the circlet on Persephone's brow pulsed with a faint green glow as the waters of the Gulf of Mexico sped by beneath us.

Persephone moaned, so I knew she was alive. I tried to reassure myself with the thought that she was immortal and couldn't die. I had to keep going until we reached Sinks Canyon.

"I hope you two know the way to Wyoming," I shouted. Lampos whinnied in reply.

Then a curious thing happened. Wet and wobbling, my arrows flew up out of the water and landed in the chariot, apparently too tired to find their quiver. "Thank you, homing pigeon feathers," I said. "I'll clean you up later."

I sang as Persephone did when we took flight. A flock of Royal Terns flew in from the right, taking position on both sides and below the chariot. The night air cooled my face while moonlight brightened the ocean ahead, illuminating the coastline in the distance. "Reach land first, and then think of getting to the cave," I told myself.

Images filled my head as I replayed what had just happened: the creature turning into a hand, covering Persephone and dragging her into the ocean; Mom's face rising from the deep. Dolphins carrying the workers to safety. Birds diving through holes created by my arrows, their wings covered in oil as they went down. My throat constricted at the thought that they'd given their lives in battle. And Indigo. She'd stopped the beast with one courageous dive, losing most of her blue tail feathers in the process.

I pushed all these thoughts from my head as Lampos and Phaeton carried us through the night. For once, my strategy of ignoring strong emotions proved useful. I refused to break down and cry. I never cried. When Mom died, I'd learned to hold my tears behind the beaver dam, determined not to let them break through. Getting Persephone back to Hades was my only goal. I refused to think about whether Indigo would be able fly after losing her beautiful blue tail feathers.

"Artemis, I don't know if you can hear me, but thank you for the moonlight. I know you're goddess of the moon, and I feel your courage carrying me back to Sinks Canyon," I said.

Inside, I was a quivering mess, but on the outside, I wanted to appear strong and resolved. Squaring my shoulders, I looked forward. The only image I could not squelch was Mom's face, easily visible to me now. I no longer worried about forgetting her.

I pictured the time in Sinks Cavern when Hades had shown me the buffalo stampeding across the prairie. He'd also shown me driving a chariot. *I must look like that now*, I thought. *Was that only two days ago?*

"You can do this, Diana." My mother's voice repeated inside my head, and I drew strength from the memory of her words.

When I was in fourth grade, my social studies homework was to memorize the state capitals, so Grams had created a game for learning not only every state capital, but also every state bird. "You never know when this information will come in handy," she'd said.

"Well, Grams, it's coming in handy now," I said out loud.

The moon was high in the sky as we reached the coast. The flock of Brown Pelicans replacing the Royal Terns helped me realize the land below was Louisiana. Just as I registered the changing of the bird guard, a new species flew in from behind and zipped to the front of the chariot.

"Nighthawks," I exclaimed. The pelicans remained on the sides and below the chariot. "Now we have two bird species escorting us," I said.

When Northern Mockingbirds flocked around the chariot to replace the pelicans, I knew we were now above Texas. But the nighthawks remained ahead, guiding us through the night.

When Scissor-tailed Flycatchers from Oklahoma filed in on either side, I marveled at their long tails and swift flight, remembering they were called a zipper, not a flock. Western Meadowlarks took over after the lengthy flight across Oklahoma. In my fatigue, I thought we were above Wyoming, but then remembered Kansas also named the Western Meadowlark its bird.

"Stupid states," I muttered. "Why can't each one pick a different bird? And why do so many choose the Western Meadowlark? They ought to make a law about that."

Lark Buntings took charge at the Colorado border, and I encouraged Lampos and Phaeton to fly faster, knowing Wyoming was ahead. By now, the moon was sinking on the horizon, and I could barely see the Western Meadowlarks surround the chariot above Wyoming as the smaller Lark Buntings flew off to the side, chirping excitedly.

The nighthawks continued to lead the rapid race through the sky.

When Eos brought the dawn over the eastern horizon, I hardly registered that fact, so great was my exhaustion. I looked at Persephone, relieved to see the gentle rise and fall of her chest. Because she was immortal, Persephone wouldn't die, but I was concerned. Indigo seemed to be sleeping, but I couldn't tell whether she was still alive.

As the rosy colors of dawn streaked across the sky, I looked below. "We're almost home, Indigo," I said. The birds separated enough for me to see the familiar sight of the meandering Sweetwater River, which meant home was near. Before we reached the rim of Sinks Canyon, the birds parted again. I had time only for a glance below at the fields on our ranch before we were above the canyon. I stopped the horses when we reached the cliff above the cave, not knowing if the rock would open.

"Hades," I whispered with my last ounce of strength. "Help me." The limestone cliff slid open, and the horses guided the chariot through the entrance. Rumbling stone indicated the door had closed behind us as we flew past the waterfall to the campsite below.

We reached the lake at the bottom, and I fought tears of relief when the horses landed on the ledge where Hades waited. "I brought Persephone back, Hades, just like you told me to do," I said before my knees buckled and I slumped against the front of the chariot, dropping the reins.

He stepped aboard and lifted me out. "Drink this," Hades said after he placed me on top of a soft blanket on the ledge. He held his flask next to my lips and cradled my head while I sipped. My body tingled from my scalp to my toes.

He returned to the chariot and carried Persephone out, placing her on the blanket next to me. Persephone moaned, but drank as Hades carefully fed her sips from his flask. "*Aqua Vitae*, water of life," he said. "Thank you, Diana. You have brought her to me just in time. This is the first time she's been tested in battle, and we didn't know what to expect."

"The monster seemed to inhale her beams," I said. "I don't know how it happened."

Hades pulled Persephone onto his lap and fed her more sips of *Aqua Vitae*. He looked at me and smiled. "You won the battle, Diana. You are a warrior."

Persephone opened her eyes and smiled at me. "Come here, Diana," she said, extending her hand.

I moved closer. "Even the strongest warriors cry after battle," Persephone said, and I placed my head on her oily lap.

Persephone smoothed my hair, and it seemed her hands pulled the tree limbs from the beaver dam in the mountain meadow, causing my tears to flow in a cleansing rush. I cried, washing my pain away. I cried for myself, I cried for my mother, and I cried for every child who'd ever lost a parent and was left confused and grieving, wondering how their mom or dad could ever expect them to grow up without the love and guidance of that parent.

It was as if Persephone had deliberately pulled the key limb from the beaver dam, and the waters of the pond in the mountain meadow rushed free, once again *naturalis unda fluens*, like the Yellowstone River, naturally flowing water. I sobbed while leaning against Persephone, who leaned against Hades, and my tears ran onto her dirty lap. When I could cry no more, my river of tears drained, I fell into an exhausted sleep.

I woke in bed in the canvas tent, clean and warm under the white bamboo blanket. Persephone sat on a green wicker chair next to the bed. "Who took off my dirty clothes?" I said, noticing her clean clothes and shiny hair.

"Don't worry. I did that," Persephone said. "We'll wash your hair when you're ready."

"The tent smells like lemons," I said. "My mom always wore lemon perfume."

"You filled the hole in your heart with memories of your mother," Persephone said.

She was right. For the first time, tears did not choke my throat when I thought of Mom. Instead, I was peaceful. I smelled lemons again and a soft breeze brushed my cheek.

"You saved me and destroyed the oil slick," Persephone said, sitting on the bed, wrapping her strong brown fingers around my hand. "You are a true warrior, Diana."

"You helped me find my mother," I said.

A chirp brought my attention to Indigo, who sat at the bottom of the bed. She hopped along the covers and settled in next to my pillow.

"Indigo, you were so brave," I said, looking at her tail. Only two feathers remained, leaving a gap in the middle.

"She can't fly very well now that she's lost most of her tail feathers," Persephone said, reaching out to place a comforting hand on Indigo's back. "I don't know what we'll do until they grow back. It takes a long time. Maybe she could stay here with Hades."

"I could take her to the ranch with me," I said. Indigo chirped again and snuggled next to my head. "Willy will help me take care of you, Indigo."

"You were also brave, Diana. Now we are warrior sisters," Persephone said. "We'll always be there for each other. The Coast Guard rescued all the workers from the rig. They wondered about the stories of the dolphins saving them, but dolphins have always helped humans at sea, so it didn't seem too unusual to them. The merfolk plugged the leak on the ocean floor, and, of course, the oil company is taking credit."

"What about Lampos and Phaeton?" I asked.

"They're happily eating hay with Hades' horses," Persephone said. "When you recover, we'll send them back to Eos."

"My mom is a mermaid," I said. The image of her face and sound of her voice filled my mind. Those memories would not fade again. "Can you believe she's a mermaid?" My eyes grew heavy, and I fell asleep with Persephone holding my hand.

When I woke again, I was completely rested. My clothes were at the bottom of the bed, clean and fresh. I dressed quickly and left the tent, stepping out to find Hades and Persephone sitting near the campfire. Indigo perched on her own rock.

"Good morning," Hades said. "Come have some honey cakes and tea."

After breakfast, we hitched Lampos and Phaeton to the chariot. Phaeton seemed to be somewhat tamer, but he rolled back his eyes and pawed the ground, calming down only when I sharply called his name.

"I'll stay here while the two of you meet with Artemis," Hades said, patting Phaeton on the rump.

I looked up, startled at his words. "We're meeting Artemis?"

"Yes," Persephone said. "We're flying to the source of the Green River to meet your sponsor, Artemis. My mother will meet us there. She'll give us a ride back here, and then you can go home to your grandmother and Willy."

"Wow," I said. "You mean this is over? I want to see Grams and Willy, but I'll miss you guys." Inside, I was conflicted. I wanted to go home but I also wanted to stay with Persephone.

"We'll meet again," Persephone said. "And it's not over yet. Today you will meet Artemis."

Facing me, Hades placed his hands on my shoulders, and his amber eyes looked deeply into mine. I smiled up at him before moving into the chariot. He waved from the ledge as Lampos and Phaeton carried us toward the cave entrance. I looked down and waved goodbye to the powerful god of the Underworld, his bronze skin gleaming in the light from the torches.

"I will see you again, Diana of the Wind Rivers. Our work is not finished," Hades called as the chariot rose past the cascading waters of the Sinks Cavern falls.

Lampos and Phaeton whinnied as they flew out of the cave into the bright morning sun, and the doors on the limestone cliff above the Popo Agie River closed behind us.

CHAPTER FOURTEEN
ARTEMIS ON SQUARETOP
MOUNTAIN

The chariot flew up and over the limestone cliff above the Popo Agie River while Persephone began to sing. Immediately, a flock of Western Meadowlarks flanked us, reminding me of the way several different birds escorted us on the long flight from the Gulf of Mexico. Their chatter filled the air and the morning sun glinted off their yellow and black wings. One bird flew parallel to me, seeming to smile as he looked in my eyes, flying quickly to keep up with the horses.

Indigo remained on the seat but chirped at the meadowlarks. After losing almost all her tail feathers in the battle with the oil slick, she had little control of her flight, preventing her from joining the flock.

"These little guys take their escort duties seriously," I said, and Persephone laughed. We flew over the Wind River Mountains. Late in the morning, a dark green forest carpeted the land below. The towering shape of Squaretop Mountain loomed in the distance, and I knew that soon we'd see the alpine lakes that were the source of the Green River.

More Aqua Pura, I thought, remembering Willy's voice when he'd told me last summer that Wyoming contained the headwaters of four major river basins.

"The Green River flows into the Colorado River," Willy had said. "These waters were once wild and free, until the white man tamed both rivers, just like the white man confined Eastern Shoshone and Crow people on reservations. Or so they think," he added with a smile, tapping his chest. "The heart of the Eastern Shoshone is free, just like stretches of the Colorado still run free on its way to the Sea of Cortez in the Pacific Ocean."

Now here I was, nearing Squaretop. It soared like a sentinel above the glacial lakes that formed the headwaters of the Green River. Close to the top of the mountain was an indentation, a grassy area nestled in rocks, and it was there we landed.

"Demeter planted this," I observed, pleased to recognize the patch of waving green grass as her handiwork.

The horses trotted closer to the rocks, and I saw Demeter. Nearby a tall woman stood next to a chariot drawn by deer. Glenda and Golden grazed to the right of the rocky area.

Persephone and I jumped to the ground. Lampos and Phaeton bowed to Demeter when she moved forward to touch their heads. The tall woman walked toward us. Realizing it was Artemis, I was overcome by shyness and moved closer to Persephone when the woman stopped in front of us.

I don't know why, but I'd expected Artemis to be slender and haughty, like Eos. After all, Artemis was more powerful, so her position merited snobbery. She was slim, but tall, with kind eyes. As she stood calmly before us, two Russian Hounds, one brown and one black, jumped from her chariot and trotted to her side. When Artemis stepped closer to me, compassion poured into my soul from the goddess of the moon and protector of animals.

Now I understood why I was drawn to every living creature and why it seemed animals wanted to speak to me, communicating intelligence and emotion with their eyes. My bond with animals came from the energy emanating from this tall, slender goddess. Without knowing what came over me, I bent down on one knee, lowering my head.

"Rise up, Diana," Artemis said.

I stood. Looking into the green eyes of Artemis, I knew I had come home. I understood the source of my connection to the planet. "I'm pleased to meet you," I said, at a loss for words.

"Welcome, Diana. Your power is growing. For the first time in three hundred years, a wild elk was sighted in the woods of South Carolina. Humans hunted the last elk there in the 1700s, but now they are returning. That is a good omen."

Drawn by her powerful gaze, I nodded, remembering the homing pigeon feathers. "And thank you for the wonderful bow and arrows."

"You're welcome. You used them well," Artemis said. "You have been named by Eos, goddess of the dawn, and she gifted you the use of her immortal horses. You've proven yourself to be a worthy warrior in training. For your courage in conquering the oil slick in the Gulf of Mexico and for saving Persephone, I present this gift."

Artemis extended her hand, uncurling her fingers to reveal a ring resting in her palm. "This ring is made of moonstone, one of my symbols. I do not give this gift lightly, but I know you will treasure it. Come forward, Diana, and hold out your hand."

I stepped closer and extended my hand. Artemis continued speaking while wrapping her strong fingers around my hand. "You have been twice-blessed with powerful protection. Your elk tooth necklace is a great gift, and now my moonstone ring will add to your defenses. The moonstone will also provide another great gift: the ability to understand animals."

"You mean I'll be able to talk to them?" Surprised at this, I looked up at her. Artemis held onto my fingers. "When I place this ring on your finger, you'll hear the voices of all animals. Don't be alarmed. At first, it will overpower you, but you'll learn to control what you hear."

"How will I do that?" I asked. The touch of her fingers calmed my nerves and released tension in my shoulders.

"You know how it was the first time you went to Denver and walked downtown with your aunt Joan and cousin Melissa?" she asked.

I nodded, wondering how she knew about my first trip to a big city. Then I mentally shrugged because it was just like the way Persephone seemed to know everything about me. "The voices of people and sounds of traffic on the street were overwhelming but I got used to it," I said.

"It's like that," Artemis said. "When you wear this ring, you'll hear the birds, deer, and elk when you're in the mountains, and when you're on the ranch, you'll hear the horses, cats, dogs, and chickens. Wherever you are, you'll hear the nearby animals, and you'll understand their speech. You'll learn to let it fade into the background, just like the voices of people in a crowded room."

"Will I ever hear the birds sing, or will they always have human speech?" I asked.

"You'll eventually be able to hear both," she said. "Your brain will adapt, and you'll hear the natural voices of animals as songs or growls and howls, but you'll also understand them in human speech, if you want to, when you're wearing the ring. You'll learn to ignore the words and just hear their birdsong. When you take off the ring, you'll just hear their animal sounds. Are you ready?"

"Yes," I said, bracing myself for whatever was coming. Poseidon had turned me into a drop of water, and I didn't know what to expect when Artemis placed the moonstone ring on my finger. I just knew it would be powerful.

Artemis smiled and slid the ring onto the ring finger on my right hand, her warm grip grounding my body.

At first, it was heavy, cold, and large, but almost immediately, it grew lighter and smaller as the band diminished in size until it became a perfect fit for my hand, snuggled against my skin. I admired the slender gold band and milky-white stone with swirling opalescent tones.

There was silence, almost a vacuum, and next came an explosion of sound that filled my ears while Artemis tightened her grip on my hand, anchoring me to the moment.

Voices: high, low, deep. All variety of sound came together when I heard the words of the animal kingdom for the first time.

"Diana knows what we're saying," a flock of meadowlarks flying by shouted.

A small herd of mule deer appeared on the right, turning and talking to each other. "She hears us," one doe said to her fawn.

"Hello, Diana," Lampos said, and I looked at the immortal horses standing a few feet away. "You have joined us." He pawed the ground with his hoof.

To my surprise, Phaeton's wild eyes calmed as he moved toward me. Bobbing his head, Phaeton spoke. "I join my brother in welcoming you."

"Diana, Diana," chanted Glenda and Golden.

"I'm here with you, Diana. It's me, Indigo!"

Indigo flew out of the chariot in a crazy zig-zag pattern and I realized Artemis still held my hand in her warm grip. She smiled, releasing my fingers. I extended my arm as a falconer does when holding birds of prey and it became a perch for a little Mountain Bluebird. She chirped, and, for the first time, I heard her words.

"Diana, you can understand me now," she said. Her voice was musical, like a five-year old girl's.

"Indigo," I said. After all that we'd experienced together, the only thing I could say was her name. She clumsily hopped from my arm to my shoulder and snuggled against my neck, rubbing the side of my face with her head.

"The ring's power will grow as you gain strength, Diana," Artemis said. "You are a warrior in training with many battles before you. I charge you with protecting the pure water, *Aqua Pura*, on our planet. You bear my Roman name, but within you the power of Greek goddesses is strong. Even stronger, however, is the power of Mother Earth. You are bound to protect the Earth throughout your life, just as your grandmother Helen has done."

When she paused, I could only nod, overcome by the moment.

"This ring contains the light of the moon, which is one of my symbols," Artemis said. "When you need its power, simply put on the ring, and ask for me, and I will help you. But now, you must pledge to protect the Earth, Diana of the Wind Rivers. This is your official naming ceremony."

Without thinking, I bent down on one knee again, placing my hand with the ring over my heart. Indigo's tiny feet gripped my shoulder. I already knew what to say. "I pledge to protect the Earth and its waters," I said somberly. "I accept my name, Diana of the Wind Rivers, and will wear this ring proudly." I looked up at Artemis, who smiled and nodded.

"You will now be known as Diana of the Wind Rivers, and no one can deny your place among warriors," Artemis said, extending her hand and pulling me to my feet. "I am honored to be your sponsor. The power of the elk protects you."

"The elk is not her only source of power," said Demeter, stepping forward and placing her hand on my shoulder. "Her power also comes from within. She is Helen's granddaughter."

"Yes, that is true," Artemis agreed. "We continue to need your help, Diana. There is much we must do to protect the rivers of the west. We still have issues with energy companies. In North Dakota, the Native Americans and other Water Protectors have gathered to protest a pipeline these companies want to build under the Missouri River. They still want to bury a pipeline under the Ogallala Aquifer in the Great Plains. Of course, Hades continues to deal with the effects of fracking, and he'll need our help, too."

Indigo flew off my shoulder as Artemis stepped forward to embrace me, and I melted into the power of her compassion. The smell of water and wind came from her hair. Our connection was strong, and the power of the Earth beneath our feet pulsed through my body. As we moved apart, I looked up at her, and felt the strength of her spirit give me confidence. "Thank you, Artemis," I said. "I won't let you down."

"I have one last gift for you, Diana. From this moment on, you will understand what Indigo is saying, even when you don't wear the ring. She will understand you, also," Artemis said. She extended her arm and Indigo landed on her outstretched palm. As Artemis placed her other hand on my head, my scalp tingled as a light zap of energy zipped between us.

"And how about you, little Indigo?" Artemis said. "Is there something you've learned on this adventure?"

Indigo careened back to my shoulder and her breath tickled my ear. "I always wanted to be blue like my father," she said. "I think that sometimes you have to lose a little blue, like my tail feathers, to become completely blue."

"You're blue inside," Artemis said. "The outer blue doesn't matter because you have courage."

"I know that now," Indigo said.

Artemis extended her arm and Indigo fluttered to her forearm. "Is that what you want? Should becoming blue be your reward for helping to bring down the oil slick?"

"I know now that my inner blue is more powerful than the color of my feathers," Indigo said in her little girl voice. "I feel stronger inside and I think that makes me a beautiful blue, like I was when I played in the spray of Oceanus with the Birds of Dawn. Being blue is in my heart, not in my feathers."

Artemis smiled and raised her arm to hold Indigo above her head. "Behold, little bluebird. Your full powers of flight are restored."

She lightly touched Indigo's tail and a cloud of blue feather dust materialized in the air. Like a milkweed pod bursting in slow motion, the blue dust drifted down to reveal perfectly blue tail feathers filling the gap-toothed look of Indigo's tail. I gasped in delight to see her missing feathers were back.

"How beautiful," Artemis said, admiring her own work.

Turning her head to look at her tail, Indigo laughed, a high-pitched, joyous sound. She flew up, circling Artemis. "I can fly easily again," she shouted. "Thank you, Artemis!"

"And what about you, Diana?" Artemis said. "Have you learned anything on this journey?"

"I learned you have to open your heart to others and welcome memories from the past, both happy and sad, even if it hurts," I said. Turning to Persephone, I smiled and her brilliant green eyes gleamed. "I also learned there's more to this elk tooth necklace than I realized."

The others joined me in laughter, although mine was hesitant at first. I relaxed when I saw Artemis throw back her head, laughing with her mouth wide open. Indigo darted around our heads, demonstrating her agility with her new navigational tool, her beautiful blue tail feathers.

"Now it's time to release Lampos and Phaeton," Persephone said when our laughter died down. "They'll fly back to Eos on their own." She started to unhitch the horses from Demeter's bamboo chariot.

I grabbed the reins while Persephone unhitched them and then removed the harnesses and bridles. After the horses were free, I hugged Lampos, wrapping my arms around his strong neck. "Goodbye, Lampos," I said.

"We'll meet again," he said in a deep voice. I stuffed my face into his warm neck, breathing in his scent. Stepping back, I looked into his wise eyes. He was so tall, I had to lean my head back. Lowering his head, he rubbed his muzzle against my shoulder. "You'll be okay, Diana."

"I can't get used to you talking to me," I said.

From behind, a warm head nuzzled my shoulder and I turned to see Phaeton. Rubbing his nose, I looked into his wild eyes, which calmed for one moment before he stepped back and snorted. I patted his neck. "Take care of your brother," I said. "Thank you for everything."

He pawed the ground with his right hoof. "You're becoming a true warrior," Phaeton said.

The brothers turned and trotted away side by side, quickly gaining speed and moving apart to spread their wings and take flight. We all watched as they became airborne and flew effortlessly into the sky, diminishing in size as they moved toward the horizon.

"We'll see them again," Persephone said.

I turned back to help put the bridles on Golden and Glenda, and we quickly harnessed them to the chariot. Demeter and Persephone stepped inside while I turned back to Artemis. "I was honored to meet you," I said. "Thank you for the ring."

"You need more training, and we have many challenges ahead, but I will see you again this summer."

"This summer?" I asked.

"Yes," she said. "Our work together is just beginning. For now, you should take off the ring. Remember, if you need help, just put it on and call my name. In the meantime, I want you to practice wearing it every day, so you become stronger in your ability to improve your selective hearing. Your goal is to move through the forest and hear each animal, but also close off the sounds when you don't need to hear animals speak." She moved toward the chariot, and I followed. "You should also perfect your ability to distinguish the voice of the grizzly bear from the voice of a wolf. A doe sounds different than a buck, and you need to know the difference between deer, and elk, and be able to distinguish an eagle's voice from a hawk. Just as you distinguish the call of the hawk from that of an eagle, you must practice hearing the difference in their voices when you wear the ring."

"How will I do all of this?" I asked.

"This summer, put on the ring and listen to the animals and birds on the ranch," Artemis said. "It will take a while for you to develop these skills. And don't forget to tell your grandmother I said hello."

"When will I see you again?" I asked.

"I'll let you know ahead of time by telling the birds, and they can tell Indigo," she said. "Then I'll come to the ranch."

"Indigo will stay with me?"

"For this summer, she'll stay on the ranch. But in the fall, she'll migrate with her family to New Mexico."

"I'll be with you all summer, Diana!" Indigo said.

"At least everyone isn't leaving me," I said. "I'm so glad we'll be together, Indigo."

Squeezing my shoulders with her warm hands, Artemis gently pushed me toward the chariot. "I'm returning to Africa," she said. "I'll keep working to help game wardens protect the elephants from poachers. You go now with Demeter and Persephone. Goodbye, Diana of the Wind Rivers."

I nodded and then rushed back to hug Artemis fiercely. "Thank you," I said. "Goodbye."

Turning, I quickly moved into the chariot and settled on the seat next to Persephone. Demeter stood in front, holding the reins and Indigo landed next me. Glenda and Golden trotted along the grassy patch, gaining speed and spreading their wings. Moving into the air, they pulled us up while I looked back, waving at Artemis.

Watching her figure become a speck on Squaretop Mountain, I sighed, looking down on the glacial lakes, *Aqua Pura*, that were the source of the Green River.

I faced the front again and reached under my bamboo vest, pulling my elk tooth necklace over my head. I took off the ring, unlatched the clasp on the necklace, and threaded the chain through the ring. Placing it over my head again, I tucked the necklace under my shirt just as a new flock of meadowlarks flew around the chariot, hiding us from the view of any humans in the mountains below. The horses headed east and slightly north, to return us to Sinks Canyon where I would say goodbye to Persephone and Demeter.

Indigo hopped onto my lap, looking up at me with eyes that seemed to understand that goodbyes were always hard for me. "I'll be going home with you," she said.

I knew I should be happy that today I'd be back on the ranch with Grams, but, somehow, I was still a little sad.

I didn't realize how important my tail feathers were until the oil monster took some of them. The palomino mares lifted the chariot away from Squaretop Mountain, and I flew above their heads, savoring the glorious flight as my new tail feathers gave me balance and power. I climbed higher, rolled over, and circled down, stopping short of the horses before jetting back up into the sky. Demeter stood in the front of the chariot, holding the reins, while Persephone and Diana sat on the bench.

"Look at Indigo go," Diana shouted.

I laughed into the wind. I'd always understood Persephone and Demeter, but the novelty of perceiving Diana's words was fresh. I knew we would become closer, because even without the ring, Diana comprehended my birdspeak.

"I'm free to fly," I shouted to Diana. After one last spiraling swoop, I landed on the seat next to her.

"Your tail feathers are gorgeous," she said, moving her fingers down my back.

Settling next to her, I fluffed my wings and leaned against her thigh, content to ride in the chariot. Listening to Diana and Persephone talk, I tuned out their words and thought about all that happened since we'd started our adventure.

I was naïve when I met Memnon in the meadow and he took me to observe Diana on the ranch. All I wanted then was to mate with one of those handsome male Mountain Bluebirds with their nest-building talent.

I was naïve like that before my first snowstorm, too. I hadn't known anything about snow, just like I hadn't known how big the world was. I'd experienced snow when we migrated to New Mexico for winter. One day, my mom and I flew into the mountains and white fluff fell from the sky. I flew up into it and tilted my body to see where the cold weight rested against my blue and grey wings.

"Mother, is this the snow you told me about?" I shouted, swooping up with my beak open. Cold fluff dropped onto my tongue.

"Yes," she sang out, flying swiftly ahead of me, her blue tail vivid in the descending white puffs. "Be careful. Stay near me in case it falls harder."

"What do you mean? I like it," I said and laughed. "It's so light I barely feel it."

"Don't lose sight of me," she said. "Stay close!"

Just after her warning, Mother disappeared as more and more white spots filled the air.

"Mom," I shouted, panic consuming my joy. Pounding my wings in the air, I zoomed ahead until her blue tail became visible again.

"I told you to keep up with me, Indigo! Snow can be deceptive," she said, her voice muffled by the swirling whiteness.

"Okay, Mom," I said, relief coloring my answer.

Just as I was no longer innocent in my understanding of snow, I no longer naively viewed the meadow as the whole world. Now I knew our meadow above Sinks Canyon was just one small place. It wasn't the whole world. That was a sobering thought. There was an entire planet out there, with oceans of water bigger than the sagebrush and grassland prairies of Wyoming. I'd thought I knew it all because I migrated to New Mexico and experienced snow, but I was wrong.

My world had expanded from meadowlarks, magpies, and eagles to birds like Wanda, the Wandering Albatross who'd given her life to protect the ocean.

Now I knew we did things for reasons that were sometimes bigger than a green mountain meadow. Wanda had. She'd given her life for a cause after watching her baby die of starvation.

The voices of Diana and Persephone fluttered over me as I remembered the story Wanda'd told me about the death of her baby.

"I wept when I realized I unknowingly killed my own child by feeding her plastic," Wanda had said. "When Poseidon asked me to join his army, I vowed to stay and help him."

I wanted to continue the fight. "I won't let you down, Wanda," I whispered to myself as we flew toward Sinks Canyon.

My experience with the oil monster had taught me that my inner blue is more powerful than my outer blue. I realized that I didn't have to hide in the bottom of the chariot again. Being blue is in my heart, and it doesn't matter if I'm not sky-blue like my father and brothers. Through her bravery, Wanda helped me see that.

"I think I've grown up a little," Diana said, her words interrupting my thoughts. I looked up at her.

"How so?" Persephone said.

"When I first met you, all I wanted was to remember my mom. And I was mad at Dad for leaving this summer. It's funny. I haven't thought about that in days," Diana said. She looked down at me and smiled. I rubbed against her hand but didn't say anything.

130

"You helped me open my heart to memories of Mom," Diana said. "I've stepped out of my own little world and realized there are bigger problems out there. I'm stronger inside because I faced the oil slick. And I realize the elk tooth necklace protects me, but it also gives me courage." She pulled the necklace from under her clothes and rubbed one of the ivory teeth. "It's warm."

"The necklace will always protect you and gives you strength," Persephone said. "I've been doing some thinking of my own," she added.

"About what?" Diana said.

"You're like a sister to me now. And you've made me think about my life. Remember what you said to me when we were headed to the Platte River to switch chariots and horses?" Persephone said.

"What did I say?" Diana asked. "That seems like such a long time ago."

"You asked me if I wanted to have children," Persephone said. "I always thought that if Hades and I had a child, she would have to stay in the Underworld. But maybe you're right. I travel between the Underworld and above ground, and so could our child."

Demeter looked back and smiled, then faced the front again to focus on driving the chariot.

Persephone glanced at her mom. "My mother has always said that, but I brushed off her ideas. Sometimes you need to hear it from someone else, I guess." She smiled when Demeter turned back. "I've been thinking that having a child might be a good thing."

"Soon?" Diana said.

Persephone laughed. "Maybe in the future. Anyhow, I wanted to tell you I've been giving it some thought. You could be like an aunt if Hades and I have children. It's something to think about."

"That's funny," I said.

"What's funny, Indigo?" Diana said.

"Well, at first, all I wanted in life was a mate and little hatchlings, but then I went off on an adventure with you," I said. "Persephone didn't want hatchlings but did want adventures. Now we've switched roles."

We laughed and then drifted into a companionable silence. Moving closer to Diana, I cuddled next to her thigh. I dozed off, listening to the wing flaps of the meadowlarks flying below us.

"There's Sinks Canyon," Diana said, startling me awake.

I ruffled my feathers and flew out of the chariot as the horses landed on the top of the cliff above the cave. The meadowlarks flew on. Demeter clicked her tongue and guided the mares to a small group of trees. Persephone and Demeter climbed out, and I flew to Demeter's shoulder, knowing it was time to say goodbye.

Diana opened the lid of the chariot seat and pulled out her gear.

"How am I going to hide this bow and quiver?" she asked. "All I have is my bike." She hopped to the ground.

"Just sling it over your shoulder," Demeter said. "Grams and Willy know you were with us, so you can tell them about it. We want you to keep it. If somebody else sees it, you can just say you were using it for target practice in the forest."

"Okay," Diana said. "How am I getting down to the parking lot?"

"We're going to unhitch Glenda and she'll fly you to the other side of the parking lot in the trees," Demeter said. "Then just walk out of the trees and nobody will know the difference. Indigo will go with you to the ranch."

"Won't someone see us flying down there?" Diana said.

"Not too many people are in the parking lot now, and we'll time it so you leave when everyone is down near the river, watching the water flow into the cave," Persephone said.

I knew what Diana was thinking. I felt the same way. Now that we had to say goodbye to Demeter and Persephone, I didn't want to leave them.

"Come here, Diana." Demeter extended her arms. I flew off Demeter's shoulder as she hugged Diana.

"You still smell like lemons and honey," Diana said. "When will I see you again?"

"Persephone and I have to finish taking care of the new spring plants and monitor the crops throughout the summer," Demeter said.

"When the September snow flies in the Rockies, I'll go back to the Underworld with Hades," Persephone said.

"Why aren't we going into the cave to say goodbye to him?" I asked, flying to Persephone's shoulder.

"Right now, he's on his way to Texas. Humans engaged in more fracking that caused numerous earthquakes, so he's trying to stabilize the underground," she said. "We have to go now, and you need to return to the ranch." She extended her arm toward Diana, and I flew back to Demeter, who lightly massaged my back while I perched on her shoulder.

"I'm going to miss you," Diana's voice was muffled as she spoke into Persephone's shoulder while hugging her.

"I'll miss you too, Diana," Persephone said. "But this isn't goodbye forever. We'll be in touch, and we'll send messages when you're with Artemis in the mountains this summer, learning how to use the ring. Maybe we can find the time to check on Mom's mountain meadow grass when you guys are there. Now, let's get you back to the parking lot."

Persephone hugged Diana one more time and then turned to me. "Come here, little Indigo, my brave companion."

I flew to her shoulder and rubbed against her check. "Goodbye, Persephone. I hope we see you this summer," I said.

"You take care of your new tail feathers," she said.

"If I'm on the ranch with Diana, when will I see my mom?" I asked.

"You can leave the ranch anytime to go see her," Diana said.

Demeter moved to the front of the chariot and unhitched Glenda. Golden whinnied and Diana pressed her head against the mare's neck. Then she gave Demeter a fierce hug before turning to Glenda, who kneeled so Diana could easily jump onto her back.

"Time to go," Persephone said, placing her hand on Diana's leg. "Take care, little sister. We'll see you sometime this summer if we can." She stepped back and Glenda flew into the air.

After glancing back at Persephone and Demeter, who stood side by side on the cliff, I followed Diana. We flew down to the trees next to the parking lot, and nobody was around when Diana dismounted and hugged Glenda's neck before stepping back to watch the horse trot away and once again become airborne.

"Now it's just you and me, Indigo," Diana said. "Let's go home."

I flew by her side as she walked out of the trees toward the edge of the parking lot where her bike waited in the rack. After glancing up at the top of the cliff, she climbed on and pedaled toward the highway. I followed, thinking that I would now meet Willy and Grams.

CHAPTER SIXTEEN
BACK AT THE RANCH

Turning my bike onto the gravel road leading to the ranch, I anticipated racing into the house to see Grams and Willy. However, when I crossed the bridge and rounded the curve in the road, I was startled to see a shiny new blue Cadillac Escalade parked in the driveway. My stomach flip-flopped as I realized Aunt Joan was here from Denver.

I moved toward the porch, and all the joy at my homecoming fizzled out. By the time I reached the bottom step on the porch, the screen door opened, and Grams moved out of the house, supporting herself with a walker.

"How was your sleepover with Jenny?" she asked loudly. "I told Joan and Melissa that you were spending the night with your friend on the ranch down the road."

Grams had a warning look in her eyes, and I knew she'd created that story to explain why I wasn't home when they arrived.

Indigo flew slightly ahead of me. "You go sit in the trees and find some insects to eat. I'll come out later and explain, okay?" Indigo took off around the side of the house. Grams didn't seem to notice.

Aunt Joan and my cousin Melissa stepped out on the porch. "Mom, you shouldn't be coming out here on your own," Aunt Joan said sharply. "Hello, Diana, we came to see you as soon as we could get here. I've been so worried about my mom. How could your dad leave for the summer? I was counting on him to help her. And why do you have your bow and arrow?"

"I was teaching my friend how to shoot," I said. "She wants to learn archery. And Dad left because he knew Willy and I would help Grams."

"Willy shouldn't help her. He's the hired hand," Joan said.

"I've been helping her," I said. "I was only gone for one night and Grams was fine."

"Let's go inside so I can sit down," Grams said, effectively diverting Joan's attention.

"All right," Aunt Joan said. "I still can't believe Evan would leave you here with a college kid and the ranch hand." She held the door open as Grams pushed her walker back into the house. "Let me help you, Mom."

"I'm fine," Grams said. "And I'm not alone. Willy's here. He's been helping me."

"That's not right. He's not even a relative," Joan said, her voice carrying out to the porch where Melissa watched me place the bow and arrow on the bench. Was it just a short while ago that I'd said goodbye to Persephone? Already, it felt like a dream.

"Nice boots," Melissa said. "Where'd you buy them?"

I looked down. I forgot I still wore the bamboo boots Demeter made for me. "Grams bought them for me in town," I said.

"I'd wear those with jeans like you are, but I'd tuck them in," she said, surprising me. She considered herself a fashion expert. "I'd like some like that."

I couldn't believe she liked these boots. They were scuffed from wearing them in the chariot and when riding Lampos to fight the oil slick.

"I think this was the last pair in the store," I said quickly. Melissa would probably want to go into town for a shopping trip. "They don't have them anymore." I moved into the house, hoping she would drop the issue.

"What brand are they?" Melissa asked, following me through the door.

"We bought them at K-mart," I improvised, knowing she would never wear clothes from that store.

"Oh," she said sadly. "Oh, well. I can find something similar in Denver, I'm sure. Those must be knock-offs from a real brand."

As we passed through the living room to sit at the kitchen table where Aunt Joan was already setting out coffee cups and creamer, I tried to deflect Melissa's attention from the boots. "You go help Grams and I'll be right back." Without waiting for an answer, I walked down the hall toward my bedroom. Once inside, I closed the door, hid my pouch with the precious bronze flask of *Aqua Pura*, and took off my boots, stashing them in the back of the closet. I put on my regular cowboy boots and went back to the kitchen. Hopefully, Melissa would forget about the bamboo boots.

All three of them were sitting at the table when I entered the kitchen. Joan poured coffee for herself and Grams. This switch to reality was jarring. *Did I really travel across the Rockies in a chariot? Did I see the ocean for the first time?* One telling piece of evidence was Indigo. I'd tell Grams about her later. I took a quick peek outside and didn't see her in the back yard, so I figured she must be off catching insects.

"Want some water?" I asked Melissa. She nodded and I joined them after filling two glasses from the pitcher we kept in the fridge.

"Okay, Mom," Joan said, getting down to business. "We came here today because I'm worried about you. When you told me on the phone that Evan left you here alone while he wanders to North Dakota to make some money, I couldn't believe it. I know you asked me not to come, but Melissa and I just had to drive up here because we're so worried." She added a small amount of creamer to her coffee. *No sugar for Joan*, I thought. She keeps herself on a strict food plan.

"I'm fine," Grams said calmly. "I'm already getting around on my own after the surgery. The doctor said I'm doing well, and I feel great. Besides, as I keep trying to tell you, Willy's here to help me."

"Grandma, that's weird," Melissa said. She used to call her Grams like I did, but not anymore. "He can't take care of you."

"Melissa is right, Mother," Joan said in her best attorney-in-court voice. Even though she didn't work anymore, my aunt loved to let everyone know she was an attorney, and using her voice was one way she did that.

I looked at Melissa and Aunt Joan. They resembled each other more than ever now that Melissa's finished her second year of college. Her dream had come true when she was accepted into the School of the Art Institute in Chicago. She'd made sure I knew she participated in runway shows and photo shoots at school. They both wore their blonde hair long but swept up in classic twists at the back of their heads. They didn't shop at big box stores or even fancy western stores in Denver. I know they purposefully wore jeans and western style shirts when they came to Wyoming, but their version was closer to fancy rodeo clothes than anything I'd ever owned. That was how they dressed coming to the ranch and "roughing it."

Their perfectly manicured nails and expertly applied make-up didn't hold a candle to Grams' tan face and strong, but wrinkled, hands. Her worn denim shirt looked beautiful on her wiry body. I knew they viewed me as a shabby, unsophisticated country bumpkin because I didn't care about how I looked. My hair and clothes had to be comfortable and sturdy for working on the ranch.

"Well, we're here to help you," Joan continued, tapping a red fingernail on the oak kitchen table.

"You don't have to stay," I said quickly.

"We're doing fine," Grams insisted.

"I don't mean we'll cook and clean," Joan said. "We need to hire someone to do that for you, Mother, and you need help showering. I hope you're not letting Willy do that. Are you? He's a man, and he's an Indian." She looked sternly at Grams, who chuckled.

"Joan, shame on you. Willy is part of this family. He's proud to be Shoshone and Crow, and I'm proud to have him here. But, no, he is not helping me shower. I'm able to do that by myself now," Grams said. "We had safety bars installed in the shower, and Diana helped me when I needed it at first. We also had home health care for a while, as you know."

"We need to talk about the future," Joan said, putting down her coffee cup and raising her chin slightly. "I think this event makes it clear you should sell the ranch and move into town where it's safe and you can live in a nice apartment."

I gasped and looked at Grams. She glanced my way, smiled, and turned back to Joan.

"Joan, I broke my hip. I did not slip into senility. I'm perfectly capable of running the ranch while Evan is gone. Even when he's here, I work as much as I can. You know I can't stay indoors for long. I have to be out with the horses, just like Diana and Willy," Grams said.

"Mother, I am serious. It's not right for you to be out here all alone, even though Diana's here," Aunt Joan said, tapping her fingernail on the table again. "Plus, she'll be going back to school in the fall."

Grams reached over and placed her hand over Joan's, quieting the nails on oak. "Joan, I have to tell you I followed through on the decision I told you about last winter." She looked at me, then continued. "I set up most of the acreage in the alfalfa fields as a charitable donation to The Nature Conservancy. When I die, they'll assume control, just as I've outlined in my Will." She leaned back in her chair and watched Aunt Joan.

I knew about the donation to The Nature Conservancy, so I wasn't surprised. However, I *was* nervous about my aunt's reaction.

At first, she was silent, but her face blanched. Then she launched into lawyer mode. "You can't do that with this property. You're giving up millions of dollars. This is prime real estate. Look at all the developments across the highway. Everybody wants to live in this area. I won't let you do that!" Her voice rose and her body followed as she stood and started pacing back and forth.

"It's already done, Joan," Grams said. "I own this land. You know that."

"What about Melissa? She should inherit something, too."

"You have more than enough money to pay for college in Chicago. However, I have left her some money in my will," Grams said. "Diana will be able to live here. The house and two hundred acres will remain in our family, and we'll retain the profits from selling the hay until I die."

"I want to see that agreement," Aunt Joan said. "Who helped you do this? You've lost your mind. We could have sold this place for millions." Her voice rose with each sentence, until she was practically shrieking.

"Joan, there are more important things than money," Grams said. "You know I've always wanted to protect the land. You and your family are welcome to come here because we still own the house and plenty of land around it. I know you're upset, but you never wanted to live here.

That's fine. But we won't sell the ranch to make millions. We want to preserve its beauty and protect Sinks Canyon State Park."

"Grandma, how could you do this to me?" Melissa wailed. "I thought I'd get part of the ranch money someday."

"I love you, Melissa," said Grams. "I did leave you some money in my will, as I said. But I know you don't love the land. You haven't even been here for over a year. You like living in cities. For the rest of your life, this will be a good vacation spot for you."

"You mean stay in this house?" Melissa said.

Now I knew why Melissa didn't come anymore. She couldn't stand our old house. What I saw as comfort and beauty in the fine wood floors and worn leather furniture, she saw as old and stinky. She didn't care that our great-grandparents built the original log cabin on this place and that Grams and Grandpa had expanded the log home over the years. The design blended perfectly with the surroundings, and the solid warmth of the logs kept out the bitter wind and held us close in snowy winters. Melissa didn't see that anymore.

I was relieved Grams had mentioned the land donation to Aunt Joan and Melissa last winter but didn't bring it up again. I knew now why it was better to wait until things were settled and the paperwork signed. I didn't feel like we were losing the ranch because I knew we were preserving it for the future.

"Well, I can see this is getting us nowhere. How could you do this without consulting me? When you brought this up last year, I didn't think you were serious," Aunt Joan said. "Plus, you never mentioned it again." She picked up her purse. "Melissa, come with me. We're leaving. Mother, I expect you to send me copies of everything."

"I'm sorry you feel that way, Joan. You don't have to leave," Grams said. She got up with the help of her walker and followed as they marched out of the kitchen, through the living room, and onto the porch.

I trailed behind, stunned, but somehow elated. *Way to go, Grams*, I thought. She'd let Aunt Joan know who was in charge. For a moment, battling an oil slick seemed like nothing next to the fury of Aunt Joan.

"We have over a five-hour drive back to Denver," Aunt Joan said once we all stood on the porch. "I will be talking with you, Mother." She turned and gave Grams a brief hug. "Goodbye, Diana. Take care of your grandmother."

Joan stomped down the steps, holding her Coach purse in one hand and car keys in the other. She slammed the car door shut and gunned the engine after Melissa got in the Cadillac.

Grams and I watched her turn the Cadillac around. She honked one last time, sticking her arm out the window to wave as they drove down the gravel driveway. A cloud of dust followed the shiny blue SUV.

"Well, that went well," Grams said. "Let's go sit on the deck and talk."

"You were magnificent, Grams," I exclaimed, turning to hug her. Her shoulders seemed frail, and she sighed, leaning on her walker. "I'll get some lemonade. Do you need help getting out there?"

"I'm an old pro at this now," she said, walking through the door as I held it open.

When I came out to the deck with lemonade and glasses on a tray, Grams was watching the birds jostling for key positions on the feeder. She turned with a smile, but her eyes looked tired. "You know, Joan didn't seem worried about taking care of me once she learned we weren't selling the ranch to developers," she said.

"I'm sorry," I said. "She did seem to lose her concern about you pretty quickly."

"She'll come around. Joan has always had a quick temper and then she calms down. I hope she does that this time."

"I hope so, too." I said. I poured lemonade for both of us. Watching Grams sip her drink, I had a new understanding of the fact that she'd lost a daughter. All my life, I'd focused on my suffering over my mom's death, but after my time with Demeter and Persephone, I understood the terrible grief Grams must have felt when her own daughter died. I looked at her with new eyes, noticing her firm jaw and the determined look on her face.

"Do you think about my mom very often?" I asked.

Grams smiled. "Every day of my life," she said. "If I didn't have you, I don't know what I'd do. Now, tell me everything that happened while you were gone."

"Where's Willy?" I asked before starting my story.

"He's working down in the barn," Grams said. "He went there in a hurry when Joan drove up the driveway. You can go see him after we talk, but first, I want to hear everything."

"When I left here five days ago, I was really mad about Dad leaving, and I rode my bike up to the cave," I said. "While I was standing there, the most amazing thing happened."

Grams leaned in, her eyes twinkling. "I knew about everything. Did Persephone give you the note I wrote?"

"Yes," I said. "That's what convinced me to go with her to meet Demeter."

"Demeter and I go way back," Grams said. "But she told you that. Go ahead and tell me everything from the beginning."

"I was standing on the boulder next to the river when the doors opened on the cliff above the cave," I said. "A black chariot and beautiful black horses flew out and hovered over the river in front of me." I began the story, knowing she believed every word.

We finished the lemonade in our glasses and drained the pitcher dry while I talked for over an hour. Grams listened intently the entire time, never interrupting, even when I told her about Indigo. "Then I rode up the driveway to the house, and my heart sank when I saw Aunt Joan was here. I'm so glad they didn't stay overnight because I couldn't wait to tell you the story," I concluded, slumping back in my chair.

With perfect timing, Indigo flew to the deck railing. She must have been watching from the trees, I thought.

"And this is Indigo, your new friend," Grams said.

Indigo flew to the picnic table and landed next to Grams' empty glass. Looking up, she chirruped at Grams.

"She's telling you hello," I said.

"Hello, Indigo," Grams said, carefully touching her back and looking up at me. "Diana of the Wind Rivers. Now you know your destiny. Not many people are lucky enough to know that at age eighteen."

"Grams, why me? That's something I still don't understand."

She sighed. "Let's go inside," she said. "I need a softer chair." Gripping the handles of her walker, she pulled herself up and squared her shoulders, heading for the patio door.

Indigo tried to follow us inside, but I stopped her at the door by holding out my finger for her to perch on. "Can Indigo come in, Grams?"

"What? A bird in the house? She'll go to the bathroom on the furniture."

"No, she won't. I'll tell her to let me know when she needs to go outside."

"Okay, but you'll have to clean up any messes she makes."

I looked at Indigo. "Grams said you can come in, but you have to go outside when you have to go to the bathroom. Can you do that?"

Indigo ruffled her feathers and chirped indignantly, looking at me and then Grams.

"Indigo said she is not a rude bird, and she would never do that. We'll give it a try." I transferred Indigo to my shoulder. Then I stacked the lemonade glasses and pitcher on the tray before following Grams inside and closing the patio door. "Stay with me," I said to Indigo, placing the tray on the counter.

Grams moved into the living room and sat on the leather sofa, patting the cushion next to her. "Come over here so we can talk. It's time you learned the truth about some things, Diana. I have to ask for your understanding."

I sat next to Grams. She touched my hand, wrapping both of hers around mine. Her grip was strong, but as I looked into her brown eyes, I could see sadness and hesitation. She sighed.

"Diana, many years ago, when I was a young woman, I met your grandfather and fell in love. I inherited the ranch when my parents died, and we lived here after we were married. He was drafted into the Army when the Vietnam War started, but he was lost in combat and declared missing in action. Then a miracle happened. They released some prisoners after the war, and he was one of them."

"I know," I said. She'd told me this story often when I was growing up. She kept her Missing in Action bracelet with his name on it in her jewelry box and told me many people still wore MIA bracelets to show their hope that, one day, their loved ones would return.

"Willy was also drafted in the war, but he came home before your grandfather. He was your grandpa's friend, so I hired him to help me," she said.

"He told me that," I said. Indigo hopped from my shoulder to my lap.

"There's more to the story," Grams said, resting against the back of the couch. "Willy and I worked long, hard hours to cut and bale the hay. As time went by, we became close and fell in love." Her grip on my hand tightened. "Willy was not married."

I gasped, which caused Indigo to flutter up to my shoulder again. "What about Grandpa?"

"He was MIA for two years by then. And I gave up hope that he would ever return alive," she said. "When Willy and I fell in love, we became lovers. Please remember, I thought your grandpa was dead."

I sat back in shock. Shock that it had happened, and shock that she used that word with me. When I was growing up, she'd helped me understand what happened as my body developed, but we didn't talk about sex in that way. It was weird to think of Grams and Willy as young lovers. I didn't want to picture that in my head. Photos of Grams from the past showed she'd been a gorgeous young woman, and her tan weathered face was still beautiful. But Grams and Willy together?

My face must have registered my feelings because Grams squeezed my hand gently, then let it go. "Try to understand, Diana. I thought your grandfather was dead, and Willy was not married."

"Okay," I said slowly.

"Imagine my surprise when the Army sent a commander and a chaplain to tell me your grandpa'd been found in a prison camp. Willy and I immediately ended our relationship. Then your grandpa called, saying he'd be coming home. They flew him to Denver and from there, he took a bus. I drove to Rawlins to pick him up at the station. The bus didn't come to Lander and we didn't have a commercial airport, so we had to drive two hours to Rawlins."

I nodded. Lander still didn't have a commercial airport. "So what happened when Grandpa came home?" I asked.

"Your grandfather was a broken man," she said. "He looked years older. I know he suffered in Vietnam, especially as a prisoner of war, but he refused to talk about it." She shook her head, sadness showing on her face. "At night, he woke up screaming, covered in sweat. He was so skinny that his collar and wrist bones stuck out. It took a long time for him to gain weight and he had nightmares for years."

"Why didn't he go see a doctor? Why didn't he get some counseling?" I asked.

"He kept it all inside and refused to talk about it," she said.

Then it hit me. I'd done the same thing with my grief for my mom. I'd kept that inside, too. Now I realized how good it felt to no longer carry that burden. "What happened next?" I asked.

"Just before he came home, I found out I was pregnant," she said, looking down at her hands. "I was pregnant with your mother." She looked directly into my eyes and smiled.

"You mean Willy was Mom's dad?" I said. I could feel my mouth hanging open.

"Yes," Grams said. "He's your real grandfather."

"Did Willy know about it?" I couldn't wrap my head around this news. I stood up, walking to the fireplace. "Why didn't you tell me? Did my mom know?" I could hear my voice rising with each question. I moved back to the couch. "Grams, what about my dad? Does he know?"

"No," she said.

This time, I grabbed her hand and held it in my own. "Who knows about this?"

"You do," she said. "I do … and Willy does."

"Why didn't anyone notice Mom was part American Indian? Why would Willy hide something like that? He's not ashamed to be Shoshone and Crow."

"You have darker skin, and so did your mom. My father was Greek, and we emphasized that Greeks have dark eyes, hair, and skin," Grams said. "Nobody questioned the fact that your mom had dark hair like my dad, and Joan was blonde like your grandpa."

"Oh, my gosh," I said. I felt sick to my stomach. "Aunt Joan is going to be furious. She won't like this at all. She's always looked down on Willy, and so does Melissa."

"She will never know," Grams said. "Nobody knows. Willy and your grandpa were still good friends over the years. Out of respect for your grandpa and Willy's wife, for he did, of course, eventually marry, we never showed our love for each other. When Elaina turned one, Willy married Sarah, the woman his parents chose for him. Now Sarah is also dead."

"Didn't Grandpa suspect something?" I asked.

"I was only a few weeks pregnant, so it was easy to tell him about it after he was home for a while. The timing was such that the baby could have been his," Grams said. "I often wondered if your grandpa suspected anything, I'll admit, but he never said a word. I tried to tell him once, as a matter of fact, but he shushed me and that was that. So, yes, I think he knew, or at least suspected. But he loved Elaina from the moment she was born. In fact, I think she helped him recover somewhat from the war, and when Joan came along two years later, our family seemed complete. We had a daughter who looked like me and my dad, and a daughter who shared your grandpa's coloring."

"This is unbelievable. I'm part Eastern Shoshone and part Crow," I said, standing again. I held out my arm, looking down at my tan skin. "I just realized something."

"What?" Grams said.

"Maybe Willy gave me the necklace because I'm his granddaughter."

"Yes," Grams said. "Now you know."

"Why didn't he give it to one of his other grandchildren?"

"You'll have to ask him," Grams said.

CHAPTER SEVENTEEN
THE VISION QUEST

I held out my arm, looking at my skin with a new perspective. I'd always attributed my dark hair and tan to my Greek great-grandfather. Now I knew Willy was my grandfather and I wasn't sure what to do or say.

"So Willy knows?" I asked again.

"Yes. When I learned I was pregnant, I had to tell him," Grams said. "Then we got word about your grandfather, and Willy and I agreed we should never let the world know. But Willy knew."

"How does he feel about it?"

"I think you should go to the barn and ask him," Grams said. "But first come here, Diana." Grams stood, leaning on her walker

I moved next to her and she took my hands in hers, gripping them tightly.

"I love you, Diana, with all my heart. I hope you believe me that Willy and I didn't know your grandpa was still alive back then. Willy wasn't engaged yet, either." Grams said.

"It's okay," I said. "I believe you."

"Are you upset?" Grams asked.

"Oh, Grams, I love you, too," I said. "I feel unsettled. This is still so new." Tears choked my throat as I looked into her eyes, trying to imagine how she'd kept this a secret for so long. As we hugged, I remembered my dad. "What about Dad? Should we tell him?"

"That is your decision," Grams said. She sat on the couch again. "Perhaps the time for secrets is over. I don't think he's quite ready to learn about Persephone and your adventure, but I think he deserves to know that Willy is your grandfather, if you want to tell him."

"Yes, I do," I said without hesitation. "You're right about Persephone and the others, but he should know about Willy being my grandfather. Will you help me tell him?"

"Of course I will," Grams said. "When he comes home at the end of the summer, I'll be right there with you."

"This is crazy," I said. "I have no trouble believing in a goddess who drives a chariot with flying horses, but I still can't believe I'm Eastern Shoshone and Crow."

"With a little Greek thrown in from me," Grams said.

"I want to go see Willy," I said,. "What will he say to me?" I was nervous. Maybe he wasn't happy about being my grandfather. Maybe he was angry or ashamed.

"He's always loved you, and he wants you to know the truth," Grams said. "Go on out to the barn."

As I left the house and walked to the barn, my stomach pitched and my heart beat faster. I entered the side door leading to the tack room where I knew Willy would be working. Even though I walked softly, he looked up from the saddle he was cleaning.

My fears about his reaction left as he opened his arms wide and stepped toward me. "Diana, my granddaughter," he said. His smile convinced me his joy was genuine.

He embraced me in a solid hug and cupped my face in his hands when we moved apart. He still smelled like Willy. Sweat, horses, and the sweet smell of hay. "You were always my little elk girl," he said. "Now you're my granddaughter as well."

"I was worried you would be ashamed of me or angry at Grams," I said, looking into his deep brown eyes. The sharp angles of his cheeks were smooth, but wrinkles radiated from the corners of his eyes. He held my hands and I saw that mine were a lighter version of the warm brown color of his.

I looked at our joined hands and realized nothing had changed. Willy had always showed his love for me in his eyes and rare smiles while teaching me how to ride a horse bareback and shoot a bow and arrow and when telling me stories of his people around the campfire at night on our trips into the Wind Rivers. Now they were the stories of my people, too. I still wasn't used to that idea.

"I always knew you were my granddaughter," Willy said. "I would never say anything to hurt your grandfather because he was my friend. So I said nothing."

"How did you hide your love for Grams?" I asked. "How could you marry another woman?"

"Sometimes we have to do what is right," he said. "Even though I loved your grandma, I had to honor the wishes of my parents and marry a Shoshone woman. I didn't marry Sarah until a year after your mother was born. Sarah and I did come to love each other, you know."

We walked out the back door of the barn and sat on the bench facing the fields. I breathed in the fresh scent of the green grass stretching before us. To the left, our horses grazed in the pasture, fenced off from the field that would provide their food this winter.

"I'll tell you the story of when our lives first began to interconnect," Willy said as I leaned back against the warm barn boards behind me. "It happened even before I met your grandmother."

I turned my head to watch his mouth and eyes as he moved into storytelling mode. All my life, Willy had told stories and I'd listened.

After a lifetime of learning from him, I trusted Willy completely. Now I looked at his face, knowing his blood ran in my veins. He was mine in a way I'd never considered before, and the sound of his voice cocooned me in warmth.

"When I was a boy, my father and grandfather taught me to hunt deer and catch fish. My friends and I hunted rabbits and birds. I went to school on the reservation and learned to read and write, but the land was always in my heart. My people— our people—believe that every living thing has a spirit of its own," he said. "When I became a teenager, I was old enough for my vision quest. You know what that is because I told you."

"Yes," I said. "It's when a young man goes into the mountains alone to fast and pray while waiting for his spirit animal to reveal itself. That animal guides and protects you for life."

"That's right." He looked at me and then turned his gaze to the fields as if seeing himself as a teenager. "In the old days, I would have walked the forty miles to the sacred place of my vision quest, but my father drove me to the Wind River Canyon. I spent two weeks alone there, hiding in the rocks when people traveled down the river on rafting trips. I didn't want anyone to see me when I was on my quest. In the days of our ancestors, we had the canyon to ourselves, but now tourists drive through," he said.

"Why did you hide from people on the river?"

"My vision quest was sacred, and I didn't want tourists to see me on this personal journey, so I walked to the top of the cliffs high above the Wind River. I climbed on paths known only to our people. When I reached the top, I fasted and purified myself with prayer, waiting for a sign from my spirit animal. I knew my spirit animal would give me strength throughout my life, but I didn't know what the animal would be. I slept and prayed for days, following the customs of our people." Willy paused and faced me without smiling.

"Did you fast the entire time?" I asked.

"I planned to end the fast after meeting my spirit animal. I hoped for a Golden Eagle, because it's a gift from the Creator. The eagle can lend its power to help people. But I kept my mind open, waiting for the animal to find me," Willy said. "After many days of prayer and fasting, I fell asleep one moonlit night. I woke up to see a tall woman landing a chariot pulled by two deer. She got out, followed by two large dogs, bigger than I'd ever seem. I thought perhaps she'd brought the dogs for me."

"Were you afraid?"

"No. Even though she was not a spirit from the legends of our people, she didn't seem dangerous. She walked toward me, carrying a bow slung over her shoulder and a quiver of arrows on her back. The moonlight danced around her, lighting up her hair and face. She was fierce, but not frightening."

"I know who this is," I whispered.

Willy nodded and continued. "As I stood, she stopped before me and told me that a girl-child would be born in the Wind River Mountains. She said that I must be her teacher and guardian while she grew, and that I should give her the elk tooth necklace when she was old enough. I gasped because my mother had given me the necklace and told me its history the night before my vision quest. She told me to always wear it, and that, one day, I would know its purpose."

"That was Artemis," I said. "She came to you on your vision quest."

"Yes," Willy said. "Artemis told me to always wear the necklace until it was time to pass it on. She then walked back to her chariot and flew away. She also told me something very important, Diana."

"What?" I asked.

"She told me that Native Americans and whites will come together to save the planet. After she left, I wondered when I would meet my spirit animal. But the next night, an elk appeared to me in a dream. The elk told me to jump on its back. We ran along the clifftops through the night, and the next morning, I found myself at the bottom of the canyon, not knowing how I came to be there, next to the river. In my hand was a small rock. I knew this rock would give me protection throughout my life and that the elk was my spirit animal," Willy said, pausing again to turn and look at me.

"We share the same animal," I said. "I've seen you pull that rock out of your pocket."

"I took my rock with me to fight in Vietnam, and it brought me safely home to the reservation," Willy said, nodding at my comment. "Then I went to work on your grandmother's ranch, and we fell in love before your grandfather came back from the war. We thought he was dead. When your mother Elaina was born, I thought perhaps she was the child I should teach and guard. But my spirit elk came to me in a dream and said I must wait because it was not yet time to pass on the necklace."

"Did you tell Grams about this?" I asked.

"No," Willy said. "I continued to wait. On the night of your birth, the elk tooth necklace glowed in the light of the moon, and I knew that you were the child Artemis had spoken of, and that you were destined for a great purpose."

"How did you and Grams hide your love for each other?" I asked. "Didn't Grandpa notice how you felt?"

"I could not dishonor your grandfather in that way," Willy said. "I continued to work on the ranch but lived on the reservation. A year after

148

Elaina was born, I married Sarah, the woman my parents wanted me to marry, and came, in time, to love her. I kept working on the ranch, but I don't think anyone suspected how much your grandma and I cared for each other."

"I never noticed anything," I said.

"Later, my wife gave birth to our first son," Willy said. He paused again and watched me.

"Jim," I said. Then it dawned on me why Willy continued looking at me. "All of your children and grandchildren are related to me. Are they going to be mad?" Willy had two sons, one daughter, and three grandchildren who were around my age.

"They already know you well. If I ask them, they will accept you as a member of our family," Willy said. "We'll figure out how to tell them." He looked thoughtful for a moment, then said, "Are you going to tell your dad?"

"Yes," I said. "Grams said she'd help me. We'll tell him you're my grandpa, but not about how I became Diana of the Wind Rivers. I just don't think he's ready for that."

"Let's go see your grandmother," Willy said.

"This is like a family reunion," I said, linking my arm through Willy's as we left the barn.

CHAPTER EIGHTEEN
VOICES IN THE FOREST

"This is the moonstone ring," I said several days later, pulling the elk tooth necklace from under my shirt and over my head. "I keep it here." I unlatched the clasp and removed the ring. Holding it between my thumb and forefinger, I extended it to Grams. The ring glowed and pulsed with heat.

"It's beautiful," Grams said softly, her eyes on the ring.

"You can hold it, but don't put it on," I warned.

Just yesterday when Indigo and I were in the barn, I'd slipped it on my finger and was instantly overwhelmed by a cacophony of voices from our horses, the chickens, geese, birds, cats, and even mice. It hit me with such force that I fell to my knees, covering my ears to block the sounds. Indigo fluttered around my head, but I couldn't distinguish her voice from the din of all the other animals. When did so many mice move into the barn? Their high-pitched voices as they called my name in unison stunned me.

"Here, Diana, here," they cried, running toward me from the bales of last summer's hay stacked at the back of the barn.

"No, Diana, look at us!" Chickens ran into the barn, flapping their wings and racing toward me. "Talk to us first!"

"Stop," I yelled.

Indigo hovered in front of my face as I kneeled on the barn floor. "Take it off, Diana. The ring. Take off the ring," she shouted at me, flapping her wings.

As I dropped my hands to the floor, gasping for air, surrounded by chickens and mice, I heard the horses calling from the pasture. "Come see us, Diana. Come run through the pasture with us."

Indigo flew closer and perched on my shoulder, talking into my ear. "Take it off, Diana. Take off the ring."

I realized the sense of her words and leaned back on my heels, gripping the ring with my left forefinger and thumb. I tugged, but the ring seemed determined to stay put. I started to sob. "It won't come off," I said.

Indigo rested her head against my cheek, softly singing. I heard tweets, not words. As she continued to sing, my breathing slowed, and a sense of calm flooded my body. I tugged firmly on the ring and it slipped off easily.

I closed my eyes, clutching the ring in my fist. Indigo continued her song. My panic receded and I opened my eyes.

The mice scurried to hide in the hay bales, and the chickens scratched in the dirt near the barn door. The horses neighed in the pasture. Sunlight streamed through the window high above the barn door, and dust floated through a sunbeam.

"Thank you, Indigo," I said. "Why did all the animals come running to me? How did they know I'd put on the ring?"

"I don't know," Indigo said. "Maybe they somehow sense it. We'd better not use the ring for a while."

"I'll wait for Artemis," I replied, returning the ring to safety on the elk tooth necklace and tucking it under my shirt. "And I'm going to ask her about how they knew me."

Now I sat at our oak kitchen table with Grams and Willy. As Grams took the ring from me, I held on to the edge of the table, the pattern of its familiar grain beneath my fingers. This table belonged to Grams' mom, my great-grandmother, and I loved the stories Grams told about doing her homework here when she was a girl, just like I had. It was the family gathering place, even though we had a more formal table in the dining room. Made of solid oak, the warm amber finish still held up after generations of use. As a child, I'd loved tracing the pattern of red rosemaling at each of the four corners.

Yesterday, I'd explained to Grams and Willy that Artemis planned to take me into the forest to practice using the ring.

Grams held the ring between her fingers, turning it left and right to admire the pearlescent stone, before passing it to Willy. When they exchanged a warm smile, I realized they were becoming more openly affectionate with each other.

Willy held the ring and looked up at me, his brown eyes serious. "This is powerful," he said, giving the ring back to me after examining it in the morning sun. He looked into my eyes, and I got the impression that he knew what had happened yesterday, but said nothing. Then he looked at Grams, who nodded.

"What?" I said. I'd never noticed how much they communicated with each other using their eyes.

Willy reached out to cover Grams' hand with his own. "I've asked your grandmother to marry me," he said. He smiled at Grams, and then they both looked expectantly at me. He placed his other hand over mine. "Now I can openly call you granddaughter," Willy said, squeezing my fingers.

"What do you think?" Grams said, clasping my other hand. They waited for me to speak, uncertain of my reaction.

I looked down at our hands. Willy's deep brown wrinkled hand, calloused from years of working with horses, Grams', tan and wrinkled, dotted with age spots, and mine, tan and smooth, lightest brown of all. I could feel their love for each other and I remembered that when I'd first met Persephone and Hades, the warmth of their love for each other embraced me in this way.

When I'd initially learned about our relationship, I'd felt awkward with Willy. But only at first, and not for long. Today, their love for each other seemed perfectly natural, and I was glad to be part of it.

"I love it," I said. "We can proclaim to the world that you are my grandfather. Will you come live in the house? When are you getting married? Will it be on the ranch?" I jumped up and hugged Willy, inhaling the familiar leather and horse smell on his clothes. Then I hugged Grams, who laughed, sounding like a young girl.

When I sat down again, Grams smiled, her eyes twinkling. "We want a small wedding at the end of the summer here on the ranch. And, yes, once we're married, Willy will come live in the house."

"What will Dad say?" I asked. "Wait, what about Aunt Joan? She won't like this."

"Joan loves Willy. Her objection won't be because he's Shoshone and Crow. That won't bother her. Her concern is status; she'll think it's wrong for me to marry the ranch hand," Grams said, shaking her head. "But she'll get used to it."

"Will she come to the wedding?" I asked.

"I think she will, but we'll have to see how she reacts." Grams said. "What do you think your dad will say?"

"I think he'll be happy," I said. "Just as happy as I am."

Through the glass patio door leading to the deck, we heard Indigo.

I opened the door and told Indigo the news. "She's happy, too," I said as she flew inside.

"Be careful with birds in the house," Grams said.

Years ago, when my horse Daisy was a three-month old filly, I'd brought her up on the deck and into the kitchen through the patio door. I thought it was cute, but Grams shrieked when she turned around. Ever since then, she'd been picky about which animals came inside. Until now, only cats and dogs were allowed.

"She'll go to the bathroom on the kitchen counter," Grams said.

"She won't," I said. "I told her she can't go in the house, remember? But we'll go out for now. Come on, Indigo. Back outside." I walked out to the deck and Indigo followed me, perching on the back of a patio chair.

"Will they have hatchlings now that they're mates?" the little bird asked.

"No." I laughed. I was still getting used to the fact that I understood Indigo's birdspeak. Everyone else heard chirping, but I heard words.

"They're too old to have hatchlings now. They'll just be two lovebirds, living happily."

Just then, a crow landed on the deck railing with a squawk. "What's he saying?" I asked Indigo.

The large bird cawed again. I could understand Indigo, but not the crow. I didn't dare put on the ring, however. Yesterday had taught me a lesson about its power.

"Thanks for telling us," Indigo said as the crow flew off with a parting comment. She turned to me. "He said Artemis will be here in one week to take us into the forest."

"Already?" I said. The remembered sound of squealing mice and shouting chickens filled my ears.

"Yes," Indigo said. She flew to the railing, sitting on the spot the crow had vacated.

The next week passed quickly. Indigo and I developed a daily routine of getting up, collecting eggs for breakfast, and riding around the pasture on Daisy. Indigo sometimes perched on the saddle horn right in front of me.

By midweek, we'd convinced Grams to let Indigo come inside the house for longer periods of time on a trial basis, especially because she wanted to sleep in my room. We proved to Grams that Indigo knew when she had to go outside.

The following week, Artemis arrived as Eos was bringing up the dawn at the far edge of the world. I thought about Lampos and Phaeton pulling her chariot across the sky. I wondered if the horses ever thought about me. Our time together seemed so long ago.

My backpack was ready with the *Aqua Pura* flask, and I wore my bamboo boots. My bow and quiver with homing pigeon arrows rested on the patio table. Indigo sat on the deck railing.

Artemis landed near the barn with a soft swoosh, the sunlight growing brighter as she neared. She alighted from the chariot and I walked out to meet her, with Indigo perched on my shoulder, just as Grams and Willy came out of the house. Her wolfhounds walked with her.

"Do you have your ring?" Artemis asked.

"Right here," I replied, pulling out the elk tooth necklace and ring.

"You tried it on, didn't you?" Artemis softened her question with a smile. "The power affects me when you put on the ring. And don't forget, you can always use it to call me as well. If I can't get there right away, I'll send an animal to defend you until I can arrive. Now you know Indigo can help you also."

"When I put on the ring, all the animals in the barn started running to me. How did they know I was wearing the ring?" I asked, mentally shuddering at the memory of my panic.

"The animals on the ranch know you. They sensed the power of the ring and wanted to talk with you. When you're in the forest, the animals will sense the ring's power, but they won't run to you until they know you better."

"Okay," I said. "I'm glad you'll be with me in the forest."

"Eventually, you won't need my help," she said.

"Why don't you have a flock of birds with you?" I asked, looking at her chariot and the golden-horned deer.

"My chariot is like a chameleon," Artemis said. "It changes colors on the bottom to avoid detection. It can look like the blue sky or a white cloud, or any other pattern."

"What about the deer? Won't people see them?" I asked.

"The chariot casts its colors forward to disguise them as well," she said. "We should get going. We have a busy day ahead."

"Okay, I'm ready." I turned to hug Grams and Willy.

"Take care of her, Artemis," Grams said, as if giving orders to a goddess was an everyday occurrence.

"I know I have precious cargo," Artemis said after climbing in and picking up the reins. "You've both taught her well," she added. "But she has more to learn."

Artemis and Willy looked silently at each other for a long time, and I remembered he knew her from the time of his vision quest. I climbed in and sat. Immediately, the does moved quickly across the pasture, rising into the air, pulling us into the sky. As I looked back, I saw Willy move closer to Grams and put his arm around her. They waved in unison.

Indigo landed on the seat beside me. Facing the front and looking over the edge, I realized I could easily see below. "We can see everything without the birds under the chariot," I said.

"Riding with me will be a new experience," Artemis said, giving me a smile.

I continued to gaze over the edge, watching as we flew above Sinks Canyon. Soon, we reached the parking lot next to the trailhead. The trail into the mountains followed the course of the river and disappeared into the forest, lost among the trees. I scooted to the middle of the seat and settled in for the long ride. Indigo moved next to me, tucking her head under her wing. We traveled in companionable silence until Artemis suggested we eat.

"I have some walnut energy bars under the bench," she said.

I found them and moved to stand in the front. We ate while watching the tops of trees pass by. Now and again, the river peeked out, glistening in the sun.

"We're going to land in that clearing ahead," Artemis said. The deer glided the chariot to a smooth landing in the large meadow. Coming to a stop near the edge of the forest, they waited while we got out. Indigo woke up and flew to observe from the edge of the chariot.

"We'll leave the chariot here and let the deer graze in the meadow," Artemis said. "Right now, we need to start working with your ring."

We unhitched the deer and pulled the chariot just inside the trees. I followed Artemis into the forest while the deer remained in the meadow.

"I want you to put on the ring now and screen out all the animal sounds except the one you want to hear," Artemis said. "It's like walking in Denver and closing your mind to the street noises so you can talk to your cousin Melissa and aunt, or like listening to an orchestra and finding the one instrument that appeals to you, such as the violin or flute. You can tune out all the nearby animals and listen to just one."

"I'm scared," I said, remembering what had happened in the barn.

"You know that when you fall off a horse, the first thing you have to do is get back on? You have to conquer that fear, right? Otherwise it becomes harder to ride your horse again," Artemis said.

"I know," I said. I'd fallen off horses plenty of times on the ranch, whether it was because the horse turned suddenly while running or whether it bucked me off. Once, I'd even flown forward off a horse when she stopped on a dime after running at a full gallop. I'd kept going, right past her head. The breath was knocked out of me and I struggled to breathe as I sat up. Willy had helped me stand and get back on the horse.

"Don't let the horse feel your fear," he'd said, and I knew the sense of his words.

I looked up at Artemis. "Okay. I'll give it a try." I inhaled deeply.

Artemis smiled. Moving closer, she put her hand on my shoulder. "I'm right here and I won't leave your side," she said.

Nodding, I took the elk tooth necklace from under my shirt and removed the ring from the chain. I gulped and slid it onto my finger. Artemis immediately grabbed my hand, grounding me as the sounds of animals and birds threatened to overwhelm me. In spite of her support, I fell to my knees again as the multitude of voices hit me.

Bird song changed to words. A family of chipmunks scurried from under a bush. I panicked, recalling the rush of animals in the barn.

"Take it off," Artemis said in my ear. I wasn't even aware that she held me next to her body. "We'll try it in small doses."

I removed the ring, surprised to find myself breathing heavily.

"It's okay," she said, her strong grip calming me. "Let's try again."

I nodded and put on the ring. This time, I was prepared for the onslaught of voices.

"Try to distinguish one voice," Artemis said. "Listen to Indigo."

"Diana, this is my friend, Memnon," Indigo said as she flew up to land on a pine branch where a meadowlark perched.

"Hello, Diana," the meadowlark said.

"I can understand you," I cried. I'd known I'd be able to, but it still surprised me.

"I met Indigo a year ago when she was a youngster," Memnon said.

Artemis and I walked closer to the tree, looking up at the two birds. I forgot to focus and the babble of other birds and nearby animals took over. Artemis tugged on my hand without speaking, and I knew she wanted me to focus.

We walked through the forest all afternoon as I explored the power of the ring. We stopped near a thicket and a doe walked out with her fawn. "Say hello to Diana," the doe instructed her fawn.

"Hello, Diana," the spotted fawn said.

"Can I pet you?" I asked, moving forward when her mother nodded.

I held the little fawn's adorable face in my hand. "You have beautiful eyelashes," I said.

"Say thank you," her mother urged.

"Thank you," the fawn said. "What kind of creature are you? Do you have a mommy?"

I chuckled and kneeled down to hug the fawn, captivated by her perfect little muzzle. "I have a dad and a grandma and grandpa," I said.

"I have a daddy, but he's not around right now," the fawn said. She nuzzled my cheek, her soft breath tickling my face. "Want to come see my thicket? I sleep there when Mommy is in the meadow."

I stood up and followed her to the thicket, leaning down to look inside. Covered in pine needles, a small indentation in the ground formed a cozy little nest.

"Come on in," the fawn said, moving past me and curling up on the nest, tucking her slender legs next to her body.

I crawled inside and sat next to her in the small area, realizing that I was able to hear the fawn and shut out the voices of all the other forest animals around us. As she talked about how much she loved the meadow, I rubbed her back.

"It's time to move on, Diana," Artemis said from outside the thicket a few minutes later.

Walking through the forest that afternoon, I lost track of time, forcing myself to focus on the ring and develop my ability to hear only one voice among many. When the voices crowded together once more and I couldn't separate one animal from the others, Artemis stopped on the deer trail.

"I can tell you're worn out," she said. "Let's go set up camp."

"Okay," I said. I took off the ring and put it back on the chain.

We followed the trail back to where the chariot waited in the trees. As we approached, the does looked up from where they grazed. After watching us for a moment, they lowered their heads to keep eating.

"Sit down and rest while I take care of things," Artemis said.

I realized how tired I was and lowered myself to a soft bed of needles under a tree. Leaning against the trunk, I inhaled the keen pine pitch smell. "I should help you," I said when Artemis walked toward me after pulling my backpack from the chariot.

"Drink some *Aqua Pura*," she said. "I'll start setting up camp."

I pulled out my flask, holding it up to look at the engraving. The elk lifted her head and looked at me, grass dangling from her mouth. She paused in her chewing and then lowered her head to resume grazing. I smiled and removed the cap, taking a long drink. My fatigue evaporated, and I started to get up.

"You stay put," Artemis said. "I'll take care of this."

"Okay," I said, replacing the cap on my flask. I leaned against the tree and listened to the birds in the trees, relieved to hear them singing instead of talking.

"Close your eyes, Diana," said the one bird I always understood. She flew down to my shoulder, rubbing her head against my cheek.

"Okay, Indigo," I said and closed my eyes. "I'll get up and help in a minute." The tree bark poked into the back of my head, but the pine smell overcame that feeling as I drifted to sleep.

***

"Diana, it's time to eat," Artemis said, gently squeezing my shoulder.

"How long was I sleeping?" I asked, standing to stretch. "The sun's setting already."

As I looked around our campsite, I realized that camping with Artemis was like magazine glamping. A white canvas tent sat on top of a green carpet covering a wooden platform. As I watched, Artemis waved her hand and released fairy lights that fluttered about.

"How did you do all of this?" I said.

Artemis smiled at me and shrugged. "I do a lot of camping, so I might as well enjoy it, right?"

I laughed. "I agree completely. Persephone could take some lessons from you."

"Oh, don't tell her that." Artemis chuckled and sent zaps of vivid purple lightning bolts to a circle of small granite boulders in the middle of the campsite. Purple and orange flames danced brilliantly in the campfire.

"I'll cook dinner while you unpack," Artemis said. She quickly moved to the chariot and removed a canvas bag. "Go on now. You can wash your hands in the stream over there."

I entered the tent, astonished to find two cots covered with soft blankets and small square pillows. Running my hand over one of the blankets, I said to the empty tent, "Bamboo from Demeter, I'm sure."

After eating the delicious soup Artemis heated on the purple and orange-flamed campfire, we sat, drinking tea flavored with honey. "Does Demeter supply all of you with food and blankets? Persephone and Hades had this stuff in the cave," I said.

"We help each other when we can," Artemis said.

We sat in companionable silence while the fire crackled. "How does it make that sound when there's no wood?" I asked.

"I added that sound effect," Artemis said. "I don't want to burn trees, but I do like a good crackling fire."

"I'm getting better with the ring," I said, watching the flames. "I'm still not sure about using it on my own."

Artemis sipped her tea and looked at me. "I'm going to be honest with you, Diana. You're a little bit spoiled. You've had your way far too long because the adults in your life feel sorry for you, so they grant everything you demand."

I looked at her in surprise. The warm cozy campsite grew chilly. "I'm spoiled?"

"Yes. But I'm here to tell you that you've got to slap yourself in the face and deal with reality," Artemis said. "Plenty of people in this world have it tough, like you. Some have it even harder. I know you lost your mom, but now you must accept the past and move on because we need you in our fight for the planet." She softened her words with a smile.

I shifted uncomfortably on my log. "I want to help but I still wonder why you chose me."

"Humans are destroying the planet and fresh water. You were born to help us. Sometimes people must follow their destiny," she said.

"I want to fulfill my duty and use the ring," I said.

"You will become better, with practice," Artemis said. "We need you to bridge the gap between animals and humans. You will be the voice that communicates animal wisdom to humans. The ring will allow you to explain the behavior of animals and their purpose in ecosystems. Humans have removed and exterminated so many species. It's only now that they—at least some of them—understand what they've done."

"How can I do all of that?" I asked.

"Remember, you're still in training. I have a magnificent and powerful animal for you to meet. This animal can have an incredible impact on the world. In fact, its numbers were once so vast that it affected all of North America."

"What animal?" I asked.

"You'll find out tomorrow. Right now, let's get some sleep," she said. She rose and rinsed our cups in the pan of water near the campfire, dousing the flames afterwards. The campfire smoked and sizzled, as if real wood burned there.

We went to the tent and settled in our beds. The wolfhounds slept between our cots, their soft breathing adding to the comfort of the tent. *Am I spoiled? I guess I do have everything I want. My horse, my saddle, and my cowboy boots. My own bedroom.* Any time I'd wanted something, Grams and Dad bought it for me, if we had the money. And, although I earned some scholarship money, Dad paid for the rest of my first year at school, and he planned to do the same in the fall.

I fell asleep listening to an owl hooting in the forest.

***

The next morning, we were up early, drinking tea with breakfast. "The animal you're meeting today once lived throughout all of North America," Artemis said. "But now its numbers are greatly diminished due to overhunting. Let's go out to the meadow so you can put on the ring and talk to her."

Artemis didn't hold my hand this time, and I wondered about this creature while I put on the ring. It had to be an elk. That was my spirit animal. Or would it be a moose? A grizzly? *I know,* I thought, *it's a wolf.*

As Artemis talked, we reached a large pond, pausing next to a stand of willows. On the other side of the pond was an aspen grove flanking the meadow and leading up to the forest, where the trees became pines.

"It will be a moose," I said. "They eat willows."

I looked for the brown color of a moose among the willows. But I didn't see one, so I sought the tawny color of the elusive cougar, and the majestic red of an elk. *I'll ride on the back of the elk like heroes in fantasy novels*, I thought. *As the elk and I talk, its sonorous voice will fill my head with the wisdom of the forest.*

Or maybe it would be a wolf. I imagined myself walking through the forest with a wolf. I'd place one hand on its massive shoulders, and the stiff fur of the wolf's coat would be coarse on top and soft underneath, like a Husky. The movement of its strong shoulders would anchor us together as the wolf imparted the knowledge of the wilderness.

Eager to see the wolf, I looked over the sparkling water glinting in the sun, but I saw no animal.

"Meet your guide," Artemis said.

I continued to scan the area on the other side of the pond.

"I'm down here," a confident voice said.

I looked down to see a two-foot-tall upright brown furry animal with

160

buck teeth protruding through her smile. "A beaver?" I said before I could stop myself.

"You expected something else?" she said, a knowing glint in her eye. "Perhaps a cougar? A grizzly? A wolf?"

Artemis laughed. "Diana, meet Zosime," she said.

"My name comes from ancient Greek and means survivor," the beaver said.

I extended my hand toward Zosime's outstretched paw, eyeing her powerful claws. She grabbed my fingers in a firm grip. "Hello, Zosime," I said. Her claws didn't hurt my hand.

"My mother named me Zosime to remind me that our species will survive," she said. "In spite of the fact that they wiped out hundreds of millions of us centuries ago, I'm still here."

"All for men's tall hats," I said.

"Right," she said. "My middle name is Benthesikyme, which means Lady of Deep Swells." She released my hand and preened her face with quick movements of her paws, looking as if she admired herself in the mirror, but none was there.

"Zosime is a brilliant, creative engineer—and a little vain," Artemis said. She smiled fondly down at the animal, who continued to smooth her face.

"I'm a water animal," Zosime said. "It makes sense that my middle name comes from the goddess of the waves. She was the daughter of Poseidon and a queen he seduced, Amphrite. My mother was named Bia. Just like beavers, Bia was overlooked by most people. Her famous sister Nike got all the attention, but Bia was the personification of might and was linked to power, force, and physical compulsion."

"You're named after great women," I said, trying to seem more respectful.

"We're changing the world, one beaver pond at a time," Zosime said. "My mother was a powerful force and taught me how to build." Suddenly, she turned her head to look at the pond. "I'll be back," she said before waddling to the pond and diving in.

I looked at Artemis, who shrugged. "She heard a leak in the dam, I think."

A furry, wet head materialized from under the water and Zosime quickly reached the edge of the pond, crawling up the bank and returning to us.

"Let's move away from the pond," she said. "When it's triggered by the sound of trickling water, I can't control my instinct to fix the dam. That's the compulsion of all beavers. We're born to build."

"You talk with Zosime while I go back to the campsite," Artemis said. "I'll see both of you later."

As Artemis walked away, I turned back to my new friend, who now walked toward a stand of aspens. I followed and sat on a fallen tree. She climbed up and sat next to me on the log. Droplets of water clung to the fur on her back as she preened her face again.

"In my defense, I have to rub my fur to spread oil. That keeps me waterproof," she said. She sat up, rubbed her belly with both paws and then went back to her face. "See? Natural waterproofing from my oil glands."

"That's terrific," I said.

"How would you feel if you were hunted for your fur? What if they cut off your scalp and left your body to rot, like they did to millions of beavers all over North America?" she said, moving her paws away from her face and looking up at me.

"I'm sorry humans did that," I said. "I'm glad you survived."

"My ancestors were killed by fur trappers," Zosime said. "Why is it that when humans see millions of animals, they want to kill them for food or profit or sport? Passenger pigeons come to mind."

"I know about them," I said. "Buffalo, too. But I don't know why people are like that."

"Did you know that your government encouraged people to kill buffalo?" she said. "They allowed people to shoot from trains moving through huge herds. People kept shooting and stopped only when their guns became too hot."

"I didn't know that," I said. "How do you know this stuff? There are no trains up here in the mountains, and that was a long time ago."

"Word gets around," she said. "Artemis fills us in on human activity."

"Well, I'm glad you're here, little Miss Survivor," I said, patting her on the back. "And I think humans are starting to realize they shouldn't destroy every species."

"Especially us," she said. "We can restore wetlands in the west. Our ponds help control flood and droughts due to our brilliant engineering feats. Our clever building creates dams that retain water and raise the water table."

"I didn't think about that," I said.

"Well, as our ponds spread out in creek beds, we saturate the grass beyond. I have a cousin in Nevada who helped restore dry creek beds after cattle overgrazed the area. They fenced off the tiny trickle of a stream and transported my cousin and her mate, who quickly created a dam using the nearby willows. After a couple of years, the pond attracted birds and other animals, effectively restoring the ecosystem of the area."

"That's amazing," I said. "We need to restore beavers to locations all over the west. But how do you know these things about places so far away?"

"Artemis," she said. "I've also helped by sending my children up and down this stream."

"You have children?" I said. "How many?"

"Well, I've had one litter of kits every year, so I've sent out over fifteen youngsters to start new ponds," she said. "Once my young ones are two years old, we send them on to create their own homes."

"You're like an army of engineers," I said.

"More like a squadron," she replied. "But we've survived the slaughter. Now the rebuilding can begin. Speaking of that, I need to get back to work. Thanks for coming here, Diana."

"Thank you for talking with me," I said as she looked up at me. "I'd better go see what Artemis is doing."

I stood up as Zosime hopped off the log and waddled back toward the pond. I followed, standing on the bank and watching her dive in, clearly more graceful in the water. With a flap of her broad tail, she disappeared.

Before walking back toward the trees, I took off the ring and returned it to the necklace.

Back in camp, I told Artemis about my conversation with Zosime. "Are they restoring beavers to wild places in other states?"

"Yes," she said. "I'm working with a group in Colorado and others as far away as England. We're releasing beavers into the wild again to repair broken water systems. It's a slow process, but very encouraging."

"I liked meeting Zosime," I said. "At first, I thought you'd introduce me to a powerful creature like an elk or wolf. Now I realize the power of beavers."

"Restoring beavers also means we can prevent declining snowpack in the mountains," she said. "When the streams and rivers flow without beaver ponds, the water rushes out of the mountains too quickly, and the winter snowpack doesn't last as long in the summer."

"It's all connected," I said.

"You can see why I gave you the ring," she said. "Humans have to work with animals to restore water systems. What you learn from talking to animals can help speed up that process. It's all part of saving pure water on the planet."

"I'll keep working on my use of the ring," I said.

"Good. Tomorrow, we're flying to Younts Peak," Artemis said. "There's someone I want you to meet. While we're there, we'll refill your flask with *Aqua Pura*."

"Another animal?" I asked.

"No," Artemis said, dousing the fire. "It's a surprise, and I think you'll like it."

***

The next morning, we efficiently broke camp after breakfast. I helped Artemis take down the white canvas tent after we'd folded the cots and blankets inside. We carried the wooden platform into the trees and leaned it against a large pine.

"It'll be here next time we come here," Artemis said. "You'll come back with me next year to see Zosime."

We loaded the chariot and Artemis whistled for the deer, who trotted from the meadow. "You go say goodbye to Zosime while I finish up here," she said.

I walked across the meadow to the pond just as Zosime swam ashore.

"We're leaving now," I said. She walked up onto the bank, pausing at my feet to smooth the wet fur on her face while she looked up at me. I put on the ring.

Sitting up on her back legs, Zosime extended her short arms toward me, her paws outstretched. "I'm glad to know you, Diana," she said, her orange buck teeth protruding from under her lip.

I grabbed her paws, crouching down to look her in the eye. "I'm honored to know you, Zosime Beaver," I said, gripping her powerful claws. "You will help heal the planet."

"This little animal and saplings will save the planet if we let them do their work," Artemis said, walking up behind us.

"We could even repair the flooding of the mighty Mississippi, if they'd let us," Zosime said.

"Let's start with *Aqua Pura* in Wyoming," I said. "I'm going to miss you, Zosime."

She moved forward and hugged my arm, wet fur and all. "You take care, Diana. I'll see you again, so we don't have to say goodbye forever."

I stroked her head and looked into her kind brown eyes. "I'm glad about that," I said.

Straightening up, I watched as Zosime turned and slid back into the water. "I'm ready to go," I told Artemis. The wolfhounds were already on board, and Artemis picked up the reins after we joined them.

The deer bounded across the meadow and gained speed. As we left the ground, I looked over the side of the chariot to see Zosime perched on top of her beaver lodge, waving one paw in the air.

"Can you lift the cloaking color on the chariot?" I said. "Zosime is waving, and I want to make sure she sees us."

"Sure," Artemis said.

She must have done something, because when the chariot circled over the pond and I waved back, Zosime stood on her hind legs and waved both paws. Then she dropped down on all fours, climbed to the bottom of the lodge, and slipped into the water with a flap of her tail.

As the chariot rose into the sky, the irony was not lost on me that I'd built dams in my heart and then learned to tear them down in order to accept the death of my mom. Now we'll build beaver dams in meadows and dry desert streambeds to retain and restore *Aqua Pura* in the mountains and plains. I'd allowed the dams in my heart to release their floodwaters so I could heal, and the dams built by beavers would restore the ecosystem, healing the planet.

CHAPTER NINETEEN
GUARDIAN OF THE HEADWATERS

I woke to cold air brushing my face. Artemis guided the deer to a soft landing on short emerald grass. A gust of winter air blew across the edges of a great snowbank packed up against the base of a rocky cliff.

"Welcome to Younts Peak," Artemis said, bringing the chariot to a smooth stop. "This glacier is the source of the Yellowstone River," she said. "You're looking at the humble beginnings of the longest untamed river in the continental United States."

"I'd hardly call this humble," I said, looking over the great expanse of snow. All around, the sounds of birds, water, and wind created a calming effect next to the massive rocks that formed Younts Peak. "It's hard to believe I was here with Persephone in the beginning of the summer."

"You came from the other direction with her. This is the north face of the peak," Artemis said. "Don't get out yet. Let's drive down to the lower edge of the glacier."

I started to stand but sat again as the deer trotted over the ground next to the snowbank. The chariot wheels bumped over clumps of grass. We traveled to where rivulets of water trickled through the snow to gather speed in a stream that rushed toward a small lake.

"That's called a tarn," Artemis said. "A small glacial lake. From there, the water races down the mountain slope, creating the North Fork of the Yellowstone. On the other side of these cliffs is the South Fork. They meet way at the bottom of the peak to form the Yellowstone, or Elk River, as the Crow people named it."

"Look," Indigo said. She pointed her beak toward the edge of the glacier where a tall woman materialized out of the snow.

"She's a glacier nymph," Artemis said as the woman came closer. We got out of the chariot and Indigo flew to my shoulder.

Taller than Artemis, the slender nymph came within a few feet of us and paused, a calm smile on her face. And what a face she had. Her periwinkle skin, pale blue with hints of lavender, contrasted with her pastel silver purple hair, which stood up all around, spiking toward the sky. Her cerulean blue eyes were the same color as Indigo's wings and tail feathers.

"I look like this from spending my entire life on mountaintop glaciers where granite meets the sky," she said, her musical voice tinkling like water over rocks. "My name is *Tixi Pagos*, which is Greek for melting ice.

I am Guardian of the Headwaters of the Yellowstone River." She bowed from the waist in greeting. "You can just call me Tixi."

"I am Diana of the Wind Rivers," I said, bowing in return. "What does the guardian do?"

"I protect and monitor the source of the river," she said. "I keep track of the amount of snowfall each winter and how much melts in the spring. The amount of water melting must never exceed the amount of winter snowfall, but every year, we have less snow. I also check the quality of the water as it melts. Nature reveals all of these things to me."

"I'm going to set up camp just inside the trees," Artemis said. "You two talk; I'll be over there."

"Don't worry," Tixi said, sensing my alarm as Artemis left. "You'll be safe with me."

As Tixi turned to watch Artemis fly away, I gasped. Transparent dragonfly wings, made of lacy ice, folded neatly against her back. They flowed down from her shoulders, ending just beneath her waist. Intricate and delicate, her wings looked like they could shatter at any moment.

"I make you uncomfortable because I look like I'm going to break, don't I?" Her striking blue eyes widened as she arched her deep purple eyebrows, dramatic against her periwinkle skin. "You know about nymphs, right?"

I nodded. "Nymphs protect trees, forests, lakes, and rivers," I said.

"I'm an Oread, a mountain nymph. We all differ according to our dwelling," Tixi said. "But I'm a very specific kind of mountain nymph. A glacier nymph. When the first snow flies in the mountains, our ice wings grow so we can swiftly fly over our glaciers, monitoring the volume and quality of the snow that falls. When the spring melt starts, our ice wings become brittle and fragile, like thin ice in a mountain river. You've seen that before on the Popo Agie River in Sinks Canyon, right?"

"Yes," I said, recalling the sight of snow-covered boulders rimmed with transparent ice in the spring, revealing the clean water racing below.

"I exist at that point just before pure ice turns to water," she said. "When the rivulets of melting water turn to small streams, I change form at the edge of the ice. My wings melt completely and I slip into the trees to spend the summer dashing through mountain meadows and over rocks hidden deep in the forest, running through glades dappled with sunshine. I dance in streams with the water nymphs and rub against the bark of trees where wood nymphs live. When the snow starts to fly in the fall, I return to the edge of the glacier and my ice wings form again."

"Why didn't I see you when I came here with Persephone?" I asked. "And why haven't I read about you in my Greek mythology books?"

"When you came to fill your flask with *Aqua Pura*, I was on this side of the cliff and you were on the other side," Tixi said. "And the reason

168

you haven't read about me in your books is that glacier nymphs are very shy, even more so than regular nymphs. Not even the Greeks knew about us."

"Does every glacier have a nymph guardian like you?" I asked.

"Yes," Tixi said. "My sister nymphs live atop mountain peaks all over the world, guarding the sources of rivers. In fact, sometimes alpine glaciers are called rivers of ice. Come walk with me and I'll show you the beginning of the longest untamed river in continental America."

She moved away and I followed. We skirted the glacier, walking on the short grasses growing next to the snow.

"This glacier has existed for tens of thousands of years. Stop and listen. Filter out the birds and the breeze. What do you hear?" Tixi stopped walking. "Close your eyes."

I stood still and closed my eyes. At first, birdsong on the breeze filled my head. Then I heard it. Water trickled over ice, melting and running down the slope. The rivulets whispered over the grass after transforming from ice to water. Gaining speed and volume, they joined the streams that raced down to form the tarn.

"North Fork is joined by another stream on the south side. They come together to form the Yellowstone. This is *Aqua Pura*, the source of the largest undammed river in the lower United States," Tixi said.

The sound of her voice pulled me away from the rushing water, and I opened my eyes.

"Let's go fill your flask," she said.

I walked along the path of the stream as it flowed toward the tarn. When we reached the bank of the lake, she paused near a rocky outcropping. Reaching into the pouch I wore like a cross body bag, I pulled out my empty bronze flask.

"May I see it?" Tixi asked.

"Yes," I said. "Demeter gave this to me. She said Hephaestus made it." I turned the flask over in my hands to look at the engraving. The female elk looked up from grazing and paused in her chewing. By now, I was used to that animation. I handed it to Tixi.

"I recognize the handiwork of Hephaestus," Tixi said. "He came here to gather granite dust from the cliffs when he made this for you. This is a very fine gift indeed. Have you met him?"

"No," I said. "I've read about him, though."

"Wait until you meet him," she said. "The Greeks described him as being ugly and malformed, rejected by his mother, Hera. They're wrong. The nymphs know his talent and inner beauty overpower his appearance. He's incredibly kind and strong."

"There's granite in the flask?" I asked. I was interested in Hephaestus, but the thought of granite dust from the cliffs at the source of the Elk

River intrigued me. "Why did he mix that with the metal?"

"That's part of the source of its power for you," she said. "Did you notice anything when you first drank *Aqua Pura* from the tarn?"

"Yes," I said. "Every time I drink it, I feel stronger. I've also seen a female elk when I drink."

Tixi nodded and looked down at the flask in her hand. The elk in the engraving pawed the ground, looked up, then leaped off the flask. As she moved through the air, she changed from a small bronze creature into a full-grown elk. She bounded around the lake, disappearing into the forest.

"Wait," I yelled. "What happened? That's my elk!"

Tixi laughed. "She'll come back. She's just having a little run through the forest." She handed the flask back to me. "Let's fill it up."

Following her, I kneeled where the tarn lapped the rocks. A short distance away, fresh water from the stream poured into the lake. Submerging my elk-less flask into the water, I gasped at the cold wetness covering my hand. After allowing water to flood inside, I held it up in the sun, water dripping down my arm.

"Drink," Tixi commanded.

I took a long pull from the flask, feeling the rush of cold water against my teeth. Gulping, I lowered the flask and smiled at Tixi. "It tastes like mountain air feels in your lungs," I said. "Biting and fresh."

She knelt and cupped her hands in the lake, raising them to sip from her periwinkle palms. "You described it perfectly," she said.

I took another mouthful and looked toward the forest, blinking my eyes. "Who is that woman?" I asked as a figure came out of the forest, walking beside a female elk. "She's with my elk."

"Go find out," Tixi said, smiling mysteriously.

I replaced the cap on my flask and walked around the lake, feeling no fear as the woman came toward me, keeping pace with the elk by her side. I was strangely compelled and comforted as I drew closer. The elk trotted quickly toward me and leapt into the air. Startled, I stepped back, putting my hands up in a defensive motion. The elk quickly shrank to the size of a small plastic toy horse, and then became even smaller as it jumped onto the flask in my hand. I looked down, and she calmly returned my gaze.

"You're back," I whispered. She flicked her tiny tail and nodded. I rubbed her head, and she pushed against my hand the way our ranch dog, Buster, did when I pet him. She lowered her head to once again graze from the bronze grass on the flask.

Sensing movement, I looked up as the woman paused in front of me. She smiled, and a flood of emotion threatened to choke me. Reaching out, she touched my face with her wrinkled brown hand. I was taller and looked down into her wise brown eyes. Wrinkles covered her face, and her long grey hair was parted in the middle and fashioned into two long braids hanging over her shoulders. She wore a buckskin dress, cinched with a beaded belt. Beautiful, beaded leather moccasins adorned her small feet.

"Diana," she whispered, cupping my cheek in her hand.

Deep emotion flooded my heart, bringing the sting of tears to my eyes. I'd never experienced such a strong connection to any human in my life. Not Dad, not Grams, not Willy, not Grandpa, not even the memory of my mother triggered this feeling. It felt like I looked into my own eyes, my own face, a mirror reflecting my soul. I reached out to touch her cheek, uncertain if this was a dream. Her warm skin was incredibly soft, like Grams' wrinkled face. The softness of old people as their skin ages and settles next to their bones. The softness of Willy when he held my hand in his.

"Do you know who I am?" she asked.

"Running Elk Moon," I said, not knowing why I was so certain. "You're my great-great-great grandmother."

She laughed and embraced me fiercely, then pushed me back to look into my eyes. "I knew of your existence long before you were born," she said. "But I didn't think I would ever meet you."

"You brought my elk back," I said, still marveling at her presence.

"The elk is your animal, just as it was mine, and Willy's," she said. "The spirit of your River Crow ancestors comes from this place. Your power is enhanced by the waters at the source of the Elk River. That is why you can see me now."

"But how are you here? How is it that I can touch you? Aren't you a spirit?" I wanted to know it all, just as I wanted to stay with her forever.

"I am always within you, Diana. When I was a young woman and first met Artemis on the banks of the Bighorn River, she told me that one day a child would be born in the time of great need. The prophecy did not lie. Artemis said that we had to get my elk tooth necklace to the Wind River Mountains in preparation for your birth. I never thought you would have my blood in your veins," she said. "Come sit with me so we can talk."

We moved closer to the tarn and sat on a boulder. The cold granite against my legs told me this was real. Running Elk certainly felt real. She took my right hand in both of hers, her skin warm and soft. "We waited a long time for your coming, Diana," she said.

"What do you mean?" I asked. "Who waited? How did you know I would need the elk tooth necklace?"

"Your coming was prophesied. Artemis told me long ago that you would be born in the Wind River Mountains, but I didn't know that you would be part of my family," she said. Although her wrinkled skin and neatly braided grey hair marked her as an old woman, her eyes held the vitality and spark of a much younger person.

"What prophecy?" I said. Willy had talked about it, but I wondered what she knew.

"Diana, many times, others have told you of your duty to save *Aqua Pura*. Persephone, Hades, and even your grandmother said this to you. Remember the note you read in Sinks Cave when all this started?" she said, smiling up at me.

A sharp pain in my left hand made me realize I gripped the flask tightly. Looking down, I saw the elk was no longer grazing, but looking up at me with bulging eyes. "Sorry," I said to her. I must have gripped so hard, I'd choked her a bit. When I relaxed my hand, she coughed and spit out the grass in her mouth. Then she grabbed some more and started chewing.

"Yes, I remember the note. It seems so long ago. How did you know about that?" I asked.

"Artemis kept me informed of your adventures," she said. "She told me to tell you about the prophecy that a girl-child would be born in the Wind River Mountains in the time of great need."

"Who made this prophecy?" I said. I felt helpless and out of control again, just like I had when I'd first flown into Sinks Cavern with Persephone. "How could they know I'd be born? None of this makes sense."

"Trust me, Diana," Running Elk Moon said. "You and I share the pain of loss, but you are healing now. When I was kidnapped as a child and taken to the white man's school, I lost my parents, just as you lost your mother. The strength of our family is in your soul, Diana. I was able to see my parents again, just as you saw your mother."

"But why me?" I asked. I knew I sounded like a whiner, but I couldn't stop myself.

"Did you know that when monarch butterflies migrate north from Mexico, multiple generations are born and die during that trip? Our family is like that. Many people have played their part in passing the necklace onto you," she said.

"How can this be?" I asked. "It just doesn't seem possible."

"My understanding of the world has grown since my fate became connected with yours," she said. "I've learned many things are possible. My spirit traveled the globe while I waited for your birth. We knew you would come, but did not know when. We waited and passed on the necklace so it would be there when you were born. What I didn't know was that you would be one of the River Crow people."

"I think I can do this, but I do wonder," I said.

"Sometimes we have to fulfill our duty, even if it's not what we want. Just like I had to be brave when I was kidnapped as a child and taken to the white man's school, you must be brave now. You must trust your inner strength and the power you gain from *Aqua Pura* on Younts Peak."

"What power do I have?" I asked.

"You must discover that on your own. In truth, we don't know yet what your full power is, but Artemis knows it is there," she said. "Just as we trusted our knowledge that you'd be born in the Wind River Mountains but had no idea Willy would be your grandfather, you must trust that you will discover your power, whatever road it takes. My spirit will always be within you, and this place will always be your source of strength. You can always return here to refill your flask."

"What's going to happen now?"

"The way of prophecies is never certain. They come to pass, but not always as we expect," she said. "For instance, as I've said, we knew Willy would give you the necklace, but we didn't know you would be his granddaughter. You must go now with Tixi, but know I travel with you in your heart."

"What about the Eastern Shoshone people? Are they part of the prophecy?" I asked.

"Your connection to the Shoshone is also strong, and the Elk River was part of their ancestral lands. You will gain strength from your people on the Wind River Reservation, but remember the Elk River and the Crow nation is in your heart also. Artemis said that native people and whites will one day come together to heal the planet. The power of that union is manifested in you, Diana of the Wind Rivers," she said. After squeezing my hand, she got to her feet. "Come, it's time for you to go with Tixi."

I looked up to see the periwinkle nymph standing near our boulder. I stood and hugged Running Elk Moon. Her buckskin dress was soft and supple, rivaling her skin. She smiled as we pulled apart. "I will see you again next summer, Diana, when you return to the source of the Elk River. Goodbye."

Before I could protest, she turned and walked away. Her form faded as she moved across the meadow. Something pushed against my hand, and I looked down to see the elk on my flask rubbing her nose against my palm. "Thank you," I whispered, knowing she was trying to comfort me.

"Running Elk Moon waited a long time to see you," Tixi said, her voice interrupting my thoughts. "Let's go see what Artemis is doing."

"Okay," I said, tucking the flask back in my pouch, still focused on my ancestor. When Tixi turned toward the forest, I gasped. "Your wings are gone!"

"I felt it while we were talking," Tixi said. Then she laughed and pirouetted. "Come run with me." She ran across the grass toward the trees where Artemis went to set up camp.

I watched her run for a moment, amazed that she'd literally turned from periwinkle to a lovely moss green. "Wait for me," I hollered and took off after her.

When she reached the trees, she paused, waiting for me to catch up. As we entered the forest, I saw Artemis in a small clearing.

"Your transformation is almost complete," Artemis said to Tixi as we walked into the campsite. "Come have some tea," she added, as if changing color were an everyday thing.

"I see you have all the amenities here," Tixi said. While she talked, her dress changed from light blue chiffon to a golden green, velvety texture, but her hair remained purple and spiked.

"I like my tea hot," Artemis said. "And my bed must be comfortable," she added, gesturing to the bamboo tent sitting atop a wooden platform covered in green carpet.

Tixi moved to the center of the campsite while Artemis poured tea from the pot she lifted from the campfire. Accepting the tea, Tixi sat gracefully on one of the three boulders placed around the campfire. "I have serious news," she said, no longer smiling.

I wondered how she could switch moods so suddenly. Only moments ago she'd run across the meadow with joy.

"What is it?" Artemis handed me a cup, and I sat on a boulder. The air was cooler now that we were in the trees. The heat from the crackling fire warmed my legs and I extended my boots closer to it, admiring the flames that burned without wood.

"I've detected particles of plastic in the newest layers of the glacier," Tixi said.

Artemis sat abruptly on the boulder behind her, putting down the teapot with a shaking hand. "That's a blow," she said. "A real blow. Are you certain?"

Alarmed, I looked at Artemis. She never seemed to lose confidence, but now her face was pale with shock. I'd never seen her like this.

"Yes, I'm certain of it," Tixi said. "I checked the newest snow amount and the water melting from the glacier. They both contain plastic particles. Microplastics. It's in the snow and water."

"What does that mean?" I asked.

"Plastic from the ocean has entered the River Oceanus," Artemis said. "Microplastics are now embedded in the water cycle. The particles travel in the water as it evaporates from Oceanus, rise in the clouds, and fall as snow on the glacier."

"I've checked with the other glacier nymphs in the United States and around the world. When snow melts in the spring runoff, it joins the headwaters of all rivers around the world. Microplastics are in *Aqua Pura*," Tixi said. "This is not good."

"How will we get the particles out?" I asked.

"Maybe we can somehow filter them out," Artemis said. "I have to talk with Poseidon and Demeter." She sighed, her shoulders slumping. "I didn't expect this. Oil spills, yes. Microplastics, no. We can't even see them. What kind of damage will this do to the planet?" She turned to Tixi. "Are you sure they're in glaciers all over the world?"

"Yes. As soon as I confirmed the particles were in this *Aqua Pura*, I sent messages with eagles to glacier nymphs all over the world, and they returned with replies from the other nymphs," Tixi said. "The particles reached all mountaintops around the world."

"We need to notify Poseidon that I'm coming to see him first thing tomorrow. I'll send a message to the sea birds." Artemis said. "Call your eagle."

"Of course," Tixi replied. Moving away from the campfire, she lifted her arms and sent a sharp, clear cry into the sky.

"An eagle," Indigo cried, flying to my shoulder, and fiercely gripping with her little black feet. Trembling slightly, she moved closer to my neck.

I looked up to see a large Bald Eagle circling overhead and spiraling down closer and closer. The eagle landed a few feet away, the wind from its powerful wings blowing my hair. Standing upright, the bird was huge, the top of its white head almost reaching my shoulder. Reaching up, I calmed Indigo. "Don't worry," I whispered. "I won't let the big bird near you." She stopped shaking, but her little bird claws poked into my shoulder.

"Greetings," Artemis said. "I need your help getting a message to Poseidon. Can you fly swiftly to the ocean and deliver the message to the sea birds?"

The bird nodded. I admired the extreme whiteness of her head feathers, which draped down to join the black and brown pattern of her neck and shoulders. Her pale yellow eyes matched the deeper yellow of her large hooked beak.

"Tell the sea birds I'm on my way to see Poseidon on a matter of great importance," Artemis said. "I'll be there tomorrow."

The bird nodded again and spread her great wings. I knew her wingspan was over seven feet, but up close, it seemed larger. With one powerful flap of her wings, the eagle flew into the sky, a piercing cry filling the air as she flew west toward the Pacific coast. Indigo's grip on my shoulder relaxed.

"Now, let's have dinner," Artemis said. "Sitting around won't get things done and we have to leave first thing in the morning."

Relieved to see Artemis in control again, I jumped up to help.

CHAPTER TWENTY
THE BLUEBIRD REPORT
THE PROBLEM WITH PLASTICS

The next morning, we flew over Younts Peak just as Eos brought the sun above the horizon on the far edge of the world. I thought of my friends, the Birds of Dawn, and wondered if I would see them again. Would the microplastics in the River Oceanus coat their wings as they flew in and out of the spray? How could Artemis and Diana remove the microplastics? What if humans kept dumping plastic in the ocean and the problem became worse? I didn't voice my concerns because I knew not even Artemis had a solution yet.

We flew west, and for most of the journey across Wyoming and Idaho, I kept up with the chariot, half wishing a flock of birds would show up. But that wasn't going to happen because this chariot had a cloaking device. By the time we reached the high plains of Oregon, I was exhausted from flying so fiercely, so I flopped on the padded bench inside.

"Come over here," Diana said, patting the seat next to her.

I hopped along the bench, and she gently pulled me closer to her thigh. I sighed and relaxed, leaning against the warmth of Diana's leg. I rarely had the chance to visit with them when we travelled, so I luxuriated in the experience as their voices enveloped me, like my mother's warm wing in the spring.

"Artemis," Diana said, "I've been thinking about what to do in the future."

"Oh? What have you decided?" Artemis said, glancing back as she held the reins in one hand. The deer seemed to fly faster than horses, and I wondered how, since horses were bigger animals. I saved the question for later because I wanted to hear Diana's reply.

"I understand now that I let my grief for Mom consume me. It's like that feeling took over my view of the world when I was growing up. I know now that she'll always be there for me and I can focus on other things, like helping the planet," Diana said.

"You've learned to think about issues beyond yourself," Artemis said.

"Yes," Diana said. "I don't know what my power is, but my love of animals and the ranch is tied up in it. In fact, I think that may be my power. I'm so connected to animals and the land that I'll do all I can to protect the planet. Can that be a power?"

"Yes," Artemis said. "You're beginning to understand that your strength comes from the Earth, and not only the land on your ranch. You know how sometimes you'll see a lone tree growing in a cliff? And when you hike to a place where you're closer to the tree, you realize it's growing straight out of the granite?"

"Right," Diana said. "I'm always surprised that a tree can survive on a cliff and still reach for the sun, growing out of rocks, branching toward the sky."

"I've perched on trees like that," I said.

Diana chuckled. "I'll bet you have, Indigo."

"Your power is like that tree," Artemis said. "You gain strength from granite and sunlight, holding on to every drop of water that falls from the sky. You gain strength from the land."

"I don't always feel strong," Diana said. "But I know I want to do this."

"Think about the way you stood on a boulder next to the Popo Agie River, challenging your fear of rapids like those where your mother died," Artemis said. "Think about the way you jumped into the ocean to rescue Persephone after the oil monster syphoned off her power. Then you stood up to the oil slick and helped bring it down. You are strong, Diana."

"I guess I didn't look at it that way. I just did those things without thinking," Diana said.

"One day, you'll feel your strength. And when that happens, you'll realize your full potential," Artemis said.

"Animals are part of my power also," Diana said. "I don't completely understand it yet, but I feel a connection to them, just as I feel connected to the land."

"Yes," Artemis said. "But you will understand one day, and then you can fully use that power to help the planet."

They were both silent for a while and I nestled closer to Diana.

"I know something that's in my future," I said.

"Tell us, Indigo," Diana said.

"Hatchlings! Hungry, hungry hatchlings," I said. "I want to stay with you this summer like Artemis said I could," I said, hopping onto Diana's leg and looking up at her. "But next spring, I want to find a mate and have hatchlings."

"That would be wonderful," Artemis said. "Baby Mountain Bluebirds."

"But what about helping Diana next summer?" I asked. "How will I do that?" I flew to Artemis's shoulder.

"Maybe you could have one batch of babies and then come help me,"

Diana said. "You told me your mom had two batches. Can you have just one?"

"Well, we do have babies in early May," I said, flying back to Diana's leg. "I could have one and then ask my mate if he minds if I leave to help you."

"We'll see if we can work that out," Artemis said. "Plenty of creatures are working moms."

"Great," I said. "First, though, I have to find a mate next spring."

"Oh, that won't be any trouble for a beautiful bird like you," Diana said, caressing my back the way I liked. We were all silent for a while, and I moved to the seat, nestling close to Diana's leg.

"I've been thinking about school," Diana said. "I've decided to become a forest ranger. When I go back in the fall, I'm going to see my advisor and start taking classes to get a degree in forestry."

"Did you declare a major yet?" Artemis said.

"No. I just took general education classes. But after this summer, I know what to do," Diana said. "Think about it. It's the perfect choice. I can work with animals while I'm in the forest and no one will know. Lots of times, I've seen rangers camping alone in the forest, so no one will suspect anything if I'm alone. I'll keep helping you and the others. It's a perfect solution."

"Well, that's a very interesting idea," Artemis said. "It just might work."

"I can help you," I said. "You won't be alone in the forest."

"Yes, Indigo, I'll need your help," Diana said. "Artemis, I've been wondering about something."

"Yes?" She glanced back.

"In all of my mythology books, you're described as goddess of the hunt. But you don't encourage hunting, right? You protect animals now," Diana said.

"That's right," she said. "My role has shifted. During the time of the Greeks and Romans, millions of animals roamed the Earth, and there was enough food for humans and animals. Now, many species are extinct, or in danger, due to human behavior. I'm trying to help maintain the balance, so my role is now protector of animals. I do, of course, realize hunting for food is necessary for some people."

"Hades told me gods are stewards of the Earth, not wizards," Diana said.

"What's a steward?" I asked, looking up at Diana.

"A kind of protector," she said.

"We're caretakers of the Earth," Artemis said. "And now you and Diana have joined us."

I fluffed my feathers and sat up on the seat. "I'm proud to help," I said.

"We're a team," Diana said.

Artemis and Diana didn't talk much after that. By the time we reached the coast, the smoke from forest fires across the state blocked our first view of the ocean. I wondered if any fires burned right now in Sinks Canyon and hoped my mom and dad were safe.

Once we were over the ocean, I immediately fell into a deep sleep where I dreamed of Wanda, diving again and again through the oil slick, her massive wings coated with oil.

"Indigo, come fly with me," Wanda shouted in my dream.

I gasped and woke up, realizing it wasn't a dream and it wasn't Wanda calling to me. Getting up, I saw a different Wandering Albatross, a younger version of Wanda, flying next to the chariot.

"Who are you?" I asked, shaking my head to clear the image of Wanda in her death dive.

"I'm Wendy, Wanda's daughter," the giant bird shouted. "Come fly with me."

"Can I go with her?" I looked up at Diana.

"Is that what she's asking you? We're almost at the garbage patch," she said. "Go with her if you want to."

I flew up to join Wendy, flapping furiously to catch up. I positioned myself to the right of her head, in awe of her formidable wingspan. "You don't even have to flap your wings to fly," I said.

"I know," she replied. "A Wandering Albatross can coast for miles on the sea wind. Poseidon said you knew my mother."

"Yes," I said. "She was a very brave bird who gave her life to destroy the oil slick."

"Poseidon told me," Wendy said. "I can tell you're getting tired. Want to ride on my back? That's the plastic island just ahead."

"Thanks," I said as I flew down and perched right between her wings. "This is better," I said, gripping her feathers with my feet.

"My mother was brave," Wendy said. "Poseidon assured me I did not have to join his forces, but I wanted to continue the tradition Mom established. She was the first bird in our family to answer Poseidon's call for reinforcements to fight the oil slick."

"My grandmother helped Demeter make Sinks Canyon into a state park," I said, proud I could offer up some family fame.

"I'd like to hear that story sometime," Wendy said. "But now we have to join the others."

I peered over the side of her wing to see that Artemis and Diana had already landed on the plastic floating island next to Poseidon's giant pink shell throne. The island moved gently as Wendy executed a perfect landing next to the chariot. I flew off her back to Poseidon's shoulder, drawn to his bluer-than-blue body.

"I've been waiting to see you since Tixi's eagle sent word you were coming today," Poseidon said. "I'm glad you let me know ahead of time because I'm starting a new experiment today and I might not have been here if you hadn't sent word."

"What experiment?" Artemis said. She urged the deer to move closer to his shell throne and then joined Diana on the padded bench in the small chariot. "Now we can all talk," she said.

"I've enlisted the help of the whales. If I need to leave, they'll keep the island intact," Poseidon said.

"How will they do that?" I asked.

"By constantly swimming around the island, they're going to keep most of the debris within the circle of the current they create," Poseidon said.

"We're going to need your new system," Artemis said. "I have grim news from Tixi Pagos."

I watched Poseidon as Artemis relayed the news about microplastics in the River Oceanus and told him how Tixi had found them in the glacier on Younts Peak. As she spoke, Poseidon turned from a brilliant blue to pale blue.

"Are you sure microplastics are all over the world?" Poseidon said, sitting up straight and rocking the throne.

"Tixi is positive. She checked with the other glacier nymphs on mountaintops around the globe," Artemis said.

"This is terrible," Poseidon said. He slumped in his throne and turned almost white.

"Don't lose your blue," I cried. "We can fix it, Poseidon. I'll help Diana." I brushed his cheek with the side of my head where I knew my feathers were especially soft.

Poseidon sat back up, his skin turning from white to pale blue. He reached up, took me in his hand, and held me up in front of this face so we could look at each other eye to eye. "If a little Mountain Bluebird is brave enough to save the world, I should take her up on that offer, shouldn't I?" As he spoke, his pale blue skin transformed into the color of the sky, deepening as he looked into my eyes. "What do you think, Diana? Are you ready to help your little friend fix this problem with plastics?" He smiled at me while talking to Diana.

"I don't know what to do, but I'll help Indigo," Diana said. "She's found her blue."

"What will we do?" Artemis asked.

"I don't know. We'll need to confer with the other gods," Poseidon said. "I knew this giant plastic trash island wouldn't stay together forever." I flew to the chariot as he picked up a plastic dinosaur from the debris around his throne. "For some reason, the toys keep floating to my throne like they want to play."

"Why are there so many plastic horses?" Diana said. "I still have most of mine from when I was a kid, but they're in a box in the top of my closet at home."

As soon as she said that, I realized hundreds of plastic horses in all sizes and colors bumped against the shell throne.

"The horses keep floating to the top. They want me to give them life," he said. "But I create horses from nature, not plastic."

"Poseidon, what's going to happen to the Birds of Dawn?" I asked. "Will microplastics coat their feathers so they can't fly with Eos?"

"They're okay for now, Indigo," he said, shaking his head. "I don't know about the long-term effects of this."

"We can't lose the Birds of Dawn," I said. "If they disappear from Oceanus, Eos won't be able to bring up the sun. They told me that."

"We'll figure out a plan," Poseidon said.

"I can help now," I said. "I want to help my friends, the Birds of Dawn."

"I'm ready, too," Diana said. She stood up, causing the chariot to rock.

"First, Poseidon and I have to form a strategy. I'll take you two back to the ranch," Artemis said. "Poseidon and I will meet with Demeter and come up with a plan. At the end of the summer, you'll go back to school to start your forestry degree, and Indigo will fly south with her flock for the winter."

"Okay," Diana said. The island rocked again as she resumed sitting, and plastic horses rubbed insistently against the pink shell throne.

Poseidon reached down and grabbed a palomino, its white mane and tail curved in plastic perfection against its smooth golden neck and rump. "You'll need horses of your own," Poseidon said, turning his intent blue gaze on Diana. He seemed revitalized.

"What? I already have my own horse. Daisy," Diana said.

"Next summer, you'll need to start training them," Poseidon said.

"You're not listening," Diana objected. "I already have a beautiful horse."

"You'll need a chariot also," Poseidon said, ignoring her and turning to Artemis. "Can you get Hephaestus on that? It needs to be a lightweight battle chariot. It should be made of wood with metal reinforcement. Maybe he'll want to use titanium."

"What do you mean, she needs a chariot?" I interrupted.

"Indigo, you and Diana need to travel on your own," he said.

"I can fly," I said.

"Diana needs a chariot to get into the mountains or over the ocean if any situations come up. Plus, you'll need to reach Younts Peak whenever you want fresh *Aqua Pura*. And for that, you'll need flying horses," Poseidon concluded with a smile.

"What's going on here?" Diana asked as Poseidon and Artemis exchanged a glance. "You guys need to listen to me."

"I'm giving you a matched pair of flying horses," Poseidon said. "Next month, we'll breed Golden and Glenda, Demeter's fine mares. I think we should ask Eos about her stallions."

"The immortal horses?" I asked.

"No, just regular winged horses. Eos has a very reputable stable," he said.

"The Birds of Dawn sing the horses to sleep every night," I said.

"Right," Poseidon said. "I'll talk to Eos. After the foals are born, you'll train them, Diana. Flying horses must bond with their owners at a young age. Next June, when you're home from school, I'll send them to the ranch with Demeter and Persephone. Then you can keep them over the summer and form a bond as you train them. Of course, Golden and Glenda will come along because the foals will be too young to be separated from their mothers." He sat back and laughed. "It's a brilliant idea that came to me just now."

"You can't send flying horses to the ranch," Diana said. She jumped to her feet, again causing plastic horses to bump against the shell. I flew back to Poseidon's shoulder.

"Why not?" Poseidon said. "Golden and Glenda will thrive on the hay from the ranch, and they can drink fresh water from the Popo Agie River to improve their milk. It's a perfect place to raise horses."

"I know that," Diana said. "But there are people around. My dad is one of them. How can I hide their wings?"

"Flying horses don't develop wings until they're six months old. No one will notice that the little ones have nubs on their shoulders where the wings will sprout," he said.

"What about the mares? They have adult-sized wings," Diana said.

"Oh, you'll figure something out," he said. "That's settled. We'll get those little ones to you right away when you come back from school next spring." He held up the plastic palomino between two fingers and looked it in the eye. "Thanks for the idea, little buddy. I feel better already, now that we have a plan." The little horse whinnied.

I looked at Poseidon in surprise. He winked at me. The others didn't seem to hear the whinny.

"This won't work," Diana said.

"Let's move on to our next task," Poseidon said, brushing aside her concerns. "Now, what kind of wood will work best for your chariot? At this point, you can even choose the color of your upholstery for the seat.

Maybe Indigo would like to get involved. What do you think, Indigo? Do you want anything special in the chariot? Maybe a little sleeping nook?"

I flew up and down, sensing Diana's alarm. "Diana doesn't want a chariot," I said.

"Poseidon doesn't give just anyone his horses," Artemis said. "You're very lucky, Diana. Don't forget he created his first horses for Demeter."

"This is impossible. They can't come live on the ranch. The neighbors will see them. What will Dad say?" Diana shook her head at Artemis.

"We'll figure it out next spring," she said. "For now, let's get you back to the ranch so I can go see Demeter on the Platte River. She should be back there now for the honey harvest in Nebraska."

"Then come here so we can discuss what we're going to do about the plastics problem," Poseidon said.

Artemis moved to the front of the chariot and picked up the reins. "Demeter and I will be back right away," she said.

The deer trotted forward on the plastic island while Wendy the albatross shouted goodbye. "I'll see you next summer," she cried.

"Goodbye, Poseidon," I hollered. "Goodbye, Wendy."

"Goodbye," Diana said, turning back to look as the chariot became airborne. "I can't keep flying horses a secret on the ranch."

"You'll love your new horses," Poseidon yelled. Then his booming laugh followed us across the ocean.

"I'll be there to help you," I said as Diana faced the front again. "Willy and Grams can help, too."

"I can't tell Dad about you right away," Diana said.

"Why can't you tell him? Are you embarrassed by me?" I asked.

"No, of course not. He just won't understand. Let's play it by ear when we get home, and I'll try to find the right time to tell him," she promised.

"My mom knows about you," I said. "Willy and Grams know about me. Why can't your Dad know?"

"He just doesn't have the background yet," she said. "Come over here."

She extended her hand and I walked across the seat. Hopping onto her palm, I looked up. "Will you tell him when the time is right?" I asked.

"Yes," Diana said. She moved her hand so I could sit next to her. "I love you, Indigo. I couldn't have made it through this without you. We'll find a way to tell Dad the truth, but it's going to take some time." She soothed me with gentle fingers, separating the top of my tail feathers in the way I loved. "I guess it would be nice to have my own matching horses."

"They might be cute," I said. "Baby birds are cute." Succumbing to Diana's touch, I closed my eyes and fell asleep as the chariot sped across the sky on our journey back to the ranch.

CHAPTER TWENTY-ONE
NO MORE SECRETS — ALMOST

When Dad opened the door of his dusty blue truck and got out, my first thought was that he was too thin. Tanned and lean, he looked older. I spotted new sun-squint lines around his eyes. His jeans were baggy and his cowboy hat was definitely shabbier, the side brims curled up with wear. He'd come home in the middle of August to help Willy and me with cutting, baling, and stacking hay. Because she was still recovering from her hip surgery, this would be the first year Grams wouldn't be able to help.

"Dad," I exclaimed, abandoning my plan to stand on the porch and await his arrival calmly as an adult. I bolted down the steps and ran into his open arms, inhaling his sweaty scent peppered with the still-present smell of soap from his morning shower. My adult dignity vanished when I burst into tears.

"What's wrong, honey?" Dad asked, pulling back from our hug, gripping my shoulders with his large, strong hands.

"I missed you," I said, embarrassed by my tears. "I'm happy to see you." I rubbed my face and smiled up at him.

"You're taller," he said, looping his arm around my shoulders as we walked back to the porch.

"I guess you're right," I said. The top of my head used to come to his shoulder, but now I was eye level with his neck instead of his chest. *Aqua Pura will do that to you,* I thought. *How can I explain my new reality to him? Maybe I won't,* I concluded. I wanted to tell him everything about my summer, but now that he was here, it seemed too outlandish. I never used to keep secrets from Dad. That was different now, too.

We moved apart and walked up the stairs as Grams and Willy came out of the house. Indigo perched on the railing and chirped.

"A bluebird on the porch," Dad said. "Look! It's not even flying away."

"Um, yeah. How about that? That bluebird has been hanging around the ranch this summer and it's used to us by now," I said, glancing at Indigo.

She flew off the railing and headed around the side of the house. That morning, I'd told her not to land on my shoulder anymore once Dad came home, at least until I could figure out how to tell him about her. I knew it was hard for her because we'd done everything together all summer.

Grams moved forward to hug Dad and Willy shook his hand.

"You're walking normally," Dad said to Grams.

"I've recovered well over the summer, but I still can't do heavy work," she said. "Let's go inside. You must be hungry."

While Dad washed his hands, I helped Grams move dinner from the stove to the table. I watched Dad eat while we talked. Leaning back, he rubbed his stomach after finishing, and thanked Grams for the meal, a habit I remembered from growing up. I cleared the dinner plates while listening to Dad talk.

We sat around the table after eating, the voices of Grams, Willy, and Dad cocooning me as I watched their faces. I wondered if any of my problems were solved. Some, but not all, I decided. Missing Dad: he's home now, so that's fixed. Losing memories of my mother: that's fixed, but I can't tell Dad about it, so that creates a new problem.

I wished I could ask Dad if he knew horses can fly.

I wondered if that might be the way to start the conversation. This was hard, and I didn't know how to resolve it. I didn't want to keep secrets from my dad.

I thought about telling him that Mom was a mermaid now.

None of it fit in with the reality of sitting here with Dad. It was too fantastical. And there wasn't any way for me to prove my story. Persephone and the others were gone, off protecting all parts of the world, and Indigo couldn't talk to anyone but me.

But I had kept one secret from Dad all these years: the level of my grief over losing Mom. Dad had no idea I'd shouted above the roar of the water crashing over giant boulders as it raced to the entrance of Sinks Canyon Cave. He had no idea I'd railed at the loss of my mom while confronting my fear of raging rivers like the one where she died.

Other than that, though, he used to know everything about me.

I imagined another conversation starter: "By the way, Dad, when you were working like a dog to extract black gold from the Bakken Oil Fields of North Dakota, I was on a flying horse above a derrick, fighting an oil monster in the Gulf of Mexico."

I didn't say it out loud.

Maybe another angle: "Dad, did you know the state bird of North Dakota is the Western Meadowlark? Speaking of birds, this is Indigo."

All of these would be great ways to start the story, but I couldn't do it right now. He was too dusty, too tired, and clearly happy to be back at the ranch. I didn't know why it was easier talking to Grams and Willy about Indigo and Persephone. Maybe it was because they'd been here when it all started, the day Dad left in June. In fact, they'd known all about it before I did.

The deal was sealed as to whether I should reveal the truth about my new ring when Dad leaned back, stretched out his legs and smiled at me. "It's good to be home, Princess," he said, using one of my childhood nicknames.

I'd loved to play rodeo princess when I was in third grade, especially after seeing her ride in the Lander Fourth of July parade that year, along with the Shoshone Princess who was Willy's granddaughter. After that, the nickname stuck.

"What's up?" Dad said. "I can tell something's going on."

I looked at Grams, who looked at Willy.

"We have some news for you, Evan," Grams said to Dad.

"I've asked Helen to marry me," Willy said, reaching out to cover Grams' hand with his own.

Dad sat up straight, a smile on his face. "Whoa! I didn't see this coming. But it's terrific news. I'm so happy for both of you." He stood, pulled Grams gently to her feet, and leaned down to embrace her in a long hug. Then he turned to shake Willy's hand. "You'll be my new father-in-law."

Watching them laugh and talk, I knew Dad's homecoming had added another layer of reality to my alter ego: Diana of the Wind Rivers seemed far away as I sat safely inside our ranch house, hearing him laugh once again. I didn't even see Indigo on the picnic table.

"There's that bluebird again," Dad said as he sat and looked outside.

"We have more news for you," Willy said.

We'd planned ahead of time that Willy and Grams would tell Dad about the fact that my mom was his daughter.

"What can top your wedding news?" Dad said, grinning at me and winking.

"Evan, this is a little more serious," Willy said.

"What?" Dad said.

I watched his face as Willy spoke.

"Helen and I want to tell you that Diana's mom was my daughter," Willy said, joining hands with Grams again.

"What?" Dad said. He looked from Willy to Grams, who nodded.

"It's true, Evan," she said. "After I thought Ben was killed in the war, Willy and I fell in love."

"But he came home from the war," Dad said. He didn't look angry, which was a relief. Just puzzled.

"They found him in a prison camp, as you know," Grams said. "Before that, we had no idea he was still alive. Willy wasn't yet married. The minute the military let me know he was alive, Willy and I ended our relationship. But I was pregnant with Elaina. I didn't tell anyone but Willy."

"It's true, Dad," I said. "They didn't know Grandpa was alive." Grams smiled at me, clearly appreciating my support.

"Ben never knew?" Dad said.

"I never told him," Grams said. "The timing made it seem like Elaina was his daughter. He loved her very much. After she was born, Willy married Sarah, and nobody else knew."

"Wait. Willy, that means Diana is your real granddaughter," Dad said, looking at me. "Clearly, you already know this."

I nodded and smiled. "It's okay, Dad. I know. And now we can tell everyone Willy is my grandfather, but we'll know the truth. We're not telling everyone else."

"Wow, this is amazing," Dad said. Then he looked at Willy. "You sly fox, you kept that secret all these years."

"We couldn't let anyone know," he said. "But now I can tell the world Diana is my granddaughter." He grabbed my hand, smiling broadly.

"We have more to tell you," Grams said, looking at me.

Now that she'd given me the opening to tell Dad about my summer, I froze. "I'll tell him more about my summer tomorrow," I said, looking at Grams. "What do you think about their news?" I shifted my gaze to Dad.

"I think it's great," he said. "Now we know my daughter is part Eastern Shoshone and Crow. Did you tell your kids, Willy?"

"We haven't told anyone about the wedding yet," Grams said. "We wanted to tell you first."

"Helen and I have decided to keep the truth about our daughter in the past," Willy said. "We don't want to bring disrespect to our families. The wedding will be enough news for the summer. I can proclaim Diana as my granddaughter, but it'll seem it's because I'm marrying Helen."

"How do you feel?" Dad looked at me. "I think your smile gives me the answer."

As he rose to give me a hug, Dad seemed more real to me than Indigo, who waited on the other side of the patio door.

CHAPTER TWENTY-TWO
THE BLUEBIRD REPORT
THROUGH THE PATIO DOOR

I knew things would be different after Diana glared at me for sitting on the front porch railing as she walked up the steps with her dad. Things got worse after that. She ignored me. Yesterday, Diana told me she wasn't ready to tell her dad about me.

"You can't sit on my shoulder and follow me around anymore," she said.

Now, while they ate dinner, I perched on the picnic table and provided them with a side view to emphasize my blue wings and new tail feathers, but nobody looked out the patio door.

Inside, they laughed and talked their way through the meal. I was invisible until they quieted down after eating, and then Diana's dad looked outside. He said something and pointed, and they all turned to look. I expected Diana to be happy when she saw me waiting, but instead, she scowled.

She didn't come out on the deck like she usually did right after dinner. They all sat inside for so long that I eventually gave up and went to find some of the full-grown grasshoppers that tasted so sweet here because they ate the alfalfa planted by Demeter and irrigated by crisp mountain water from the Popo Agie River. I caught and ate seven in quick succession, but even their crunchy outer shells encasing soft creamy innards didn't eliminate my bitterness over being ignored by Diana.

Maybe it was time for me to go home. I said as much to Diana later that night.

We were out on the deck as the sun was setting. Everyone else was inside, but they moved from the kitchen table to the place Diana called the living room. I could see them from where I perched on the picnic table after returning from my lonely grasshopper feast. Diana saw me and came out, carefully closing the patio door.

"Indigo, I have to tell you that we can't talk together anymore when Dad's around. I can't tell him about you right now," she said, facing me with her back to the door.

"You told me that yesterday. I'm going back to my family so we can migrate south for the winter anyhow. Should I even come back here in the spring?" I said, tilting my beak up. I knew that was harsh, but I wanted to hurt Diana the way she'd hurt me today.

"Oh, I'm sorry, Indigo," she said, moving closer.

I noticed she still kept her back to the door so her dad couldn't see that she was talking to a bird.

"I just can't reconcile what happened this summer with Dad coming home. How can I tell him?" she asked.

"Maybe you can't," I said. "Maybe you won't tell him about me."

"Oh, Indigo, you're part of my life now. I want him to know about you. I'm proud of you and I love you, just like I love him," she said. "I have to find a way, and it might not happen before I leave for school or before you return to the meadow for your migration."

I didn't know what to say, but I did feel better after she sat with me until the sun went down, her fingers following the contours of my body all the way up to the ends of my tail feathers, just the way I liked.

"Diana, since we met Tixi Pagos, I've been wondering about something," I said.

"What?" she asked, pausing in her stroking.

I rubbed my head against her finger and turned to face her. "If there are microplastics in the River Oceanus, what happens when the Birds of Dawn fly through the river's spray as I did with them when we were there?" I looked up, waiting for her reply. Several days ago, I'd told her about my entire body turning cerulean when I darted through the rainbow spray with the other birds.

"I don't know, Indigo. I'm sure they'll be okay, but I don't know how it will affect them," she said. "I remember you asked Poseidon about it, and he didn't have an answer, either. We have problems we just can't fix right now. But we do have each other. Artemis and Poseidon will put together a plan, and we can help them next summer."

Diana was very busy all the next week. She spent time doing the usual chores with her dad, but I felt better because now she didn't mind that I followed along, trying to hang out in the background. Her dad noticed me, however.

"I've never seen anything like it," he said one afternoon as I followed them through the pasture while they rode horses, checking the fence lines.

Diana had told me earlier that they had to make sure the wire with twisted metal weapons was securely attached to the wonderful bird perches they used to hold the wires in place. She said it was called barbed wire, but I called it animal killer because I'd seen dead antelope hanging on the metal weapons when I migrated south last fall with the flock. My mother said they were caught when they tried to leap over the fence.

"That bluebird is always around," Diana's dad said.

"I think it moved to the ranch this summer," she said. "She seems to like us."

"She?" He looked sharply at Diana.

"Yes. I can tell she's female because of her coloring," Diana replied.

"Right. You just seemed to know her or something, the way you said that," he said. "Regardless, she is a pretty little bird and I'm glad she's here. Maybe she's your guardian. She came here to take care of you when I was gone."

"What?" Diana said quickly.

"You know, a guardian bluebird. That's a thing," he said.

"Oh, right," Diana said, looking at me with a smile. "This bird has been hanging around all summer. Maybe she is my guardian."

"Tell him about me. Tell him about me now," I shouted, but she shook her head and looked away. I knew her dad would just hear chirping, not my actual words.

"I'm going to miss you, honey," her dad said. "I can't believe I have to take you back to college in three weeks."

What would I do when Diana is gone? Suddenly I realized the summer was slipping away.

"But first, we have the wedding," Diana said.

***

The next few days passed quickly, in spite of the fact that Diana didn't tell her dad about me. On the morning of the wedding, I flew away from the ranch because, during the night, I'd dreamed about a special gift I could give Grams and Willy.

As I flew above the canyon, I wondered why I'd waited this long to go home. Did Mom miss me? I thought about her as I looked down on the trees. What would she say? Would she notice my new tail feathers? My excitement grew as I approached the home meadow.

When I flew above the familiar place, I was struck by how dry the meadow seemed. I'm already spoiled by Demeter's mountain meadow grass, I realized. I headed toward my parents' nesting tree, wondering how they would react when they saw me. As I drew closer, I was almost hit by bluebirds on a mission. It seemed no one had time to notice me. Bluebirds zipped by and I recognized the intensity of their flight as they raced back and forth across the meadow, scaring up bugs for their hatchlings. Then I remembered. By now they would be fledglings, having already taken their first flight. None of the zipping birds paid attention to me.

When I reached my home tree, Father sat on a branch, feeding three young birds. They all turned to look at me and quickly turned back to

Father. Clearly, food was more interesting to them now. Suddenly, Mother flew up with a grasshopper in her mouth. I couldn't help but notice that it was smaller than those I'd been eating on the ranch. Tough meadow bugs. They didn't have access to the fine hay on the ranch.

I peeped, and Mom noticed me. She tossed the grasshopper to Father. "Take this," she said briskly and flew to my side. "Indigo! You came home," she said, rubbing her face against mine.

"Mother, I missed you," I said, close to tears.

"You've grown," she said, putting her wing around me briefly.

"I guess I have," I said, noticing that I was larger than Mother. I used to fit perfectly under her wing, but now she was smaller. "I've been drinking *Aqua Pura*."

"Let's move over there and talk," she said. Turning to Father, she asked him to take over for a while.

I followed her to a nearby tree where we perched side by side. The other birds continued to race across the meadow with food for their young, but Mother seemed content to focus on me.

"Tell me all about your adventures," she said.

I settled in next to her, fluffing my feathers and hunkering down on the branch. "When I left here at the beginning of the summer, I had no idea what to expect," I said.

Mother listened intently as I told my story, interrupting periodically to ask a question. "These are my new tail feathers," I said after reaching the end of the story.

"They're quite beautiful," she said. "Indigo, you seem so confident now. You've really grown up."

"I'll come back when Diana goes back to school," I said. "Then I'll stay until it's time to migrate. But first we have the wedding."

"I'm so happy for Grams," Mother said. "I've never met her, but my mother told me so much about her."

"Mother, I need your help with a gift I have for Grams' wedding," I said. When she nodded, I told her my idea.

CHAPTER TWENTY-THREE
THE BLUE SURPRISE

Grams called Aunt Joan the day after we told Dad about the wedding. I was glad Joan and Grams had more or less resolved their differences over donating the ranch land to The Nature Conservancy before we dropped another bombshell. I sat at the kitchen table with Grams, smiling as I anticipated my aunt's reaction.

"Joan, I want to tell you some exciting news. Diana's here and we have you on speaker phone," Grams said.

"What is it, Mom?" Joan said. "Is everything okay?"

"Yes," Grams said, smiling at me. "I want you to know Willy and I are getting married." There was silence on the other end of the line, and then Joan's sharp intake of breath filled the kitchen. "What do you mean, Mom? Our Willy? The ranch hand?"

"Joan, you know he's our friend, not just a hired hand. And, yes, our Willy," Grams said. "Soon he'll be my Willy." Grams flashed an impish grin at me, clearly enjoying herself. I knew she liked to rattle Joan's perfect world just for fun.

"You're marrying him?" Joan's voice rose an octave. "Mom, he's the ranch hand. What will people think? He's lived in the bunkhouse all these years. They'll think the worst."

"Willy's been my friend since before you were born. He was also your father's friend," Grams said.

"Mom, this isn't right. Are you sure about this? Diana, what's going on?" Joan said.

"They're very happy, Aunt Joan," I said, smiling at Grams. "You should see them together."

"Mom, I'm going to hang up right now and call you back in a while," Joan said in clipped tones. The phone went dead.

"Oh, boy," I said. "Now you've done it, Grams."

Grams laughed. "She just needs time. She'll come around. It might take a few days."

"Is she mad because Willy's from the reservation?" I hadn't thought Aunt Joan was like that, but I remembered the comments Melissa'd made about Willy years ago.

"No, that doesn't bother her. She's upset because she thinks it won't look good that I married our ranch hand," Grams said. "Remember, she was worried about what people would think?"

"I'm glad it's not that, because I don't want her to be mad if she ever learns about me," I said. "Joan might not want to tell people her sister had a different father."

"She won't have to tell anyone about that," Grams said. "She'll never know."

Grams knew her daughter well; two days passed before Joan called back.

"Hi, Joan. Diana's here also, just so you know you're on speaker phone," Grams said.

"I needed to get used to the idea of you getting married," Joan said. She sounded calmer now. "Are you sure you want to do this? Does Willy want to become part of our family?"

"He already is," Grams said. "He's been part of our family for years."

"I know," Joan said. "I just have to get used to the idea that he'll be my stepdad."

"Well, take your time getting used to it," Grams said. "But the wedding is in two weeks, at the end of August. Just as soon as we finish putting up the hay, we'll put up tables in the yard for the wedding."

"So soon?" Joan said. "How can you plan a wedding that fast? Don't you want to send out invitations?"

"Well, it's on a Saturday, so we know most of our friends can make it. We're going to call people and follow up with details in the mail. I just hope that you, Dan, and Melissa can come. Are you free in two weeks?"

"I have to look at my calendar and call you back," Joan said. "Goodbye."

"Now she's all mad again," I said.

"No, she's just frustrated. Joan likes to be in control, and she's not right now," Grams said. "But I think they'll make time to come."

Thirty minutes later, Joan called. "Hi, Mom," she said. "We had plans that weekend, but I can change them. Luckily, Melissa isn't leaving for college yet, so she'll come with us."

"That's wonderful," Grams said. "Willy and I want all of you here for the wedding."

"How can you plan a wedding so quickly?" Joan said again. "Can I help you?"

I was sure my face mirrored Grams' surprised look. "You don't have to do that, Joan. Diana and I can plan the wedding. It will be a simple affair right here on the ranch. But thank you, honey. We'll get everything we need from town. I've already started talking to the caterer and hardware store, so we have food, tables, chairs, and a tent," Grams said. "This is a very casual wedding with about a hundred people."

"What about music and dancing?" Joan said. "And the cake?"

"It's all under control," Grams said. "We'll have a buffet in the tent and dancing afterward. We already have a D.J. The local bakery's making the cake. We just want to celebrate with friends and family."

"What about flowers?" Joan said. "Mom, let me take care of the flowers. I want to do something. What are your colors?"

Grams laughed. "At my age, the last thing I worry about is colors. I do have a cream lace dress. I planned to use tiger lilies from the ranch. They're in bloom now."

"Orange flowers," Joan said. "That actually sounds nice. Orange and cream. I'll take care of that. It will be my gift to you and Willy, okay?"

"Well, that is a nice gift," Grams said. "You go ahead and take care of the flowers if you want to. All I need is a bouquet."

"I'll call a florist in Lander right away," Joan said. "We'll come the day before the wedding. I'll make a hotel reservation right now."

"Thank you, honey," Grams said.

"Mom," Joan's voice was hesitant. "I *am* happy for you and Willy. I just had to get used to the idea."

"That means a lot to me," Grams said. "I'm glad you're coming."

"I'm glad, too," I said.

"Diana, you let me know if you guys need help with anything, okay?" Joan said. "We want this wedding to be nice."

"I'll let you know," I said. "Thanks, Aunt Joan."

After Joan said goodbye, Grams and I looked at each other. "She came around, just like you thought she would," I said.

"Joan has a good heart, but she wants to project a certain image to the world," Grams said.

"You mean like having a nice wedding?" I said.

"Yes. Having her old mother marry the ranch hand wasn't part of her world view, but she's slowly accepting it. And, yes, she does want a nice wedding. She'll order more than a bouquet for me, but that's okay. I'm sure the flowers will be outstanding," Grams said.

True to her word, Aunt Joan immediately took care of ordering the flowers. She called back to tell us it was all taken care of, and the florist would even deliver the flowers.

***

On the day before the wedding, the rental company erected the tent, creating a festive mood in the back yard. In the pasture, the horses perked up their ears at all the activity. The local hardware store delivered white wooden chairs, a wooden platform for dancing, and tables for dining. A bevy of tech guys set up stereo equipment. Grams had hired a crew of workers to arrange the white chairs for the ceremony on the lawn in two sections of fifty chairs each.

Inside the tent, the workers set up tables for the wedding supper. After the meal, they'd take down the tables and prepare the tent for dancing.

At dawn on the morning of the wedding, Willy, Grams, Dad, and I walked through the pines and down to the river to collect water for a traditional hand-washing ceremony. Willy carried a wooden bucket that my great-grandpa'd made. Dad carried a shallow pottery bowl I'd made in high school art class.

"There's that bluebird again," Dad said when we reached the bank of the river. Water lapped the boulders under the pines. Dad pointed to a nearby branch where Indigo perched.

"I see her," I said. "Maybe it's a different bird."

"I don't know," Dad said. His attention shifted to Grams as she started to speak.

"This is not something Willy's family does, but some say it's a Native tradition," Grams said. "We'll collect the water and then you'll say your part, Diana."

She said that for Dad's benefit. Last night, she'd come into my bedroom to tell me about the hand-washing ceremony. "Would you pour the water over our hands during a special ceremony tomorrow morning? Having Diana of the Wind Rivers bless our marriage with pure water from the mountains above our ranch would make me so happy. I have a short script for you to read, and I'll tell you what to do tomorrow."

"I'd love to do that," I said. "What about Dad? Won't he suspect something?"

"I'll just tell him that you're pouring the water. I won't tell him why, obviously. Diana, at some point, you'll have to tell him the truth," she said. "But not now." She hugged me close.

"Grams, I'm so happy for you and Willy," I said as we moved apart.

"Thank you, sweetie," she said. "I'm happy, too."

Now, Grams, Dad, and I watched Willy walk onto a boulder next to the riverbank. He leaned down to submerge the bucket under the flow of cold water.

"Using water from the Popo Agie River that runs through our property adds meaning to this ceremony," Grams said as Willy lifted the dripping bucket. He moved off the boulder and we all followed him up the bank to level ground.

"This pure water is an important symbol," Grams said as we paused under a pine. "It started as mountain snow feeding Christina Lake, the source of the Popo Agie River. For thousands of years, the river has traveled into Sinks Cavern and emerged down the canyon, flowing through our ranch on its way to Lander Valley."

"My ancestors drank water from this river," Willy said. "I will now pour it into this basin Diana made in high school. Our families will unite through the purity of the water."

Indigo flew to a branch above us, but Dad didn't say anything. He was used to her now, and I was glad she was here. Dad placed the shallow bowl on the ground, and Willy filled it with water from the bucket.

"Diana, you pour," Grams said.

I leaned down and picked up the bowl. The outside was fired clay, and the inside was glazed blue, shimmering under the pure water.

"Slowly pour water over our hands," Grams said.

I followed her direction after she and Willy held out their hands.

"I love you, Willy, but I also loved my husband Ben, and his memory will stay in my heart," Grams said, rubbing her hands together as I slowly poured water from the basin.

"I loved Sarah in the same way," Willy said as the cold water flowed over his brown skin. "She will remain in my heart as you and I move forward. As I wash my hands with you, Helen, this cleansing will help us transition into our future."

"As Diana pours water over our hands, we honor our past relationships, but purify our future together," Grams said. "We keep Ben and Sarah in our hearts but make room for our new life together."

Even though I had the script in my pocket, the words came to my lips without thought. "I bless this union with my love," I said. "May the past embrace you and carry you forward into your new lives. The mountain-born water from this basin will bless your union. As the water flows over your hands, it will give you a fresh start in your marriage."

Grams then reached down to pick up two towels she carried with her. Dad and I watched as she and Willy dried each other's hands.

"With the drying of our hands, we begin our future together," Willy said. He carefully dried Grams' hands and looked up at her with a smile.

Tears flooded my eyes as I watched them clasp hands. They then turned, embracing us with their love.

As the others walked back to the house, I trailed behind, wondering how much our lives would change after the wedding. Not much, I decided watching Willy envelop Grams' hand in his. We'll just be happier.

"I'm going to see my flock this morning," Indigo said.

"What?" I turned from watching Willy and Grams. "Why leave now?"

"I just want to see my family," she said. "I'll come back today."

"You don't want to miss the wedding," I warned her. "Be back on time, okay?"

"I will," she said. "I'll see you this afternoon."

The ranch was a busy place that morning as Aunt Joan, Uncle Dan and Melissa arrived after spending the night in a hotel in Lander.

"You and Melissa are in charge of helping your grandmother get ready. Melissa, you take care of her make-up. Diana, you can help her get dressed," Aunt Joan said. "I'll be outside if you need me." She left us alone in the kitchen.

"I thought you guys might not come," I said to Melissa. "Was your mom mad about Willy and Grams getting married?"

"She was hopping mad at first," Melissa said, her blonde hair shining in the morning sun streaming through the patio door. "You should have seen her. Dad was home the day you guys called. She blew up. Mom doesn't yell too often, but she did that day."

"What made her call us back? She was pretty calm two days later," I said.

"First, my dad helped her. He pointed out that Willy and Grams were better off together and could take care of each other. Dad also reminded her that Grams is old enough to know her own mind," Melissa said. "I think it's sweet that they're in love."

"I remember years ago you said Willy was stinky," I said, deliberately reminding her of that.

"Well, I kind of went through a snobby phase," Melissa said, looking at her hands and then back at me. "I learned a lot when I went away to design school. One thing I learned is that it's a big wide world out there with lots of different people."

"Yeah, I learned a lot my first year of college," I said. "I'm glad you think the wedding is okay."

"Well, another thing Mom told me is she realized a long time ago that she couldn't control Grams. Mom said that we should at least make this a nice wedding because Grams is more interested in putting up hay than planning a wedding."

I laughed. "She's right. Grams would rather ride a horse than think about wedding flowers."

"Look at this," Melissa said. "I brought all the makeup we might need. I'm going to start on you, Diana."

"Oh, no," I said, standing up. "I don't wear makeup."

"Well, today you will. Now be quiet and sit down," Melissa said. "I want to help, and I'm good at this." She stood up and pushed me back in my chair. "You've already showered, so we can take care of your makeup now and then we can focus on Grams."

I don't know what Melissa did, but when she finished with my eyes and face, I had to admit that she'd done a good job. The eyeshadow, eyeliner, and mascara weren't overdone, and seemed to emphasize my eyes. "Thanks," I said when she put the last brush down.

"You look beautiful," she said. "You should wear makeup all the time."

"I don't know if the horses care if I have makeup on," I said. "But thanks for doing this. I do want to look nice today."

Melissa took charge of corralling Grams in her room after a quick lunch at noon. "Let's do this, Grams," she said with a smile.

Surprisingly, Grams submitted. I enjoyed watching Melissa take charge, thinking she was a mini-me of her mom.

The wedding took place under the cottonwoods on the back lawn where the ranch nestled against the base of Table Mountain. The ceremony was scheduled to start at two in the afternoon. By one-thirty, the guests were filling the chairs set up on the lawn. Earlier, the florist had draped a chain of flowers made of bright orange tiger lilies and deep purple asters along the backs of the chairs in each row. I smiled and greeted friends and Willy's family members as they seated themselves. As two o'clock neared, I wondered about Indigo. Would she make it back in time?

I took a last look at the guests. Sitting on the left were predominantly locals from town, and on the right side of the aisle sat Willy's family and friends from the reservation. Some of Willy's family members on his mother's side had even come from the Crow reservation in Montana. I could sit on either side of the aisle, I realized.

Just as I prepared to walk up the aisle and sit in the front row, Indigo landed on the fence on the right side of the lawn. Behind her followed an entire flock of bluebirds, many of them completely blue males. They lined up on the wooden rails, causing some guests to point and talk. I wondered what Indigo was up to. I started counting the birds and reached twenty when Melissa began playing the violin from where she was stationed in front of the guests, a short distance from where Willy stood.

I walked up the aisle with Robert, one of Willy's grandsons. I wasn't really in the wedding, but Aunt Joan had decided I should have an escort. I felt elegant in my new dress, which was light blue with a swoop neck and capped sleeves. A light chiffon layer over the dress added flair, and the fluttery hem brushing against my calves was perfect for dancing. The chain on my elk tooth necklace matched my silver post earrings, and the silver belt cinching my waist tied it all together. Today, I didn't hide the necklace.

When we reached the first row of chairs, Robert and I smiled at each other and parted to sit on our respective sides of the aisle. Before I could even sit, Melissa began to play "The Wedding March" and we all turned to look as Grams walked up the aisle with Dad, only a slight limp left over from her hip surgery. Soon after finding out about their plans, he'd announced that he wanted to give away the bride. Seeing them caused a sharp sting of tears in my eyes.

Grams wore an elegant but simple cream-colored dress with a lace overlay on the bodice and a chiffon skirt that flowed around her legs. She carried a bouquet of orange tiger lilies. A ring of white flowers and greenery graced her head, making her look like a young woman from a distance. Her eyes remained on Willy as she walked up the aisle. She smiled at me before handing off her bouquet.

Willy looked magnificent in a western turquoise shirt, black pants, and his black cowboy boots, which he wore only on special occasions. A large chunk of turquoise adorned his bolo tie, made of shiny black leather encased in silver tips. Of course, he wore his dress cowboy hat, black with a beaded band circling the crown. I'd helped him brush it off this morning. Attached to his cornflower boutonniere was a blue feather. *How did he get that?* I wondered.

Willy's cousin, who was a minister on the reservation, performed the ceremony. Just as Willy and Grams kissed, the entire flock of bluebirds flew off the fence, following one another in a line. Starting low to the ground, they circled the kissing couple and spiraled into the sky, one after the other, following the lead bird, Indigo. She led them back to circle Willy and Grams one more time and then they flew up again, filling the space above the couple with blue joy. As the birds flew over the trees, all the guests clapped and cheered, and I heard several people exclaiming.

"Where did those birds come from?"

"Trust Willy to have birds at his wedding!"

"How did they train those birds to do that?"

From where he sat right next to me, Dad looked over and raised his eyebrows. "How did you do that, Diana?" he said. "I know you've got something going on with this bluebird thing."

"I had nothing to do with it," I said. "Honestly." This time, I wasn't keeping a secret. I'd had no idea that Indigo planned this surprise. Luckily, there wasn't time to keep talking because Grams and Willy joined hands and walked back down the aisle while we all stood again and clapped.

As soon as Grams and Willy reached the end of the aisle, the minister said," Everyone should now join the couple in celebrating this wonderful event with a meal in the tent."

People mingled as they headed toward the tent, where Grams and Willy were greeting guests. White tablecloths adorned round tables with place settings and floral centerpieces. The buffet table set up to the side was flanked by servers in white bar jackets, ready to begin the process of feeding the crowd.

Before I could join the line to hug Willy and Grams, Aunt Joan's long fingers gripped my arm and her voice hissed in my ear. "What is your grandmother up to with that bluebird thing?"

"I don't know what your mother's doing," I said. "But wasn't it beautiful?"

"Yes, it was," she said, her voice softening. "But I'm still going to find out what's going on."

Later that night, after the last guest left, Aunt Joan, Uncle Dan, and Melissa gathered up their things before returning to their hotel in Lander. They planned to leave from there in the early morning to drive back to Denver. Aunt Joan confronted Grams during our goodbye hugs at the door.

"Mom, does this bluebird event have anything to do with that woman who used to come visit on the ranch when I was a child? You know, the woman who wore those flowing clothes and had braided hair wound around her head?" Aunt Joan said. "Whenever she came here, I had a special feeling about her. Today, that same feeling hit me when the bluebirds flew around you and Willy. What's happening here on the ranch?"

Aunt Joan and my mom had seen Demeter years ago, I realized. Why hadn't I heard about it before?

Grams' voice was neutral. "I don't know what you're talking about, dear. What bluebird thing? I was kissing my new husband and didn't notice. Although many people told me about it during the reception," she said. "And that woman who came years ago was my good friend Debbie from California. She hasn't been back in a while."

Melissa made a choking sound and covered her mouth, clearly holding back her laugh. There were no disagreements in Aunt Joan's house because everyone followed her rules, so I was sure Melissa rarely heard anyone sidestep her mom.

"I'm still going to get to the bottom of this bird nonsense. But right now, we're leaving for town. You were beautiful today, Mom," she added in a softer tone.

"Thank you for the lovely flowers," Grams said, hugging Joan. "You made this a very special day for me."

"It's my gift to you and Willy," Aunt Joan said, turning to hug him. "Willy, I'm glad you married Mom."

"We'll take care of each other," he said.

"I know you will," Joan replied. "Now that you're my stepdad, that doesn't mean you can tell me what to do."

"I wouldn't even try," he said. We all laughed. I was relieved Joan could make jokes now.

After they left, Willy and Grams headed to Willy's cabin where they'd spend the night. They'd already decided to take a honeymoon trip in the fall, rather than right now.

"Let's look at the stars," Dad said. "I'm not quite ready to call it a night."

"Okay," I said, following him onto the deck after turning off the kitchen lights so we could see the stars better.

"Are you happy Willy is your real grandpa?" Dad asked when I sat down.

"Yes. I feel funny about Grandpa. He'll always be my grandpa, but now Willy is, too," I said.

"You're right. Your mom would be happy, too, if she knew," he said.

"I'm glad," I said. *I can tell her sometime*, I thought. *I think I'll see her again.*

"Look at that moon," he said.

As we looked up in companionable silence, I figured this was a good time to tell my secrets, so I said, "Did you know Artemis is the goddess of the moon?"

CHAPTER TWENTY-FOUR
A WHINNY ON THE WIND

Of course, I didn't tell Dad about Artemis. In the end, I couldn't find a way to tell him the truth about Indigo and our adventures. It would have all sounded too farfetched. The weekend following the wedding, Dad drove me back to school. During the three-and-a-half hour drive from Lander to Laramie, we talked about Grams and Willy, the ranch, and his time in the Bakken Oil Fields outside of Williston, North Dakota.

"It's a dry, dusty boomtown on a broad flat plain far from the mountains in the distance," Dad said. "There's no extra apartments or rental units right now. Farmers turned their fields into trailer courts with electrical hookup. Companies are making money as they frack the oil out of the bedrock."

"What's it like living there?" I said.

"Williston is booming, and the pipelines are flowing with oil. The grime of it coats the sagebrush on the edge of town, and I'm glad I don't have to work there in the winter." His eyes left the road for a moment, and he turned to glance at me before facing the front again. "I'll probably go back next summer, just to give you a heads up."

"I don't want you to go again, but I know it pays well," I said. "Can you come back before we start haying, so we can take a pack trip next summer?"

"We'll see how it goes," he said.

When we were an hour away from Laramie, I told Dad about my plans for the future. By then, we were driving past Elk Mountain, a lone feature jutting up from the high plains leading to Laramie. When I'd first moved here last fall for school, it had taken me a while to get used to living with mountains in the distance, rather than right next to me, like they were on the ranch.

"I'm going to major in forestry," I said. "I want to be a forest ranger."

"You do?" he asked, glancing away from the highway to look at me with a smile. His eyes returned to the road.

"Being a ranger means I can spend time in the mountains, and you know that's what I love," I said.

He nodded and looked over at me again. "I think that's a good idea, Diana. You'll make a good ranger, and you already know how to survive in the mountains. Maybe you can get a job near Lander."

"I'd like that. Then I can live on the ranch when I'm not in the mountains," I said. "It's a plan, anyhow."

"It's a good plan," he said.

Dad spent the night in Laramie and drove back to Lander the next day. Before the first day of class, I met with my advisor and declared forestry as my major. The next three years would be challenging, but I could handle it.

***

On a Friday afternoon in mid-September, I caught a ride home with friends from high school. Several people from Lander were at the university and it was easy to find someone making the long drive. I came back to say goodbye to Indigo before she flew southwest with the rest of her flock for the winter.

I was at the ranch by seven and spent the evening with Grams. Willy and Dad were scouting out places for a hunting camp near Big Sandy, the area where I'd met Artemis on Squaretop Mountain in June. They'd be home in time for dinner tomorrow night.

The next morning, I was up early and rode my bike to the Sinks Cave. At this time of day, no tourists were in the canyon. Vibrant gold aspen leaves highlighted the early first snow coating the rim. I left my bike at the edge of the empty parking lot and walked past the visitor center, now closed for the season. Following the path to the river, I stood on a boulder, watching the flow of water as it passed into the cavern.

Listening to the sound of rushing water, I looked at the entrance to the cave where water raced underground, and then looked left to see the dry overflow channel, showcasing huge granite boulders. The cave entrance was now fully exposed, revealing an open area carved out of the limestone. A high ceiling and sandy bottom demonstrated the power of the water over the years where it had created an amphitheater of sorts at the base of the cliff.

The rush of water from the spring run-off was gone because the winter snowpack in the mountains melted by August. The cycle began again with the first snowfall high in the mountains, where over two hundred feet would accumulate over the winter.

I pictured Tixi Pagos at the source of the Yellowstone River. By now, her moss green skin would be back to periwinkle and her winter wings formed as she monitored the first snowfall in the mountains. I wouldn't see her again until warmer June weather triggered the spring melt, sending water racing from the mountain peaks into the glacial tarn.

While I started my new classes, the gods and goddesses worked around the globe to protect the planet. Demeter and Persephone initiated planting in Australia, where it was now spring. Hades continued to monitor fracking in Texas, and Poseidon swam with the merfolk as they explored deep water trenches to determine the extent of microplastic pollution. Artemis returned to Africa to work with a group of female park rangers protecting elephants and lowland gorillas. Everybody had a winter job. I knew my work with the gods would resume next summer.

I smiled at the thought of next spring, which would bring not only the melting of Tixi's winter ice wings, but also the birth of a new god or goddess. Persephone was pregnant. While she took care of her child, I would train the baby winged horses Poseidon has promised to send to the ranch in June.

I looked up at the sound of geese honking. They flew above the southern rim of the canyon, disappearing overhead. The river marked their passing as it gurgled into the cavern, its volume normal and mild. I was no longer afraid of this river, or any river. From now on, every time I stood on this boulder to remember my mom, her image and voice would come easily to my mind.

"Diana, I'm here to say goodbye," Indigo said, appearing at the top of the limestone cliff overlooking the river, the very same limestone that had opened when Persephone first flew out of the cave.

"Hello, Indigo. I've missed seeing you," I said as she perched on a tree next to the boulder where I stood.

"I brought the flock," she said. As she spoke, an entire flock of Mountain Bluebirds flew over the edge of the cliff and down to our boulder.

Without hesitation, the blue stream of birds flew in a line, just as they did at Gram's wedding, but this line was longer. I laughed and held up my hands as blue wings created a breeze around my body, starting at my feet, and spiraling to my head, then moving back up to the top of the limestone cliff.

Surrounded by the blue breeze, I inhaled the scent of water on limestone, and reveled in the sound of blue wings. All the while, Indigo perched on the aspen next to us, singing at the top of her lungs. Embraced by blue, I was part of the flock as each bird chirped when it flew around my head. The soft breeze of feathers fluttered my hair. I twirled around on the boulder as the wave ended when the last bird soared past my ears and back up the cliff, turning green pines to blue as they landed in trees.

"I have to go now," Indigo said. "We're starting our migration today."

"Be careful," I said. "You're flying a long way."

"I will," she said. "This is my second time flying to the southwest, but the elders in the flock know where to go."

"I love you, Indigo." I said. "I promise I'll tell Dad about you this winter."

"I hope you find a way," she said. Leaving the aspen, she flew to my shoulder and rubbed her head against my cheek. "I love you too, Diana."

With a little push off with her tiny feet, Indigo took flight and soared toward the blue mass in the pines at the top of the cliff.

"Safe travels," I shouted as she left.

"Take care," she called back. When she reached the top of the cliff, the entire flock rose into the sky and headed southwest, leaving me alone on the boulder with the sound of water gurgling into the cave.

Scanning the sky for more birds, I heard the whinny of a horse carried on the wind, reminding me that Persephone would return in the spring so we could tackle the problem of microplastics. That issue had no easy solution. As the sun moved higher above the rim of the canyon, I returned to my bike and pedaled back to the ranch.

At the dinner table that night I looked at Willy and Grams before turning to Dad. This would be a good time to get him ready for next summer when Poseidon sent the new foals to the ranch.

"Hey, Dad," I said. "How do you feel about flying horses?"

About the Author

Nona Schrader experienced the beauty of the Wind River Mountains while growing up in Lander, Wyoming.

After completing her B.A. and M.A. in English at the University of Wyoming, Nona moved to Wisconsin to teach. She retired after 26 years and now enjoys writing her nature blog and the *Aqua* novel series.

In the summer, Nona relishes trips to Wyoming, which contains the headwaters of four major river basins in the western United States. The beauty of pure mountain water inspired Nona to use her love of Greek mythology to convince others to protect water on our planet.

Aqua is her first novel